Malt ME

I'm given a second chance at happiness...there's no way
I'll let him take that from me.

Book 1 in The Liquor Cabinet series
Liquor has never been so disturbingly saucy

College. It's supposed to be both exciting and daunting. For me, it turns into a nightmare.

Now everyone looks at me with pity, treating me like I'm glass. I don't blame them. Not a lot of people can survive what I have. But I refuse to let the darkness swallow me whole, to let the monster win.

I'm given a second chance at happiness, and I won't allow the horrifying memories to take that away from me. He's already taken too much.

But turns out he wants more. The devil won't stop until he's consumed every part of me.

He wants another chance to own me, possess me, and then ruin me if he wants to. But there's no way I'll let him.

I am Mackenzie Merlot. I am strong. I am a survivor.

And this time...he'll lose.

Malt Me, book 1 in the Liquor Cabinet series

Edited by Karen Hrdlicka, Barren Acres Editing

Cover Designed by Tash Drake, Outlined with Love Designs

 Created with Vellum

AUTHOR NOTE

Some of the chapters repeat themselves, as they are given from both points of views. I have added extra and tweaked them, so that these scenes are not exactly the same.

The legal drinking age is Australia is 18.

This book contains Australian slang as it is set in Australia and uses Australian spelling.

Here is a glossary to help you out:

Missus – Wife/Girlfriend/Partner
Arvo – Afternoon
Headjob – Blowjob
Undies – Panties
Franga – Condom
Singlet – Tank
Trackies – Track pants

Thongs – Flip Flops
Hinterland – Mountains
Esky – Cool Box/ Cooler
Ambo – Ambulance Officer
Up the duff – pregnant
Obs – vitals – blood pressure, temp etc.
Maccas – McDonald's
Bottle-O – Liquor store
Mines – that is mine
Brewski's – alcoholic beverages

THE LIQUOR CABINET SERIES

Liquor has never been so disturbingly saucy

Malt Me (Book 1)

Tequila Healing (Book 2)

Wine Not (Book 3)

The Final Shot (Book 4)

The Liquor Cabinet: Series boxset

ALSO BY DL GALLIE

THE CASTAWAY GROVE COLLECTION

Love has arrived in the Grove

Oasis

Unequivocal Love - Coming 13th October

Five Words - Coming January 2020

I've Loved You Since Forever - Coming April 2020

————

THE UNEXPECTED SERIES

When it comes to love, expect the unexpected

The Unexpected Gift

The Unexpected Letter

The Unexpected Package

The Unexpected Connection

coming November 2019

————

STAND ALONES

Out of Nowhere

Antecedent

Seven Nights

Titanic Tales, a charity anthology (no longer available)

Gone Coastal, a sizzling summer beach anthology

Leave Me Breathless: The Lilac Collection

To my husband, Troy,

For giving me the confidence to take this leap
and for always loving me, especially when I am being
irrational

PROLOGUE

STANDING ON THE MEZZANINE LEVEL LEANING ON the timber railing, my foot resting on the wire cable I look down and realize that we did it; we bloody did it. Our dream of opening a brewpub has actually come true. I never imagined the path to get to this point would have been as rocky as it was, but despite it all, here we are.

Malt Me is officially open and it's currently full, yes it's at maximum capacity on opening day. The beer is flowing, the kitchen is pumping out orders, and it seems like everyone is having a blast. You cannot wipe the smile off my face; I'm glowing with pride and achievement.

Looking towards Jordan my heart flutters, just like it did all those years ago when we first met. I see that he is just as happy as I am, if not happier. He looks up at me and smiles. After all these years, his smile still makes me weak at the knees. He takes the checker plate stairs that wind along the side of the room, two at a time. He saunters over and wraps his tanned muscular arms around me, lifting me up into a hug, spinning us around, "We did it,

Kenz, we really did it." Lowering me down, he places a soft kiss on my lips that quickly turns heated.

I step back, gently pushing him in the chest, "STOP! We have to be professional." He pouts, so I place a quick kiss on his lips and whisper into his ear, "Later, I promise to make all your dreams come true." I wink as I pull back.

"Kenz, all my dreams have come true. I have the girl of my dreams in my arms and we are standing in OUR brewpub."

He bends down for another kiss and from below I hear Mike yell, "Get a room, you two!"

"Fu...whatever, Mike, if I wanna kiss my missus, I'll kiss my missus." Turning his attention back to me, Jordan says, "Come on, baby, lets go play boss and mingle"

"I'll be down in a sec, I just wanna stay here for a moment and take it all in. I still can't believe we did it, Jor. There was so much in our way and at times, I wasn't sure I wanted to do this and then Clint happened." He goes to interrupt me, but I put my finger on his lips to stop him. "I'm not dwelling on that, Jor, but it happened. It's a part of who we are and a major part of this journey. I just want to enjoy this moment, cause I'm still amazed that we did it. Now, go and have a beer to celebrate and tell Mike to behave. I'll be down in a sec to celebrate with you, promise."

Jordan leans down, giving me a quick peck on the cheek, "Don't be too long, Kenz." He winks at me and walks away. His wink still sends shockwaves to my girly parts.

When he gets to the top of the stairs, he looks over his shoulder and says, "I love you, Kenz, and I promise to look after you and our beers forever." I laugh as he jumps down the stairs, and when he gets to the bottom, he yells, "Beer me baby" and throws his arms wide. I cannot help but laugh, like really laugh.

"Wait for it!" Mike yells, and then I snort. Yes, I snort laugh for everyone to hear and laughter erupts from down below.

I take a bow and since everyone is looking at me, I clear my throat, "While I have your attention, Jordan and I want to thank you all for being here today, at the grand opening of our baby, Malt Me. The journey here hasn't been smooth, but we got here, thanks to the support of many of you. We both thank you all so very muchly. BUT I want to give a special shout out to my partner in crime..."

Mike interrupts and yells, "Naw shucks, Kenz, you don't have to thank me!"

"As if, Mike. As I was saying before I was rudely interrupted, I want to thank Jordan. We would not be here today if it wasn't for his love of beer and his passion for everything beer; specifically one awesome drunken decision that was made at the Oktoberfest all those years ago. Jordan, I love you so very much and I'm so so proud of you. Together we are going to make beautiful beers and live hoppily ever after." Everyone below laughs at my beer joke but to Jordan and I, it's our mantra. "So, if everyone can raise their drinks and toast Jordan. Congrats on making your dream come true baby."

"You mean our dream!" he yells.

Below everyone says, "Cheers, to Jordan and Kenzie." They all start congratulating Jordan and waving for me to come down. I walk towards the stairs with a huge happy smile on my face. I look down at everything and freeze, something by the front doors catches my eye and I stumble. Before I know it, I'm tumbling down the stairs.

Vaguely I hear someone yelling "Kenzie!" Then it all goes dark...again.

1

KENZIE

...Seven years earlier

THIS PAST SUMMER HAS BEEN AMAZING. I FINISHED high school before Christmas and had a fantabolous week long holiday with my bestie, Sarah Bryant, for schoolies; we went island hopping in the Whitsunday's. I finally turned eighteen and to top it all off, I was accepted into the college course that I had my heart set on.

Today I'm moving into my first apartment and this time tomorrow I will officially be a college student. I was accepted into Stratton's School of Business and I will be completing my diploma of Tourism Management, which is twelve months in length. If I enjoy it, I can transfer my credits to university and complete a Bachelor of Tourism.

I found a cute apartment, a short ten-minute bus ride from the city center and college. Thankfully I have my inheritance from Dad to help with expenses. There are six apartments in total and mine is number two; they are in a two story red brick with the apartment being on one level and the garage and laundry underneath. As it's my first apartment, the majority of my furniture I had to buy. It's being delivered later today, so apart from my clothes and personal items, all the heavy lifting is taken care of.

Hoping I'd get an uber hottie to deliver my stuff; luck wasn't on my side and I ended up with a balding beer bellied rough nut, who stinks, just my luck. Thankfully, he gets everything unloaded pretty quickly and placed into the rooms I want, now all I have to do is put it all together. I love to hate *IKEA* flat packs. I love that they are cheap, but hate having to put them together.

I quickly change into my grey trackies and fluro pink Wine Time Finally singlet, grab a bottle of wine, and I decide to start with the bedroom stuff first. After all, I'll need to get a good night sleep in order to be fresh and ready for college tomorrow. Pouring a glass of wine, I try and decipher the bed instructions when my phone starts to play *Love Shack* by The B-52's. I glance at the screen and see Mum's smiling face looking at me. "Heya, Mum"

"Hi, Mac, how's the unpacking going?"

"I'm drinking wine."

"That good, huh?"

"I'm starting to wish I had paid extra and gotten them to put it all together for me. Why am I such a tightass?"

"Language, honey, but if I can put a BBQ together, I am sure you will be fine with a bed and a few shelves"

"I know, I know, I'm just not in the mood for it tonight." We both laugh "I've decided that I'll put my bed together tonight and then work my way through each room. Enough about my flat pack hell. How are you?"

"I'm good, missing my baby girl."

"I'm eighteen, Mum, not really a baby anymore, but I miss you too. You know you can always move here. There is nothing really keeping you guys there, and Skye can always go to school here, in the city!"

"I don't want to disrupt your sister's schooling, she was doing really well at the end of last year. She has decided she wants to be a nurse."

"For this week?"

"Mac, that's not fair. You were just as indecisive as her. If I remember correctly, you were going to be a chef, remind me again what you are studying?"

"Fair enough, Mum, I was just teasing. Look, I'd love to chat, but I really need to get this done and get a good night's sleep. My first class is at 9:00 a.m. tomorrow. Tell Skye I love her, I'll give you guys a call tomorrow night and let you know how my first day went."

"Sounds good, baby girl. Good luck with the furniture and I'll chat to you tomorrow. I love you, Mac. Your dad would be so proud."

"I love you too, Mum and I hope he would be. I still miss him." Tears rise to my eyes when I say that.

"I miss him too, honey, and I know he would be because I'm very proud of you. I'll chat to you tomorrow."

"Thanks, Mum, I love you."

"Love you too, baby girl."

After hanging up, I grab my family photo out of a box and I sit and stare at it, a lone tear cascades down my cheek. I still miss Dad, even though he died five years ago. One minute he was mowing the front lawn, and the next, we are organising his funeral. He had a bleed on the brain, also known as an aneurysm and the ambos were unable to revive him. There's not a day that goes by that I don't think of him. I stare at the photo. "Love you, Dad," I whisper, as I kiss my finger and place it on his head. I put the frame on my chest of drawers, the only non-flat pack item. Grabbing my wine, I take a sip, turn up the tunes and dive in.

It only takes me three hours to put together my bed and shelf. I'm putting away the last shirt and *Baby One More Time* by Brittany Spears comes on, I grab my brush and sing at the top of my lungs, shaking my booty around my new bedroom. This has been a great day. I quickly grab a shower and put on my new, silk, Peter Alexander PJ's before jumping into my newly built and made bed. I'm pretty proud, as I managed to get the draws and the intricate headboard shelf thingy put together with only one tantrum, and I didn't damage the chocolate brown timber either.

I snuggle under my sunflower comforter that my Mum and sister bought me for my high school graduation present. I still can't believe Mum and Skye got me this; I pointed it out months ago when we had a girls' shopping day. When I went back into Talking Pillow to get it, they'd just sold the last one; little did I know it was Mum and Skye who purchased it. It's the softest Egyptian cotton, and it's covered in sunflowers with a bluish green background. The thousand thread sheets are a buttery yellow, with blue accents that match the comforter. My mum always says you need to sleep like the dead and to do so you need comfort. She's a total sheet snob, and I have now inherited this trait too. I snuggle down, looking forward to the new adventure that starts tomorrow.

My alarm goes off at 6.30 a.m. and I'm so excited. Jumping up, I race to the kitchen, and turn on my coffee machine; while the coffee is brewing I grab a quick shower. For my first day of college, I settle on my Wrangler jeans that hug my curves and make my ass look amazing. A wine coloured sleeveless shirt with black lace at the top, which I pair with my black Diana Ferrari ballerina flats. I look in the mirror and I'm pleased. I look sophisticated, yet sexy. Perfect for my first day of college.

Pouring my coffee into my travel mug, I grab my bag, lock up and I walk to the bus stop. I catch the 115 express into the city, and depending on traffic, I should arrive with plenty of time to spare. Traffic is light for a Monday morning so I don't have to rush. The bus arrives early enough that I head to the Java Lava Cafe, which is next door to the college and grab another coffee, I'm totally addicted to coffee...and wine.

After my coffee, I head to college. Walking up the front steps, I admire the building. I've never seen so many windows before; they're that reflective stuff, which has always fascinated me for some weird reason. Gazing towards the building, I bump into someone while my neck is craned and I fall flat on my ass.

Looking up, I see the hottest guy I have ever seen, he has an electric smile, likable lips, bulging biceps and the most mesmerizing blue eyes. His sandy blond hair is short on the side with a waved fringe, and I imagine myself running my fingers through it, while biting those luscious lips.

"Um, sorry. I wasn't watching where I was going," I say, as a slight blush creeps onto my cheeks, due to my inappropriate thoughts.

He puts out his hand to help me up, and I wrap my fingers around his. I feel an electric current sparks between us when our hands touch and he helps to pull me up. I feel sad when he drops my hand. "No worries, I probably should not have stopped in the middle of the walkway. I'm Jordan McRoberts." He lifts his hand to shake.

Reaching my hand out, I grip his hand and shake. "Nice to smash into you, Jordan, I'm Mackenzie Merlot." I feel the same spark that I felt moments ago. Letting go of his hand, I push my golden blonde hair over my shoulder and smile.

"Pretty name for a pretty girl."

I snort laugh at his comment and can't help but smile. "That's the cheesiest line ever, dude, but thank you for the compliment. I'm really sorry about bumping into you, I was mesmerised by the building and all the windows."

"It's partly my fault too, I should have been paying attention and not playing on my phone."

Stepping around him, I look over my shoulder. "I hope to see you around." I shamelessly wink at him as I walk up the stairs into the building.

———

Heading to reception, I fill out more paperwork, finalise my registration, get my amended timetable, and head to my first class. I walk into the classroom and I take a seat in the middle. My gaze moves towards the seat next to me. There's this guy sitting there, staring at me. He has wavy, dark brown hair that hangs just below his ears, and his eyes match the darkness of his hair. *Great, I'm sitting next to a weirdo.* I consider getting up and moving seats but he looks over and smiles. His smile lights up his face and he looks less creepy now. His smile makes his dark eyes pop and sparkle, making him less of a weirdo and spunky, a Patrick Bateman from *American Psycho* kind of spunky.

"Hey, I'm Clint MacNicholson," he says in a deep rough voice.

"Hi, Clint, I'm Mackenzie Merlot." Putting out my hand to shake his.

He takes my outstretched hand and returns the shake. "Nice to meet you Mackenzie."

The lecturer, Michele, walks in and gets straight into it. No pussyfooting around. "Welcome, everyone. I'm Michele. When you enter this classroom you are on Michele time. All phones are to be switched off. If I see or hear one, it's mine and I have lots of friends in China, so be prepared for an excessive bill." Everyone laughs, but by the stern look on her face, I don't think she's joking.

This teacher is hardcore and kind of badass. We're given our first assignment; we have to write a travel magazine and we are partnered with the person sitting next to us. Looks like I'm working with Clint. I later find out that Michele owns the college and is a total ball-buster, but the best lecturer around.

My first day flies by, and by time I get home, I'm

exhausted. *Welcome to college life*, I think. Before having my shower, I call Mum and Skye to give them a run down of my day. After my shower, I climb into bed and fall straight to sleep. I'm so shattered that I don't even read. Usually, I need to read to make me sleepy.

2

JORDAN

TODAY IS THE FIRST DAY OF COLLEGE AND I'M SUPER excited. My childhood friend and best buddy, Mike Mustange, and I are attending the same college. I'm studying business and marketing, as I'd like to run a bar one day. I love all things beer related and I hope to turn that into a career.

As I'm walking up the college steps, I vaguely hear someone calling out to me, I look over to see Mike waving. "Earth to Jordan. Hello ... anyone home?" I was totally lost in thought, thinking about my encounter with Mackenzie. Everything else faded away, and I was consumed with thoughts of her, even though I only spoke with her for about a minute.

She is the most gorgeous girl I have been near; dazzling green eyes, long golden blonde hair and the most kissable lips I have ever seen. When she placed her silky smooth hand in mine for me to help her up, I felt a spark. My cock twitched, sparking to life just from her touch. It was like a scene from the movies where fireworks explode and everything around you fades away, leaving just the two of us staring at each other. My heart rate accelerated, just from her touch. I didn't want to let go of her hand and break our contact, but if I didn't, she'd think I'm a creeper. So I reluctantly let go of her hand.

We did our introductions, and her name was just as beautiful as her face. I could feel my cock starting to harden, and from the discomfort I said the dumbest line ever. *Seriously, what was my cock making my brain do?* I've turned into a complete pussy, so glad Mike wasn't here to witness my pussiness. She snort laughed at my cheesiness; it was refreshing to see her not hide it, and I hoped she didn't think I'm too cheesy or a douche.

As she walked off, she winked at me. Her wink went straight to my dick and my pants became really uncomfortable and tight as my cock pressed against my fly. I subtly adjusted myself as I watched her walk off. Being male, I had to check out her ass and its one mighty fine ass. Her jeans hugged and accentuated her curves. I imagine holding onto her ass as she wrapped her legs around me, and I sank my teeth into her shoulder before kissing the life out of her.

I shake my head to clear those dirty thoughts, but her ass will stick in my mind for a longtime to come. Shaking my head, I reply, "Sorry, dude, I was just thinking."

"Ouch, did it hurt?" he says.

Reaching out, I punch Mike in the arm. "Whatever, douche, let's get to our first class. I hear the lecturer is super strict and I want to make a good first impression." I slap Mike on the back and we head into our first day of college.

3
———

CLINT

I CAN'T BELIEVE MY LUCK WHEN I LOOK UP AND SEE who walks into my first class...the hottie I saw when I was walking out of registration. She has the most amazing green eyes and her ass is incredible. Thoughts of gripping her ass as I plow into her enter my mind. I smile at that thought, and it's also when I decide that she is mines. Wriggling in my seat, I adjust my dick, which, seems to have a mind of its own where this hottie is concerned. I can't take my eyes off her as she makes her way across the classroom. As luck would have it, she sits next to me. After she sits, she turns her head in my direction. I smile.

After I introduce myself, she smiles and it lights up her face. I feel my cock twitching again. I'm thankful for the table blocking it.

When she takes my hand to shake it, I feel all giddy. Her hand is ever so soft, and I imagine what it would feel like wrapped around my cock, gripping it tightly, stroking up and down. Wriggling in my seat again, I discretely adjust my growing cock.

I want to know more about her, she is so mesmerising. I haven't felt like this with anyone since high school, not since Laura. Just as I'm about to ask her another question, the lecturer walks in. *Damn it.*

Turns out this class isn't going to be as easy-going as I was hoping, as the college owner is the lecturer. Just my luck, so much for an easy semester.

Mackenzie and I get paired up for our first assignment, and I thank the heavens that I'm partnered with her; everyone else in this class is a bore.

Is it fate that Mackenzie and I are paired up?

Are we destined to be together?

All signs are pointing to yes, Mackenzie Merlot will be mines.

4

KENZIE

OVER THE NEXT FEW WEEKS, CLINT AND I MEET UP after class at The Java Lava and on weekends, at my apartment to get this magazine assignment completed. We smash out an amazing magazine and I'm really proud of the final product. All the work we put into it really paid off. We manage to get a ninety-three out of a hundred, which is pretty good for our first assignment. To celebrate, Clint and I agree to head to the, Dirty Duck, after class. The Duck has become the local for the Stratton college students.

I finish at 2:00 p.m. and wait for Clint outside the building. Looking up, I see Clint walking towards me and I can't help but smile. I tell him I'm just ducking to the bathroom and then I'll be ready to go.

"Tik tok, hurry up," he says, as I race to the bathroom.

It's quiet for a Thursday, or it could just be that it's 2:00 p.m. and most people are either at work or still in class. Clint and I grab a booth in the back. The Dirty Duck is your typical college bar, wooden high-top tables in the middle. Red cracked and peeling vinyl booths along the back wall. There are pool tables to the left as you walk in and the bar runs the length of the room with bathrooms off the right. The lighting is dim, but enough that you can see. The neon signs along the walls and the backlights from the bar provide extra lighting.

Heading to the bar, I order us a jug of beer and some nibblies. The Buffalo wings here are the best, not too spicy just perfect. Once I'm seated back at the booth, I pour us each a beer and raise my glass. "To us, for acing our first major assignment. Cheers!"

Clint raises his glass and shouts, "Cheers," before we clink glasses.

After taking a sip, I look towards Clint. Pointing at him I say, "You know what? You and I make a pretty good team. Here's hoping we get another assignment together before the year is out."

Clint raises his glass again "To us, the kick ass combo that is M and C."

"Cheers to that," I say holding my glass in the air.

The afternoon flies by and before I know it, I'm kind of wasted. I haven't been this drunk in a long time, it feels good to let loose and feel kind of numb. The past few weeks at college have been pretty full on. I know I'm wasted, as I can't stop giggling, which results in me snort laughing. Everyone in turn laughs at me, which only makes me snort again; it's a vicious laugh/snort cycle. Some of the other students join us when their classes are over. We consume way too many jugs of beer, eat a gazillion wings and dance the night away.

Clint and I return from the dance floor after dancing

for a few songs. Just as we sit down, he leans over, tilts my chin up, and kisses me. His lips are soft and it's not bad for a first kiss. I wouldn't mind doing that again, so I lean over and I kiss him again. This time, when he pulls away, my lips are tingling. I smile and lean into him again. I whisper in his ear, "You know, I've thought you were kind of hot since our first day in class." I nibble his ear lobe and kiss along his jawline, pressing my lips to his once again. Running my fingers through his silky soft hair, I gently tug on the ends, as I slip my tongue into his mouth. Our tongues gently caress one another, as our hands explore each other.

Clint groans into my mouth before pulling back, gazing into my eyes he whispers, "You know what, Mackenzie? I thought you were pretty hot too. From the moment you walked into that classroom, I was secretly hoping you'd sit next to me."

I think it's all the beer, or the high from getting such a good mark on our assignment but I kiss Clint passionately, again. Grabbing Clint's hand, I entwine our fingers and softly whisper, "Let's get out of here."

Leaving the bar, we manage to grab a cab straight away, which never happens...especially on a Thursday night. We're back at my place before we know it. We go up the back stairs, enter through the kitchen, and head into the lounge room.

I place my bag and keys on the breakfast bar, and Clint wraps his arms around me from behind, holding me close to him. I feel his cock hardening against my ass, as he nibbles on my neck and earlobe. I moan and start grinding myself against him, his cock getting harder.

Spinning around in his arms, I kiss him intensely, devouring his mouth, our teeth crushing together. He deepens the kiss as he turns us, pushing me up against the hallway wall.

Grabbing the hem of my shirt, I lift it over my head and drop it on the floor. I unzip my navy blue skorts and am left standing there in my satin purple bra and matching undies; internally high fiving myself for dressing sexy this morning. Clint eyes me up and down. "Fuck me, your gorgeous," he says, before he kisses me deeply. I run my hands up under his shirt and around to his back. Moving my hands down, I grip his ass, pulling him closer. I grab the bottom of his shirt and lift it over his head. Raking my eyes down his chiseled chest, I moan and dart my tongue out to moisten my lips. Reaching for his hand, I tug and walk down the hall to my bedroom.

We reach the end of my bed and I make quick work, removing his jeans and boxer briefs. I push him back and begin to crawl my way up his body. Grabbing my arms, he pulls me up so I am straddling him. I rest my arms either side of his head, my hair creating a curtain around us, leaning forward I kiss him passionately, our tongues meshing together. He sits up, snaking his arms around my waist, quickly removing my bra. The straps fall down my arms and he takes my nipple into his mouth. He bites down before sucking the tip between his lips, gently raking his teeth over my hard peak; the pain is quickly replaced with the most delicious pleasure. Moaning, I throw my head back. Not wanting to be selfish, he takes the other nipple into his mouth and repeats the same process, which has me once again throwing my head back in ecstasy as I shamelessly grind my pussy into him.

He literally rips my undies off me and flips us over, so he is now on top of me. He grabs a condom and sheaths his rock hard cock before stroking it a few times, not once removing his eyes from me. In one stroke he thrusts deep into me and I moan. I draw him down towards me and rub my tongue over his lips before I slip into his mouth. Our kiss becomes more passionate and I embrace him tighter. Grabbing my left leg, he places it over his shoulder and begins to thrust in and out. I've never felt pleasure like this before.

"Ohh, Clint!" I moan.

He continues to move in an out and his pace quickens. Before I know it, I feel my whole body tense as my orgasm rips through me like a tsunami; tingles wash over me from head to toe as the most amazing feeling ripples through me. I see fireworks behind my closed eyes...this is the most intense orgasm that I have ever had. It's not long before I feel Clint spasm inside of me.

Lowering my leg, he falls on top of me. "That was fuckin' amazing Mackenzie."

All I can manage in response is, "mmhmm."

He lies on top of me for a while; I can still feel his heart frantically beating and his hot breath on my shoulder. I wrap my arms around him, and slowly rub my hands up and down his back while we both catch our breath. Easing off me, Clint removes the condom and chucks it into the bin next to my bed. He lies back next to me and I snuggle into him, running my fingers back and forth across his chest, gently tugging on the smattering of light brown hair. We both drift off to sleep in the early hours of the morning.

———

I wake alone the next morning and I feel a little sad until I see a note on his pillow with a sunflower. I can't help but smile that he remembered sunflowers are my favourite flower.

MACKENZIE,
YOU LOOKED SO BEAUTIFUL SLEEPING. I DIDN'T
WANT TO WAKE YOU.
I WILL CALL YOU THIS AFTERNOON. I'D LOVE TO
SPEND THE EVENING WITH YOU.
CLINT

Rolling over onto my back, there's a huge smile on my face and I get excited thinking about seeing Clint again tonight. My girly bits tingle just thinking about a repeat performance from last night. I roll onto my side, smiling and fall back to sleep.

A few hours later, I wake when I hear a noise outside my bedroom window. I peek through the timber blinds but I can't see anything. I climb out of bed, head to the bathroom, and run myself a bath. While the tub is filling, I grab a bottle of wine out of the fridge. *It's 5:00 p.m. somewhere.* I soak in the tub to ease my muscles; sore from last night's extracurricular activities, I ache all over.

Reaching for my Kindle, I lose myself in my book, *Break Open* by A.M. Gillham. It's an Aussie version of

Sons of Anarchy and these guys are hot and the story is addictive. I eventually realise the water is cold and I'm pruned. This soak was just what I needed; I feel so relaxed right now. Grabbing my fluffy purple bath sheet, I dry off. I'm in a lazy mood so after I hang my towel up I grab another glass of wine and jump back into bed with my Kindle. I must have fallen asleep again because when I wake up, Clint is sitting on the black and grey chair in the corner of my room. I shit myself, as I wasn't expecting anyone to be here.

"Damn, Clint, you scared the shit out of me," I scold, holding my hands to my chest to calm the erratic beating of my heart.

"Sorry, Sweetcheeks." He smiles. "You looked so beautiful sleeping, I didn't want to disturb you."

"It's all good. I just wasn't expecting anyone to be in here when I woke up. Wanna come join me?" I pull the covers back, raising my eyebrows seductively as I reveal that I am still naked from my bath.

His eyes light up. "Shit, had I know you were naked, I would've joined you as soon as I got here. " He quickly strips off his green cargo shorts and charcoal grey T-shirt before jumping onto the bed. He grabs my face and kisses me; I can feel this kiss all the way down to the bottom of my toes. We don't make it to dinner, or breakfast, or lunch the next day. Man, does Clint have some stamina. Thankfully, I have Sunday to recover before college on Monday.

———

Over the next few weeks, Clint and I become insepara-
ble, spending all our free time together. He and I get
along really well together, I just wish he and Sarah got
on. He's always putting her down, and then he snaps at
me when I defend her; not sure what the issue there is.

One Friday after class, Clint and I stopped in at the
Duck for an end of week drink. While I grab a booth,
Clint heads to the bar to get us a jug of beer. I've just sat
down when I get a text.

SARAH – *Yo bitch, girls nite 2 nite. I'll be at
yours at 7*

ME – *Bestest idea you have ever had. See you
then XO*

SARAH – *Whatevs. See you soon XO*

Putting my phone back in my bag, I look up to see
Clint walking across the bar and I can't help but smile.
He really is good looking and he only has eyes for me. I
feel special when I'm with him. He places the mugs and
jug down before pouring us each a beer. While he is
pouring, I tell him about tonight, "Sarah just texted me
and we are having a girls' night tonight, so I'll have to get
going after this jug."

Clint stares at me. "What about me? You just going to
leave me high and dry?" He takes a sip of beer before
adding, "You are such a fucking selfish bitch at times
Mackenzie." He finishes his beer, before slamming it

down on the table, making everything rattle. He grabs the jug and refills his mug.

I'm dumbfounded by his actions, one minute I'm checking him out and feeling good, the next I start to question everything. I finish my beer and tell Clint I'll see him over the weekend.

Sarah and I have a great night together, as we always do. We dance for hours, laugh and drink way too many cocktails; it's never a dull night when Sarah and I get together.

Late Saturday arvo, still feeling worse for wear, Clint comes over. He walks in and I smile. "Hey, baby, how was your day?"

"You look like shit."

"Well hello to you too. Sarah and I had a great night, thanks for asking."

"Don't be smart with me."

"Looks like someone got out on the wrong side of the bed this morning. What's crawled up your ass?" I walk over to him and wrap my arms around his waist for a cuddle. He shoves me aside and sits on my couch. Shaking my head, I snarikily say, "Please sit down." I walk into the kitchen and I grab us a beer each, I pass Clint his as I sit down on the opposite end of the couch. Taking a sip, I look over at him, "Are you okay? You seem off."

"Just leave it Mackenzie, I'm fine," he snarls. He finishes his beer and slams the empty on the coffee table before abruptly standing up. "I can't be around you when you're like this, Sarah is such a bad influence on you. I knew I shouldn't have let you go out with her. I'm out of here." He stands up. "Later, bitch." Slamming the front door on his way out.

Open-mouthed and shocked, I sit staring at the front door. *What the hell was that all about?* This is the second time he has acted like this, I'm not sure I like this version of Clint.

5

CLINT

Oh My God, sex with Mackenzie is out of this world. Who knew she was such a devil in the sack? I really picked a wild one this time. I can't help but smile when I think back over this past weekend. I snuck out early Friday but not before leaving a note and flower for my girl. I wanted to give her some time alone, I'm nice like that.

I couldn't stay away, right now, I'm peeking in her window, watching her sleep. I slip, knocking over the crate I'm standing on. The noise startles her awake. I manage to duck out of sight, just as she lifts up the timber blinds to have a look around. I stay hidden until I hear the water start to run in the bathroom. I take this chance to head home and freshen up before I come back over.

Later that afternoon, I let myself into Mackenzie's apartment with the key I took when I left this morning. She is back in bed sleeping, so I sit on the chair in the corner and again, I watch her sleep. She is so beautiful, I smile to myself and I think how happy we are going to be together. My cock is starting to get hard staring at her. She starts to stir and when she opens her eyes, I frighten her.

God she's beautiful when she sleeps.

She pulls the covers back and she's naked.

Fuck Me!

My eyes rake over her beautiful body, pausing at her amazing tits before I look to her face; she is winking at me seductively.

I quickly strip off my clothes and jump onto the bed. I grab her face and passionately kiss her, pulling back to stare into her beautiful green eyes. I quickly roll on a condom and pin her to the bed. I fuck her hard and fast. We spend the next twenty-four hours in bed and they are the best hours of my life so far.

The next few weeks are amazing. Mackenzie was meant for me and I for her. I'm so glad I found her. I thought Laura was the one when I met her in high school, but her leaving me was the best thing to happen.

She is *nothing* compared to Mackenzie...My Sweetcheeks.

———

I spend as much time as possible with her, only letting her spend time with her best friend, Sarah, when she begs me. I really don't like that bitch, but I always get what I want, so I guess letting her out now and again will be okay.

Later in the term, we are paired together for another assignment in Michele's class. This time, we have to create an all-inclusive tour and come up with the marketing plan; again we kick ass. Mackenzie and I are a great team, in and out of the bedroom.

6

KENZIE

THE JUNE LONG WEEKEND FOR THE QUEENS'S birthday is fast approaching and it's time for Sarah and my annual, long weekend, girls' getaway. We take turns arranging the weekend away; this year it's her turn to plan it. I always get scared when it's her year as she can be pretty wild at times; which is one of the many reasons I love her so much.

We started this tradition when we were thirteen; somehow we managed to convince our parents to do this for us. This year's will be amazeballs; as for the first time there will be no parents. We really were lucky to have parents who were happy to do this for us. I have no idea what she has planned this year and that scares me. Sarah can be crazy when left unsupervised. Even though I'm scared, I'm also super excited to see what craziness she comes up with.

Grabbing my phone, I text her to discuss the finer details, like what to pack and maybe get a hint on where we are going but she is currently locked up tighter than

Fort Knox, and the not knowing is really frustrating me. I'm such a pushover; I always cave and tell her what we are doing and where we are going.

ME – *Yo bitch, what do I pack for the weekend? And where are we going?*

SARAH – *Togs and winter woolies*
SARAH – *PS. Not telling*

ME – *WFT woman? That gives me no clue whatsoever*

SARAH – *I know :P I'll pick you up Thursday afternoon after class. I'm really looking forward to this weekend. It feels like forever since I have seen you. You are all loved up with Clint. You know, if you two get super serious, he is going to have to learn to share*

Sarah's text gets me thinking. Have I been neglecting everyone? I reread it to make sure I read it right. Am I so wrapped up in Clint that I have become one of those girls?

ME – *I have not been that bad. I can't wait for this weekend.*

SARAH – *Me neither. Love you XoXoX*

ME - *Love you too XoXoX*

I throw my phone on the couch and Clint waltzes in, he looks pissed off. Walking into the kitchen, I give him a kiss on the cheek. "Hey, baby."

He storms past me, shoving me out of the way; I bang my hip on the corner of the breakfast bar and wince in pain. He plonks himself down on my charcoal grey, suede, L-shaped couch; he grabs my phone as it was digging into his leg. He looks down and glances at the screen. "Who the fuck are you saying, 'love you' to?" He air quotes love you.

"It's just Sarah. We are finalizing our girls' weekend."

"What girls' weekend?" he spits.

"I told you, Sarah and I go away every June long weekend."

"Well, where are you going?" he shouts at me,

"No idea, it's her year to plan. All I know is I need to pack togs and winter woolies."

"Well, I don't want you going!" he shouts. "You never asked me if you could go." He slams his fist down on the coffee table.

"Excuse me?" I turn to face him with a shocked expression on my face "You are not the boss of me, and if I want to go away with my friend, I will." I state matter-of-factly, with my hands on my hips.

"Like hell you are, you belong with me." He slams his fist down on the timber coffee table again and throws my phone. It slides across the monochrome rug onto the floor in front of the TV cabinet.

"I what?" I stare at him dumbfounded.

"You heard me, bitch, you're mines and mines only." He spits through his teeth, in a tone I have never heard him use before. My body tenses, I start to get a horrible feeling, as fear courses through my veins.

"I am no ones, and with an attitude like that, I think you can leave." I bend down, pick up my phone, slide it into my pocket, and walk back to the kitchen to grab a glass of wine for myself.

Clint jumps off the couch, grabbing me by my upper arms, gripping tightly, slamming me up against the wall. The very wall that we first made out against, all those months ago, making the pictures rattles. He grabs my face roughly, squeezing my chin tightly, he glares into my eyes, and through clenched teeth spits, "You are mines, Sweetcheeks, and I say you are not going away with that slut." Raising his right hand, he backhands me, his hand colliding with my left cheek. My head slams back into the wall with a thud. He let's go of me and I slide down the wall. I start to cry.

My head is throbbing, I rub the spot that hit the wall, with such force that I was sure the pictures were going to fall down this time. I'm scared out of my wits; I look up towards Clint, who is hovering above me. "I...I think you should go."

"Whatever, Mackenzie." He storms out slamming the kitchen door as he goes. I hear him yell, "And there's no way you are going away next weekend!"

Sitting on the floor, I hug my knees and begin to sob. After I don't know how long, I stand up, shaking like a leaf. I lock all the doors and slowly make my way to the bathroom. I run a hot shower to try and wash away everything. I slide down the cold tiles, the hot water cascading over my body. Wrapping my arms around my knees, I sit there and cry, resting my forehead on my knees. When the water runs cold, I climb out, dry myself off and climb into bed.

Lying in bed, I stare at the ceiling; my mind starts thinking about everything.

Have I changed since dating Clint?

Have I neglected everyone?

Why has Clint changed?

I don't understand this change in him. I'm so confused. I start to doubt everything that I know about Clint, about myself, about everything. I start to cry again, and eventually, I cry myself to sleep.

———

Before I know it, my alarm goes off. My alarm song of choice at the moment is *Barbie Girl* by Aqua. That song puts a smile one my face, and for a moment, I forget about all of my worries. Jumping out of bed, I head to the bathroom to get ready for college. Looking in the mirror, I notice a huge purple bruise on my left cheek where Clint hit me last night. Gently I run my finger along my cheek, and then I notice marks on my arms from when he grabbed me. I gasp in shock, I cannot go out in public like this. Grabbing my phone I ring in sick and leave a voice-mail for Sarah, cancelling our lunch date; we were going to meet up in between classes today.

Feeling pretty shitty, and not up for doing anything, I change into my comfy grey Bonds trackies and LA Kings jersey. Heading to the kitchen, I make myself a coffee and plonk myself on the couch. I go over everything that has happened in the last twenty-four hours to try and make sense out of it.

I'm so confused right now.

Making myself another coffee, I grab my Kindle and try to lose myself in my book but I can't concentrate. I keep reading the same line over and over. Eventually, I give up reading and turn the TV on. I end up watching watch some random cooking show.

A few hours later, I wake up to banging on my front door; my heart freezes thinking that Clint is here. I realise that I'm not sure I want to see him. Cautiously, I walk over to the window and peek through the timber blinds, seeing Sarah standing there with two coffees and a brown paper bag. She must have left work to come see me. She is in her black slacks and a white sleeveless silk top with a big flowey bow at the front. I unlock the door an open it. "Bitch, there better be an orange poppy seed muffin in there to go with my caramel latte."

Sarah is smiling but her face immediately drops, "Kenz, what the fuck happened to you face?"

Subconsciously, I reach up and rub my finger across my cheek; I completely forgot about the bruise. "I, ah, bumped into the kitchen door."

"Nice try, want try and improve that lie?" She pushes past me and comes inside. I wince when she bumps my upper arms, thankfully she doesn't notice. Sarah sits on the couch, tucks her legs under her, and she places the coffees and muffins on the coffee table. I feel her staring at me. Watching me like a hawk as I walk over and sit next to her. Finally, I look over at her and I can't hold back the tears. She pulls me into a hug and gently rubs my back in circles, just like she used to when we were younger. She whispers, "Shhhh."

Leaning into her hug, I cry in her arms for a while. I sit back, sniffle, and wipe my nose on my sleeve as I tug away from her; earning myself a look of disgust from Sarah; she hates when I wipe my nose like that. She's staring at me with raised eyebrows, waiting for my explanation. Sitting back on the couch, I snuggle into the corner with my purple nana blankie. "It's nothing, Sarah, just leave it."

"Kenz, that is not nothing." She points to my face. "Did Clint do this?"

Staring into my lap, the tears start to fall again, "Sar, he's changing. He's not the guy I started dating at the beginning of term. He's always so angry, he appears everywhere I go, he's always waiting for me here. Apparently I'm his, and the latest is, he doesn't want me going away with you this weekend for some reason. I told him I'm going whether he likes it or not. That's when he shoved me against the wall and hit me."

"That fucker." She jumps up and startles me. "Shit, sorry, chicky." She sits down next to me and wraps me into a hug, "Listen to me, Mackenzie." She pulls back to stare directly at me.

"Wow, you called me Mackenzie. You only do that when I am in trouble."

"Mackenzie Merlot, you listen to me and you listen goodly. You need to think long and hard as to whether you want to be with Clint. You have changed. We never see you anymore and he is always with you, like always. I was actually surprised he wasn't here now, but after seeing this." She spins her finger around my face. "I know why."

"But..."

"No buts, lady, you need to look out for you. I seriously think this weekend away is just what you need." Sarah jumps up excitedly and squeals in excitement, "I have an idea, let's blow off the rest of the week and take off now. You need to get away to clear your head and me being the uber, awesome bestie will happily accompany you earlier. Plus work is slow and I'm totally bored out of my brain."

I sniff and wipe my nose on my sleeve, again, earning another scowl from Sarah. "Okay, that actually sounds really great. I think extra time away is just what I need."

"Squee, I'm so excited," she squeals.

"Hang on, we will have to wait till tomorrow, as I have a presentation due..."

"Well that sucks donkey balls," Sarah interrupts me but I put my hand up to silence her.

"If you let me finish, my presentation is due first thing but I should be done by eleven. You can then pick me up from college, like we planned, and we can leave straight from there."

"Woo-freakin-hoo. Okay, I'm going to head home make a few changes to our weekend plans and pack. You finish your assignment and I will see you out outside the college tomorrow at eleven. No later, or I'm stalking in there and dragging your ass out."

"Thanks, Sar, I can always count on you to make me feel better."

"Happy to help, Kenz. That's what best friends are for. Make sure you text me if you finish earlier."

Sarah and I chat for a while and it's just like old times. Before she leaves, she gives me a crash make-up course to cover the bruise on my face. I suck when it comes to make-up, so I really appreciate this help. It reminds me of our makeovers we used to do when we were twelve.

A few hours later, we walk arm in arm out to her car, it feels good to be with her again. She gives me a big hug and tells me to call her if I need anything. I wave as she drives off; I check the letterbox on my way back inside and get excited when there is nothing. *No bills*, I think to myself.

Feeling a lot more relaxed after my visit with Sarah; I head back inside. After locking the front door I turn around I see Clint standing in the kitchen. I freeze and stumble back into the door.

"Hey, Sweetcheeks."

Hesitating a little, I reply, "Hey, C." I race over to the couch, sit down with my purple blankie that Nan knitted for me, cover my legs, and I curl up into myself. I feel really uncomfortable having him here. "What are you doing here?"

"I missed you in class and I was worried, Sweetcheeks."

"I'm fine, I just wasn't feeling very well this morning. Sarah stopped by with a coffee and a muffin. I'm feeling a little better now." I take a deep breath a quickly add, "She and I have actually decided to extend our weekend away, we are now leaving tomorrow after my presentation."

"I thought I told you that you are not going," he snarls through clenched teeth. I notice his hands, fisting by his side.

"And I told you that I was, this isn't up for discussion. If you have a problem with it, then I think you need to leave."

Clint grabs the dish rack throwing it against the wall; cutlery, glass and plate fragments fly everywhere. I sit there open-mouthed and frozen; my heart racing with terror. I'm unable to move for fear that he will pound on me next. Fortunately for me, he turns punches the wall near the kitchen door and storms out. Before he's out the door he yells over his shoulder, "Fuck you, bitch!" and storms off.

I sit there on the couch in shock. After a few minutes, I get up and lock all the doors; I also put the deadlock on. I lean against the front door, close my eyes, and take a deep breath. I look to the kitchen and see the enormous mess that Clint has caused. Shaking my head, I walk to the kitchen and begin to clean up the devastation after his outburst.

Walking past the stereo, I turn it on and crank the music to drown out all the white noise and any thoughts that keep appearing in my head right now. Grabbing the dustpan and brush, clean up the mess and add new cups and plates to my shopping list.

Girls Just Wanna Have Fun by Cindy Lauper comes on. Normally I would sing at the top of my lungs and shake my booty around the room, but I'm too frazzled right now. If that song doesn't excite me, then I really am in a funk.

With the weight of the world on my shoulders, I head to my room to start to packing for my trip away with Sarah. While packing, I forget about all my Clint worries. As soon as I'm finished, I lie on my bed and pull up the covers. I start to think about what I'm going to do and I start to cry again. I don't have a friggin clue on how to handle this. On one hand, I think I'm falling in love with Clint, but on the other, I'm scared to be alone with him.

I let out a frustrated sigh and shout, "Fuuuuck!"

Kicking off the comforter, I head into the bathroom to clean my teeth. Looking up into the mirror I don't recognise the girl reflecting back and it's not because of the huge, now almost blackish purple bruise. I feel lost. Alone. Scared. I finish cleaning my teeth, and before heading back to bed I recheck all the doors are locked.

Once everything is secured I climb back into bed. Grabbing my Kindle from the nightstand, I read for a bit to lose myself. However I can't concentrate, I keep thinking about what I'm going to do.

Eventually, I drift off to sleep.

Around 2:00 a.m., I startle awake and feel like someone is watching me. I turn on the bedside lamp but my room is empty. I shake my head and tell myself I'm going crazy. I lie back down and fall asleep again but I still feel like someone is watching.

7

CLINT

AFTER A LONG DAY, I HEAD OVER TO MACKENZIE'S and when I get there, I'm in a pissy mood. Waltzing into her apartment, I storm past her, shoving her into the bench. She smiles, but I'm too pissed for niceties, so I sink down onto her couch to finally relax. *A head job would be great right now.* Her phone is digging into my leg so I grab it, glancing down to see a text ending with, 'love you.'

Now I'm really pissed. My mood darkening by the minute. Why is my Sweetcheeks saying "love you" to someone when she hasn't even told me yet? I bet the bitch is cheating on me.

Thank fuck it's only that slut Sarah messaging her about a girls' weekend, but I don't fucking think so. She is not going away with that tramp; she is such a bad influence AND to not know where they are going, that's just crazy.

What if I need to reach her?

Why is she not thinking about me in all of this?

She goes on and on and on about this fucking weekend, I've told her several times that she isn't going, why isn't she listening to me? Why is she being like this? I can't believe she is talking back to me; she's never done this before, I'm seriously going to loose my shit in a minute.

"Like hell you are, you belong with me." She has really pissed me off now. She's still back chatting so I slam my fist down on the coffee table.

The final straw is when she shakes her head at me and tells me that she isn't mine. Think again, bitch; you are mines...forever. I snap and slam the bitch against the wall. I roughly grab her face and stare directly into her eyes and spit, "You are mines, and I say you are not going away with that slut."

With the rage simmering, I slap her across the cheek and her head slams back into the wall. I let go of her and she slides down the wall, crying. I fucking hate when bitches cry. She rubs her head and looks up at me with sad, puppy dog eyes and asks me to leave, as if I want to fucking stay here anyway.

I throw my hands up in the air. "Whatever, Mackenzie."

I storm through her kitchen, slamming the door on my way out. I'm halfway down the stairs when I bellow, "And there's no way you are going away next weekend!"

Jumping into my car, I throw it into gear, and drive home.

———

The next day Mackenzie isn't in class, this is the first class this year she has missed. I start to worry about my Sweetcheeks. I decide after this class, I'll head to her place to see if she's okay; after all, I'm a caring and nice boyfriend. I think I'll get her some sunflowers on my way over too, flowers always cheer chicks up...and open their legs.

Pulling up at her apartment complex, I realise I forgot to get the flowers but they are soon forgotten when I see that slut Sarah's car out front. I head down the driveway when I hear her and Sarah walking out. I quickly race up the back stairs, the door is unlocked so I let myself in and wait. A few minutes later my Sweetcheeks comes in the front door, I inwardly sigh when I realise that she is okay and nothing terrible is wrong.

She's blabbering on about going away and I start to fume. Looking at her dumbfounded, does she not remember our conversation last night? She continues to back chat me, I'm a little turned on by her feistiness. I unclench my fists, which I didn't realise I had clenched. I turn and grab the dish rack, and with all the anger coursing through my veins, I throw it against the wall. That stops the bitch in her tracks, she sits there frozen as I punch the wall in anger. It hurts like a bitch but I am too pissed off to care right now. I roar, "Fuck you bitch!" and I storm out.

I get in my car, and like most times when I am pissed off, I drive. I drive around for hours. It's the middle of the night and I find myself back at Mackenzie's place. I try and unlock the door but she has it deadlocked and I can't get in; Goddamn *it*.

Walking around to her bedroom window, I peek in; my beautiful Mackenzie is sound asleep, the moonlight glistening on her silky soft skin, illuminating her gorgeous face.

Seeing her sleeping, looking so alluring, makes my cock harden. I walk over to her front steps, stroking myself through my cargos. I lean against the railing and yank my cock out as I continue to tug and pull on my shaft.

Closing my eyes, I imagine it's my beautiful girl's hand wrapped around my engorged throbbing cock. After a few more strokes, I explode all over her steps, with a contented sigh, marking my territory. Slipping my now limp cock back in my cargos, I blow a kiss to my girl and whisper, "Sweet dreams, Sweetcheeks," before quietly walking back to my car and driving home.

8

KENZIE

Setting my alarm earlier than usual, I hop up and use the techniques Sarah showed me yesterday to cover the bruise on my cheek. I also wear a long-sleeved silk shirt to cover my arms. I get to town early so I grab a coffee from Java Lava and go over my presentation one more time.

My presentation goes extremely well and I get 97.5 out of 100, the highest in the class so far, YAY ME. Seriously, I am digging this course and my lecturer Michele is amazing. She really knows her stuff, hence why she probably started the college and has turned it into a world-renowned institution.

She's become a great mentor to me also, not only with school stuff but personal stuff too. I thank her and mention that I'll be away for the rest of the week as I'm heading away with my bestie for the long weekend. She tells that's a good idea and to have a great time and I quote, "Don't do anything that will get you kidnapped, killed or arrested, you're too pretty for jail." She is seriously the coolest person I have ever met. We both laugh as I turn and leave.

Skipping out of the building, I literally, skip into Jordan, again. He's just as hot; if not hotter than the first time I bumped into him. I'd know, with all the times that I've bumped into him since college started. "Shit, dude, I'm so sorry. You must think I'm such a klutz. This is like the fifth time I have run into you this year,"

"Actually, it's about the tenth but who's counting?"

"Obviously you are, Jordan," I laugh, pushing my hair behind my ear.

He starts to laugh too but looks concerned, he reaches out to touch my cheek. "Mackenzie, what happened to your face?"

"Shit," I mumble, I thought I managed to hide the bruise with my make-up this morning, but I guess up this close it's hard to hide. "I, ah, ran into a door." Just as I say that, I see Sarah pull up and I thank her for being on time. "That's my ride, I'll catch ya later. " I run towards Sarah's green Toyota Corolla and jump in, "Hey, bitch, ready to ride?"

"Umm, who's that Hottie McHottie you were just chatting to?"

"That's Jordan, I think he goes here or works nearby. I keep running into him. Like literally running into him, he must think I'm such a klutz."

"Please, the way he watched your ass as you ran to the car, I bet he's thinking about how he can get you on your back and be buried balls deep inside of you, while you scream his name as you have the best orgasm of your life."

"Sarah!" I shout and whack her arm, "You are so crude and FYI, Jordan does not think of me like that." I look out the window and see him staring at us; I smile at him and wave goodbye. "Besides, I'm with Clint."

Sarah doesn't acknowledge that comment, she indicates and we take off but her comment about Jordan liking me sets my mind racing, giving me butterflies; I can't help but smile as I think about Jordan...great, now there's another item to add to my ever-growing list of concerns.

9

JORDAN

I'm so glad that I have a late start today; I'm really not in the mood for adulting today. Stopping at the corner store, I pick up a packet of Chicken Twisties and a Diet Coke. *The breakfast of champions.*

Just as I am about to open the glass doors, my arm is grabbed, and I'm flung around. "Back off, asshole, she is my girlfriend." I look up into the wild eyes of the dickwad himself, Clint.

"Excuse me?" I growl.

"I said, back off, she is my girlfriend and I don't appreciate you ogling her like a piece of meat. She is mines."

"Okay, dude, whatever." I shrug free and walk inside to see Mike waiting for me. As I'm walking up the stairs, I start thinking about Mackenzie, again. Whenever I think about her, I can't help but smile. She is the most beautiful girl I have ever laid eyes upon. Today her long blonde hair is down, framing her gorgeous face, her lips are a cherry red colour. What I wouldn't give to kiss those lips, but I can't as she is dating that dickwad, Clint; lucky bastard.

When she crashed into me, again, I inwardly smiled, like I do each time she bumps into me. She says something about being a klutz but I'm lost in her green eyes, sparkling in the sunlight. *God, she is beautiful.*

I can't believe I turn into a blabbering tool when I'm around her. Did I really just confess to counting the number of times she's bumped into me? Why do I become pathetic around her? Thankfully, she just laughs at me. She has the most amazing laugh, and if you get her going, she snorts; it's really cute.

Glancing over at her, I see a bruise on her cheek. Without thinking, I lift my hand to brush the bruise, gently caressing her cheek. When I ask her what happened, her face changes from her happy smile to sadness and hesitation. I quickly pull my hand back and wonder who did this to her? I bet it was that douche she is dating.

She lies to me but before I can reply or ask her any more questions, a car pulls up out front and she says, "That's my ride, I'll catch ya later."

I stare at her ass as she skips off, her denim jeans clinging to her perfect tight butt. As usual, my cock starts to twitch when I watch her ass as she walks away.

Walking over to Mike I slap him on the back. "Hey, asswipe, how's it hanging?"

Mike grabs his crotch and replies, "A little to the left." We both burst out laughing. "What did 'I'm a dickwad' grab you for?"

"He told me to stay away from his girlfriend, she bumped into me, again, on her way out."

"If she was my girl, I'd tell you to stay away too. She is mighty fine if I do say so myself."

"As if you'd stand a chance with her. Besides, I ran into her first therefore as part of our aforementioned bro-code, which was established when we were ten, I get first dibs," I smugly reply before quickly adding, "Not that I'm interested or anything."

"Right, dude, not interested. Come on or we will be late, and Mr. Denon will be pissed."

Is it that obvious that I'm interested in Kenzie? I think to myself as we head into the lecture hall. I've been interested in her since the first time she bumped into me...but I missed my chance. Now she's with that asshat.

10

KENZIE

Sarah and I are driving back into town after six glorious days at *Peppers Ruffles Lodge & Spa* in the Gold Coast Hinterland. We wine, we dined, we drank, we pampered and most of all, we chillaxed; it was just what the doctor called for. Looking over to Sarah, I smile, "Sar, thanks for extending our weekend. It was just what I needed."

"I'm happy to help, besides this has been the best six days. I think we need to extend our long weekend, into a weeklong getaway from now on. I haven't felt this relaxed in forever, and I must also add, you look much more relaxed too."

"I am, and if I'm honest, I haven't thought of Clint once. I'm such a bad girlfriend,"

"You are not a bad girlfriend." She, hesitates, and then adds, "Can I be honest with you?"

"When have you not been honest with me?"

"True." Reaching over she squeezes my hand, takes a deep breath, "There's something about Clint that irks me. I can't put my finger on it. Are you sure he's the one you want to be with? What about that other hottie?"

I know she is referring to Jordan but I can't let on about my feelings towards him, she would never let it go. "Which hottie?"

"The one you keep bumping into, Justin?"

"You mean Jordan?" My cheeks flush when I say his name and think about him. "What about him?"

"Well, for starters, you just turned fifty shades of pink when I mentioned his name just now, and this past week, you have spoken about him and not Clint, who IS your boyfriend."

"I did not," Pausing, I add, "Did I?"

"Ya ha, you did. Look, if you want to be with Clint, I'll support you. And if you want to be with Jordan, I'll also support you. Just promise me you'll think about this, I want you to be happy. I want me bestie back. You haven't been you lately, except for the past six days. I finally saw my, Kenzie, this past week."

"I promise to think about it. But truthfully, I'm totally confused right now." Lifting my feet up, I rest them on the dashboard, lean forward, and sigh, "Why can't we live at the spa forever. Be pampered everyday, drink margaritas, and chillax?"

"Well, for one, we aren't billionaires..."

"You just about are. You're lucky your dad is uber rich. I know I have my inheritance, but you literally have no worries in the world."

"No, that's Daddy, not me, and I refuse to mooch off him, but I know what you mean. I work just as hard as anyone else, but if Daddy wants to spoil me, and you by default, I'm not going to say no."

"And that right there is why I love you. You have such a generous heart. I'm so glad you guys moved in all those years ago. Sarah, you are my sister from another mister and I'm so honoured to call you my best friend."

"Naw, I love you too, Kenz. Even though people always mistake us for lovers when we go away together."

In unison, we both shout. "Bitch sistas for life!" Before, we both burst out laughing.

"Seriously, Sar, thanks for this week away. I have to say the highlight for me was our sunset horse ride. That was the most spectacular sunset, I have ever seen." Remembering the sky, I can't help but smile; it was filled with magnificent oranges and pinks; very romantic, especially with the hamper of bubbly and antipasto that Sarah arranged for us.

"I'm happy to assist. I think the highlight for me was the dinner and drinks that first night. I've never eaten such an amazing meal. That creamy garlic mushroom sauce was to die for and the chocolate lava cake was the bomb". *My mouth waters as I remember how amazing that meal was, the word foodgasm comes to mind.*

"Sarah, you really out did yourself with this retreat. Pretty sure that my credit card will hate me this month and I'm positive that my liver needs a holiday, but my body feels amazing. I also have pretty nails; and pretty nails make everything perfect." *I silently add, my mind is relaxed; albeit confused as to what I am going to do but I am relaxed.*

It's almost 8:00 p.m. when Sarah drops me off. I flick

on the lights and dump my bags on the floor, deciding that I'll deal with them later. Grabbing a bottle of water, I sit on the couch and smile, as I think about the last six days; they were totally amazing. Sarah really out did herself this year. Undecided on what I am going to do, I change into my PJ's and climb into bed. Even though it was a relaxing week, I'm shattered.

———

Before I know it, my alarm is blaring and its time to get up and head to college. My alarm song choice at the moment is *Israel's Sun* by Silverchair, the base get me up and going each morning. Jumping out of bed, I head to the bathroom and take a long hot shower. After putting my hair up into a ponytail, I forgo make-up, as the bruises have faded but I do add a touch of lip gloss. I decide to wear the new sundress I bought while away, from this cute little boutique up in the hinterland. Looking in the mirror, I decide to add a jacket, since the bruises on my arms haven't yet completely faded. The dress is black and white with spaghetti straps and comes to mid-calf. I pair it with my Nine West black wedge sandals. Looking at the time, I realise I'm running late, so I make a mad dash to the bus and get there just in time. As I take my seat on the bus, I sigh, no coffee for me this morning, ugh.

As I'm racing into the building, I see Jordan across the street. I smile, wave, and wait for him. He crosses the street, saying "Hey, Mackenzie, did you and your friend have a nice trip?"

"Oh My God! It was seriously amazing. We tried

every treatment on the spa menu. I don't think there is one spot on my body that hasn't been pampered. The cocktails were amazeballs and the food was to die for. I think I gained 10kg."

I notice his eyes rake over my body, I feel those damn butterflies appear and I can't help but smile. "You still look amazing to me, and you also look a lot more relaxed then the last time I saw you."

I blush at his comment, but it also causes the butterflies in my tummy to intensify and flutter. He looks at me with compassion and kindness, it makes my smile grow.

"That door must have hit you pretty hard," he snidely adds.

I look up at him, and I'm pretty sure he knows the door story is fake. "Yeah, it did. I'm such a klutz, as you know, with all the times I'm falling for you."

"Falling for me, hey?"

"Umm, I meant into you." I feel my cheeks heat and turn a shade of pink, I look towards the ground in embarrassment.

We walk into the building together, and I'm laughing when I look up, I see Clint. He looks over and smiles but as soon as he sees me with Jordan, his expression instantly changes to rage. He stalks over to us and shoves Jordan in the chest, "Dude, I told you last week, she's mines. Now get the fuck away from my girl." He pauses, before looking directly at me and snarling. "She. Is. Mines."

I look to Jordan and he is staring at Clint. Jordan then gazes towards me and I shake my head, subliminally telling him to let it go. "I'll catch you later, Mackenzie, glad you had a great time away."

Sighing in relief, he walks around Clint, up the stairs, and I see him walk into the lecture room on the right. *Huh, I guess he is a student here.*

Clint grabs my arm roughly and drags me towards the street, and then down the alley near the college. "Ouch, you're hurting me, Clint."

Managing to yank my arm free, I step back, rubbing where he was squeezing. He shouts, "What the fuck is going on with you and that asshole?"

"W..w..wwwhat?" I stammer, looking at him dumbfounded.

"Don't play dumb with me, Sweetcheeks, you were fucking him this weekend, weren't you?"

"What the hell?" I yell, "You know I went away with Sarah, why would you even say that?"

"Don't lie to me, you little bitch. You chicks are all the same. Get what you want and then leave. Everyone always leaves me."

"Clint, I don't have to put up with this." Spinning, I turn to leave, but he grabs my arm, nearly ripping it out of its socket when he turns me around to face him.

"You are mines and mines alone. "

"NO, I am not yours!" I pull my arm free and stalk away. After a few steps, I turn back and point directly at him; I stare into his soulless brown eyes. "You know what Clint? I'm done. I can't do this anymore. I don't like the person you've become, and most of all, I don't like the person I've become. I wish you the best." I turn around and I walk back into the college.

Of course, being Monday morning, Clint and I have our first class together but he doesn't show, I sigh in relief. I find it really hard to concentrate in class, and normally, it's my favourite.

After class, I head to the Java Lava Café for a much-needed coffee. Having just placed my order, I'm digging in my monstrous Guess handbag for my wallet, when the person behind me says, "And add a hazelnut latte, full cream milk, and a double chocolate brownie to that order too, please." They hand over a twenty to pay. I spin around ready to seethe and see Jordan standing there, smiling. His smile stops me in my tracks and then he winks at me. Pretty sure my ovaries went boom.

After staring at him for a few seconds, I smile. "You didn't have to do that."

"It's my pleasure, Mackenzie, but there is an ulterior motive to me buying you a coffee."

"Here we go, what's your condition?"

"You have to have it with me." He winks at me again before smiling smugly at me.

Ovaries: boom...again.

Cheekily, I reply, "I guess I can lower myself to have a coffee with you," winking as I walk past him to the end counter to wait for our coffees.

We grab our food and drinks, and head to a table by the window. Grabbing my coffee, I lift the lid take a deep breath of the caffeine goodness that I am about to enjoy and take a sip. My eyes close and I savour the flavour, letting out a little pleasurable moan. When I open my eyes again, Jordan is staring at me; the look in his eyes is intense but electric. "Who knew drinking coffee could be so erotic?"

My neck and cheeks immediately heat, I lower my head in embarrassment. He reaches over and lifts my chin; I feel a spark as soon as his fingers touch my skin, leaving my chin tingling and warm. He looks directly into my eyes. "Don't be embarrassed, that was the hottest thing I've ever seen, Kenz."

"Umm, that doesn't make me feel any better." Jordan lets go of my chin, and I feel naked and alone, missing his touch. He grabs his coffee, and copies what I just did. I burst out laughing. He opens his eyes and looks at me, trying to contain his laugh, but he can't hold back. We are both laughing and before I know it I'm snorting. He is laughing at me for snorting and it becomes one vicious laugh/snort cycle, as it usually does the first time I snort around someone.

We eventually compose ourselves and manage to have a normal conversation, with no awkward silences. It turns my shitty morning around. He tells me about his course and how he hopes it will lead to a job managing a bar. Jordan is so passionate about beer. It's a total turn on, seeing him so enthusiastic about it. At one point, I zone out and imagine him pinning me to the couch, kissing the life out of me. Yep, I'm going to need a change of undies, as that mental make out session was hot.

As we are finishing up, I look out the window and see Clint glaring at me from the corner. If looks could kill, I'd be dead right now, as would Jordan and everyone in a five-kilometer radius. Jordan notices the change in me and he looks to where I'm staring, and then looks back to me, "Is everything okay with you two?"

I look at him, then I look back to where Clint was standing but he's gone. Looking back at Jordan, I feel my eyes start to water. "Ummm, I broke up with him this morning."

"I'm sorry to hear that." He reaches across the table and gently gives my hand a reassuring squeeze.

"He's not the person I thought he was, the way he spoke to you this morning was one of the final straws. I was so embarrassed."

"You have nothing to be embarrassed about, Kenz. He's a douche, plain and simple."

"Don't be like that, you sound just like him. This week away with my friend Sarah, made me realise that I didn't like the person I'd become while I was with him. I didn't like the person he was becoming either. It's for the best," pausing, I add, "I think."

"Well, he's a fool for pushing you away. If you were mine, I'd do everything in my power to keep you happy and smiling." I can't help but smile at that statement. "Much like you are now," he adds.

Again, I blush at his words. "I bet you say that to all the girls."

"Nope, only the pretty ones."

Looking up, I see he is intently staring at me. I smile back at him and think to myself, *he is the kind of guy I need to be dating*. My phone pings with a text, bringing me back to reality. Reaching into my bag, I slide the screen and see it's a text from Sarah.

SARAH – *Morning bitch. Thanks for a great time away. I think our annual weekend needs to become an annual week...but no fucking horses*

I laugh as I read her text. I quickly reply,

ME – *Sounds like a plan...the horses stay*
ME – *I broke up with Clint this morning*

SARAH – *I'll bring wine and choc chip cookie dough, be at yours in an hour. Love you XoXoX*

ME – *it's a date, see you then. Love you too XoXoX*

I look up to see Jordan staring at me. "Sorry, that was Sarah. I just told her Clint and I broke up, and we now have a date with wine and Jerry."

"Jerry?"

"Ben and Jerry's Jerry."

"Righto," he laughs.

"I have to go meet her now, but thanks for the coffee and chat. Next time it's on me," I say as I stand up and clean away our plates and cups.

"On you, hey?"

"Oh My God, not on me on me, but on me, you know my treat"

Jordan laughs, "You are too funny, Kenz, I can't wait to have coffee on you." He winks at me as he says this. My cheeks heat and I giggle like a schoolgirl. Jordan and I walk out of the coffee shop; I head to the bus stop to go home and he goes back to college.

————

Sitting on the bus, I think about my coffee with Jordan; my heart rate increases when I think of his smile. I had a really nice time with him and was so relaxed. Smiling to myself, I remember him calling me Kenz, the way he wraps his tongue around the Z is kind of hot. I'm now imagining other things he can do to me with his tongue and his hands. Clenching my thighs together, I blush when I realise I'm having dirty thoughts on a public bus. My cheeks turn a deeper shade of red and I become hot under the collar.

Deciding to get off the bus a stop early, I duck into the local bottle-o. I'm winning as they have my wine on sale, two for one, so I grab four bottles and race home to chillax and unwind with Sarah. I want to forget all about this morning, well not the coffee with Jordan part.

Placing the wine bottles on the front steps, I notice a stain on them. "I'll clean that off on the weekend," I mumble to myself. I'm digging in my bag for my house keys, when I feel someone behind me. I recognise Clint's cologne, but before I can turn and acknowledge him, he whacks me across the back of the head and I black out.

11

CLINT

THIS PAST WEEK WITHOUT SWEETCHEEKS HAS BEEN tough, I miss her so much. Doesn't she realise that she and I are meant to be together? I can't and will not let her go.

I'm looking forward to today, Mackenzie and I have a class together first thing on Mondays. After class, I'm going to take her to the Dirty Duck, where we are going to get super drunk. Then, I'll take her back to her apartment and fuck her silly. I get hard just thinking about her sweet, sweet pussy.

Looking up, I see her walking in with that asshole that hangs around her like a bad smell, and they are laughing. My blood starts to simmer as I stalk over to them. With all my might, I shove the asshole in the chest, I should pound him into the pavement for laughing with *my* Sweetcheeks.

The pussy has no balls.

He doesn't say anything.

He doesn't fight back.

Pussy.

My blood boils when he looks at my Sweetcheeks and smiles.

Who does this fucker think he is?

I so badly want to beat the shit out of that asshole right at this minute, instead I grab Mackenzie's arm, dragging her towards the street, and down the alley near college. I'm going to find out what the fuck is going on between her and that douche hole, once and for all.

It occurs to me that this weekend she was away with him and not Sarah. Deceitful fucking bitch!

She keeps denying it but the bitch is lying to me, I just know it.

Why do they always lie?

Do I look stupid or something?

Why do they always do this to me?

Reaching out, I roughly grab her, spinning her towards me. I growl between clenched teeth. My blood boiling with fury.

"You are mines and mines alone." I angrily shout.

She pulls away and when she turns back around, our eyes lock; it's magical. My cock hardens seeing the anger in her emerald green eyes boring into me. I'm lost in her beautiful eyes when she shocks me by breaking up with me. I don't think so, she is mines.

She storms off, leaving me standing here in shock. There is no fucking way I'm letting that bitch break up with me. I turn and punch the wall in frustration, I'm too pissed off for the lecture. I decide to skip class and head to the pier to think. I always go there when I need to think, or I drive around but I'm not in the mood for driving today.

Why does this always happen to me?

Why do they always leave me?

I'm a nice guy.

I'm fantabolous in the sack, and my cock is quite impressive, if I do say so myself.

Why do they always leave me?

———

As I sit at the pier, I think about Mackenzie when it hits me. I know what I have to do. I race back to the college to talk to her, but I see her and that douche in the Java Lave Café together. I fucking knew it! I knew she was with him this weekend and not Sarah.

She looks over at me and her beautiful face lights up when she sees me, but I'm so pissed that she is with him. I can't be near him, or her, right now, I need to calm down. I decide to go to her place and wait for my Sweetcheeks.

On the way to her apartment, the perfect plan comes to mind; I'm going to take her away, it will be just the two of us, together forever. Sitting in my car I wait for my Sweetcheeks to arrive home. When she gets here she doesn't see me, so I decide to surprise her.

She places her bags on the steps, so she can dig in her ginormous handbag for her keys. *I will never understand why chicks need such a big handbag.* I sneak up behind her and whack her across the back of the head. She collapses into my arms and I catch her before she hits the ground. I'm caring and nice like that.

She groans and screams when she opens her eyes, why is she wailing? Something inside of me snaps when she starts to scream. Pulling my fist back, I punch her over and over, I can't stop.

I tell keep telling her, "You are mines."

I keep punching and kicking her, repeatedly, hoping that it will click in her mind that we are meant to be together. I wish she would stop screaming, fucking bitch.

Sarah and her nosey neighbour arrive, and they are shouting at me to stop but I can't. I need Sweetcheeks to know how much I lover her, to remind her that she is mines. That we belong together...forever.

She groans and I swear I hear her say, "Baby, I love you." I pause, mid-swing and smile. Turning around, I smile and want to show these assholes that she does love me, but there is nothing but anger radiating off them.

Old mate from next door pulls me off her and I stumble down her stairs. Sarah races over to Mackenzie. I sit there frozen until I hear them call ooo. I decide to leave Sweetcheeks with her friends, I'll come back later to see her.

Blowing her a kiss, I turn and run off.

12

KENZIE

When I wake up, I'm in a hospital bed, with a drip in my arm, a throbbing head and my body aches from the top of my head, to the tip of my toes. Everything is foggy; I blink a few times for my eyes to adjust to the light when all of a sudden I remember. Everything comes rushing back to. I start to scream as I remember Clint hitting and kicking me at the apartment.

The door to my room flies open and in rushes a nurse and a doctor. Their words are all muffled as the fear I felt earlier courses through my body. They pump something into my drip, causing my body to immediately relax. My eyes become heavy, and I drift back to sleep.

A few hours later I wake up and I see Mum and Skye huddled together on the green pleather sofa. Mum looks over at me and smiles; she shifts Skye off her and comes over to my bed. She sits on the edge and grabs my hand, squeezing it.

"W...where am I?" I stutter, "W...what happened?"

"Honey, you're in the hospital. You were attacked. Do you remember?"

I'm stunned at what Mum tells me, but after a moment of silence, I nod my head and start to cry. Mum stands up and wraps her arms around me. I wince from the discomfort, but I really need a Mum hug right now, so I push through the pain.

Pulling back, I look at Mum and sadly whisper, "I remember Mum," The tears start to fall again. "I remember it all. Clint attacked me at the apartment. Sarah and Mr. Neil saved me."

Panic sets in again when I start to think about Clint, "Wh...where's Clint?"

"He took off when Sarah and Gavin arrived but the police picked him up earlier this evening and he's currently in jail. The police want to speak to you but the doctor said not today. They'll be coming by tomorrow to get your statement." I just nod my head, too shocked to speak. You read about this happening, but you never think it will happen to you.

I'm starting to get sleepy again when the door to my room opens and in walks a nurse. Smiling, she says, "Hi, Mackenzie. I'm Paula and I'll be looking after you."

"Hi, Paula!"

"On a scale of one to ten, how would you rate your pain right now?"

"I'd say an eleven." Laughing at myself, I lift my hand and rub the back of my head gently before adding. "My heading is killing me, my face hurts, my ribs are aching. Everything hurts."

"I'm not surprised honey, the doctor has prescribed

endone for the pain. I'll go and get them for you and I'll be right back." Paula returns a few moments later and hands me the pills and a cup of water. Swallowing the tablets, Paula leaves and I lay back down.

Skye comes over and sits on the end of my bed, rubbing my leg gently. "So glad you're okay, Mac. When Mum got the call, it felt like Dad all over again. We jumped in the car and got here in record time."

"I'm sorry that I made you worry."

"Don't be sorry, I'm just glad he didn't do more damage. Who knows what would have happened had Sarah and Mr. Neil not intervened? Besides, us Merlot's are tough, it takes more than one asshole to bring us down."

"Language, Skye," Mum scolds.

Skye and I both laugh.

Paula comes back about half an hour later. "Sorry, ladies, but visiting hours are over. You can come back tomorrow morning and see Mackenzie."

Mum and Skye both give me a hug and tell me they will be back in the morning.

Sleep eludes me, each time I close my eyes, I relive the attack. It's about 1:00 a.m. when the night nurse gives me something to help me sleep. I drift off quickly but wake up an hour later in a cold sweat, my heart racing. Tears pouring down my cheek, I see his evil face every time I close my eyes. Staring at the ceiling, I wonder, if I'm strong enough to deal with this?

———

Early, the next morning Mum and Skye are back to visit me. The doctor does his rounds and I am to be discharged later in the day. They decide to go to my place and pick up a change of clothes for me.

Not long after they leave, there's a knock at my door; Sarah pops her head in. As soon as she see's me, she bursts into tears and races over to my bed. She sits in the chair next to the bed, grabs my hand and sobs, I lean forward and rest my head on hers and together we cry. A movement by the door frightens me, I look up to see Jordan standing there. He has one hand in his jeans pocket and the other is holding a tray of coffee. He smiles at me. "Hi," is all he manages to say and for the first time in twenty-four hours, I genuinely smile.

"Hi yourself." I manage to squeak out.

He walks towards the bed and places the coffees on the tray table. He is staring at me and I feel really self-conscious. I let go of Sarah's hand, discretely smoothing down my hair, I look towards the bed as I must look like a mess. My heart rate increases, and I feel my cheeks flush. When I look up into his eyes, a sense of calm washes over me and for the first time since the attack, I relax.

Sarah blows her nose and it sounds like a foghorn. She throws the tissue towards to bin in the corner and misses. She then turns to me. "You scared the freakin shit out of me woman. I got to your place, heard a scream, and raced down the path. Clint was on top of you and he was kicking and punching, mumbling to himself, "You are mines." She pauses to make sure I'm okay, I nod and she continues, "Mr. Neil came out, grabbed him and shouted at Clint to stop. He ran off and Mr. Neil called triple zero while I went to you. The police and an ambulance arrived pretty quickly, you were whisked off here and we gave our statement to the police, and..."

I sniff, "I'm so sorry, Sar."

"Don't apologise but if you ever do that again, I will punch you in the vagina." I cringe at her choice of words, but oddly enough, it also causes me to smile. Man I love this woman, even when she is being totally inappropriate. "Shit, sorry, babe, but please don't ever do that again."

"Not planning on ever doing that again. Trust me."

Turning my head I look out the window, I notice it's a dreary, dark and overcast day outside. *Much like I'm feeling now*, I think to myself, as I look back over at Jordan. With a smile, I say, "Not that I'm not glad to see you, but what are you doing here?" Looking between Sarah and Jordan, I'm confused as to how they got in contact, and also a tad jealous that Sarah has been spending time with him. "How do you two know each other?"

He smiles and takes a seat on the windowsill, and goes to answer but Sarah butts in, "After I had finished with the police at your place, I had to do something. So I headed to the college, hoping that Clint was there so I could kick his ass. I did a Kenz move and smashed into Jordan. He could see the distress on my face and asked what was up. I remember he was the guy checking your ass out before we went away." Jordan and I both blush at this comment, but I'm secretly thrilled that he's embarrassed about it. "I told him what happened when I got to your place, he and I then searched around the city for Clint, but we had no luck. I felt to stupid and helpless."

"Sar, you are not stupid. If anyone is stupid, it's me. You warned me about Clint, several times, but I didn't listen. This is entirely my fault."

In unison they both shout, "NO!"

Before Sarah can reply, Jordan says, "This is not your fault, Kenz, this is that asshat, Clint's, fault. Don't you ever say this was your fault."

Smiling at them both, I nod in agreement, but deep down I know this is my fault.

Reaching out, I grab one of the coffees, take a sip, and moan.

"What is it with you, coffee, and moaning, Kenz?" Jordan says with a grin.

I giggle, shrugging my shoulders, I smile and take another sip of this amazing brew. As I savour that sip of coffee, I think to myself, *I really like him calling me Kenz.* I glance over at him as he is taking a drink, I check him out and smile. Hiding my grin behind my coffee cup, I continue to smile but Sarah sees. She grins back at me and winks. That butterfly feeling from when we had coffee the other week is back, with a vengeance.

I'm lost in thought when the door opens, Mum and Skye walk in with my bag and another tray of coffee. Skye nudges Mum. "Told you Sarah would have bought coffee, she is just as much of an addict as Mac is, if not more." Sarah and I look at each other and shrug our shoulders in agreement and laugh.

It's true, we are. If I could drink coffee intravenously, I totally would.

Mum eyes Jordan sitting on the windowsill, then looks at me and smiles. "Mum, Skye, this is Jordan, a friend from college. Jordan, this is my mum, Margaret, and sister, Skye."

Standing up he puts his hand out to shake Mum's hand. "It's a pleasure to meet you Mrs. Merlot and Skye."

"Please, call me Margaret. Mrs. Merlot is my mother-in-law and I'm nothing like her."

The conversation is flowing and its comfortable, not awkward like it was with Clint. Jordan gets along really well with Mum and Skye, which makes me happy. No one, except for me seemed to get along with Clint.

There is a knock at the door, it opens and in walks two police officers. "I'm Officer Ferguson, and this is my partner, Officer Jones. Are you up for a chat Ms. Merlot?"

"Please, call me Kenzie and yeah, that's fine."

"Do you want everyone to stay?" Officer Ferguson asks me.

Nodding my head, "Yes, if that's okay, I'd like them to stay."

"That's fine. I'd like you to know that Clint MacNicholson has officially been charged with assault causing grievous bodily harm. He made bail earlier this morning but there is a domestic violence order (DVO) in place. He cannot come within fifty meters of you, except for the court appearance. Someone from the department of prosecutions will be in touch and they will inform you of dates and anything else that they need."

I sigh in relief that he has been charged, but I'm also scared that I will have to face him again in court.

"We will need your recount of what happened yesterday."

Mum sits on the bed next to me, squeezes my hand and whispers, "You can do this Mackenzie. I'm right here."

Mum's words of encouragement give me the strength that I need to give my statement. Officer Jones sets up a recorder, I take a deep breath, close my eyes and begin.

"I had just gotten home and I was digging in my handbag for my house keys. I felt someone behind me and I knew it was Clint, I smelled his cologne. He whacked me on the back of the head and I fell into his arms, I blacked out. Then I remember screaming in agony. He was punching and kicking me, each impact harder than the last." The tears are pouring down my face by this point. Sarah hands me a glass of water, I take a sip. Taking a deep breath, I try and slow my rapidly beating heart. The fear I felt yesterday is bubbling to the surface. I'm not sure that I'll be able to finish. Taking another deep breath, I manage to continue. "I remember screaming for him to stop but he didn't. He kept repeating, 'You are mines' over and over and over. Eventually, I blacked out from the pain and when I woke up I was here."

Reaching over, Officer Jones turns off the recorder. "That timeline of events matches up with the other witness statements." He digs into his pocket and hands me a card. "Here's my card, if you think of anything else or have any other questions, please do not hesitate to contact me."

"Thanks Officer."

Mum escorts them out of the room and after closing the door, she comes back to the bed. Wrapping her arms around me, she whispers. "I'm so proud of you, baby girl."

"Thanks Mum." I sniff.

I excuse myself to have a shower. Even though I'm in a crappy hospital shower, with zero pressure, this is the best shower that I have ever had. Digging in the bag, I pull on the denim shorts and sunflower shirt that Mum packed and make my way back into the room. I bump the bed trolley as I'm getting back into bed and wince in pain, "Shit...fuck...shit." I grab my side. Jordan is there to push the table away and help me back into bed.

Mum looks at me. "Mackenzie, language."

"Sorry, Mum, but that really freakin' hurt." She glares at me again over my language.

The doctor walks in and asks everyone to leave, so he can check me over once more before discharging me. Everyone slowly shuffles out, and he proceeds to poke and prod me like I'm a piece of meat. He's happy and I'm allowed to go home. He recommends that I follow up with my local doctor in a week's time. He also gave me details for a therapist to talk to.

Everyone shuffles back in when the doctor leaves, and I say, "Let's get me out of here." Jordan carries my bag and we all make our way to the car park. We say our goodbyes, gentle hugs all round and Sarah and Jordan agree to pop over tomorrow. They head to the left, while Mum, Skye, and I head up a level and make our way back to my apartment.

———

Mum and Skye stay with me for the next week until I can do most things myself. You don't realized how much you use your ribs until they hurt like a bitch when you try to do anything. Sarah is over for breakfast the morning they leave and as they pull out of the driveway, I start to cry. She carefully pulls me into a hug, and ushers me back inside. She demands I lay on the couch as she heads into the kitchen. She returns with a bottle of wine and a tub of ice cream. I look at her and smile; she knows just what I need, when I need it. I don't even care that's its 10:00 a.m. and I'm drinking wine. After what I've been through, I deserve it.

We spend the rest of the day on the couch drinking wine, eating ice cream, and watching *One Tree Hill*. This is just what the doctor ordered.

13

CLINT

Something snaps when I get to Sweetcheeks' house, I don't mean to hurt her. After Sarah and nosey Mr. Neil intervened, I take off. I drive around and around until I calm down.

Before heading home, I stop by my Sweetcheeks apartment but she isn't there. I wonder where she could be?

Stopping at Maccas, I get a feed and head back to my place. When I get home the police are here. Oh no, something must have happened to Mackenzie and that's why she wasn't home.

The Officer walks over to me, "Are you Clint MacNicholson?"

"Yeah. What's it to you?"

"You are under arrest in relation to the assault of Mackenzie Merlot. You're not obliged to say or do anything, unless you wish to do so, but whatever you say or do may be used in evidence. Do you understand?"

"I understand." I mumble as I'm handcuffed and escorted to the squad car.

We arrive at the station and a few hours later, I am formally charged with assaulting Mackenzie. I'm not allowed to see or be near my Sweetcheeks; that's going to kill me.

A few weeks later at my court hearing, I manage to get a glimpse of her, she looks so beautiful, my cock comes to life. It breaks my heart that I can't touch her. When I see that she was with that slut and asshole, my blood starts to boil.

"She. Is. Mines." I growl under my breath.

My lawyer persuades me to plead guilty. Luck is on my side and I'm only to serve two years. Sweetcheeks bursts into tears when I'm sentenced. Her reaction proves to me that deep down, she still cares for me. As they lead me out of the courtroom, I look over at her and smile.

One day, we will be together again, Sweetcheeks, one day.

14

KENZIE

...6 weeks later

FOR THE LAST SIX WEEKS I HAVE ONLY SEEN THREE people: my therapist Jeannie, Sarah, and Jordan. I've only left the house for my doctor appointments or therapy. I started to buy my groceries online and get them delivered, so I don't have to leave home. I feel protected this way, locked in my little cocoon, safe and sound. A plus, I'm saving heaps without the impulse buys, so it's win/win. My local bottle shop, *Dan Murphy's*, also delivers so I don't even have to go out and get my wine and beer either; hashtag winning.

The only time I was truly frightened at home, was when I got a locksmith in to change all the locks, add window locks and another deadlock to the front and back doors. He was running late, neither Sarah nor Jordan could be here, so I had to do it by myself. The hour he was here was pretty rough but I survived; just. I sat on the couch and didn't move a muscle. My eyes followed him every time he came into the lounge room; I'd hold my breath until he left the room. As the minutes ticked by I slowly started to crumble and freak out, my heart pounding with every second he was in my apartment. Sweat was beading on my brow. When he said he was finished, I nearly passed out with relief.

As soon as he left, I completely lost it. Racing around, I deadlocked all the doors and windows before heading to my bedroom. Hiding and rocking in the corner, I knew I had to call Jeannie. When I dialed her number, I could barely breathe. My chest tightening as the panic attack set in.

After a few moments, she had calmed me down: my breathing returning to normal and the tightness in my chest disappearing. She told me that it was a massive step that I allowed a man alone into my house, and I should be proud of myself. After hanging up, I sat for a little longer going over what she said. She was right, I *am* strong. I can go on with my life, without fear.

A few days later, I'm chatting with Jeannie, and we decide it is time I get back to my everyday life and routine, which includes college and seeing my friends, in public and not at my apartment. I admit to her that without the support of Jordan, I don't think I would be as strong and confident as I am. I finally tell her about the time, a few weeks ago when Jordan popped over between classes. He found me in a heap in the corner in my bedroom. I'd been to the letterbox and a delivery guy tapped me on the shoulder. I completely freaked out. Jordan sat with me for the whole afternoon. He even let me watch *The Hills*, and he hates that crap. He has seen me at my weakest moment and not once has he made me feel afraid or inferior.

He's become my person...my rock.

I'm not one hundred percent sure I'm ready to go back to real life just yet, but I can't keep sitting at home, dwelling on what happened. If I do, I'd be letting him win, and Clint does not get to win.

I refuse to let him win.

I'm stronger than that.

I am a survivor.

After I returned from my appointment with Jeannie, I decide there is no time like the present. Pulling on my big girl undies, I call Michele. While I'm waiting for the call to connect, I smile. T*oday I take back my life; Mackenzie Merlot is back!*

After the call connects, I take a deep breath and explain that I'm ready to come back to college and asked if it's okay. She says I'm more than welcome to come back, she also reiterates that Clint has been expelled from the college, and there are rumors circulating around about what happened.

Due to the circumstances of my absence, Michele has given me an extension on the two assignments I missed, and she is confident that I will be finished in time to graduate in October, with the rest of the class. If not, I will have to wait until March.

———

Sarah and Jordan are at my apartment, and we are having

Indian takeaway and a few beers. Taking a deep breath I say, "So, I'm going back to college tomorrow."

They both look at me and don't say anything. I'm starting to think that they don't agree, when Sarah turns to Jordan. "Cough up, buddy, told you she'd be back before the two month mark."

Shaking his head, he grabs his wallet and hands over fifty dollars. Looking at me, he says, "Even though you just cost me fifty bucks, I'm glad you're getting back out there"

"You guys bet on me? Seriously?"

They both reply, "Yep."

Sarah comes over, hugs me, and whispers so Jordan can hear, "Thanks for winning me fifty bucks, but even if I didn't win, I'm happy you are getting on with your life. I would hate to see assface douche hole win."

"Assface douche hole, I like that. Has a good ring to it. Jeannie and I were talking yesterday and I think it's time. As you said, we don't want assface douche hole to win."

Jordan smiles at me. "I'm so proud of you, Kenz. Do you want me to pick you up in the morning?"

"Thanks, Jordan, but I'm going to catch the bus. To get back to the old me, I need to keep to my original routine and the bus is it. I will take a coffee break, if you are free? After all, I still owe you one."

"Coffee it is then," he says, with a big smile on his face, causing those butterflies to once again take flight.

After dinner, we decide to watch *Prison Break*. It's about 10:00 p.m. when they both leave. Grabbing the rubbish, I walk them out. After saying our goodbyes, I race back inside, lock all the doors, and jump into a steaming hot shower. I put on my navy blue satin pajama shorts and Wine Time Finally singlet, and I snuggle in bed with my Kindle, reading the next book in the Break series.

———

Today is my first day back at college: my emotions are all over the place. I'm excited and scared but most of all, I'm confident. The first face I see when I'm walking into the building is Jordan's. He sees me, waves, and rushes up to me. He envelopes me in a bear hug and I smile into his chest. "It's so good to see you here at college, with you hair done and wearing actual clothes, Kenz." He is trying to hold back a laugh. I look up at him in shock and then I laugh too because he's right. For the last six weeks, I've lived in trackies and a singlet, with my hair piled up in a topknot. If I were having a good day; I'd also put a bra on.

Still laughing, I reply, "Hardy har har, Jordan." I can always count on him to make me laugh; he really has been my rock over the last six weeks.

He smiles and I swear my ovaries explode, just like they did on the first day of college. I smile at that memory. Draping his arm over my shoulder, we turn and head in for our first class of the day.

The first week back at college was tough but I survived. It was the pity looks and the whispers that got to me, but Jordan and, his best mate Mike Mustange, were always there to assist me. I've gotten to know Mike much better since my attack and I love to hate him. He's my 6-foot-1, bald-headed teddy bear with a goatee, and a heart of gold. He comes across all tough and macho, but he's a big softie underneath his grough exterior. Pretty sure they each have a secret, 'Kenzie is in distress' beacon because they were always there when I needed help.

Jordan and I are hanging out more and more and for the first time since the incident, I'm genuinely happy and content. Every Friday we end up at the Joker; the Dirty Duck holds too many memories and I'm not ready to deal with those yet. Sarah and her new boyfriend, Josh, always join us. We become the four amigos, or five if Mike tags along.

———

Jordan and I officially started dating a few weeks before I graduated. I managed to catch up and get everything finalised so I can graduate with my class on schedule.

It took me a long time to decide that I wanted to date Jordan, in the back of my mind I kept thinking, what if it happens again? Deep down, I know he's not Clint, but it's still there, niggling at me. It wasn't until Jeannie made me realise, that my fear won't immediately disappear, there will be set backs, like the deliveryman incident, but it was all part of the healing process.

At a session with Jeannie one afternoon, that was when I realised I can't keep living in fear. By living in fear I let Clint win and I am stronger than that. See I can even use his name now, even though assface douche hole has a great ring to it. I remember her words from that day clearly, "You are the owner of your emotions. You control everything. You are the only one holding you back." Those words really stuck with me.

Once I finally admitted my feelings for Jordan, I fell for him and I fell hard. For the first time in a longtime, I feel free, happy, and safe, and I knew I would survive.

My new motto is "I am Mackenzie Merlot and I'm a survivor."

15

JORDAN

It is so nice to see Kenz smiling again, like really smiling. Even though we have only been hanging out for a few weeks, I can already tell the difference between her fake and her real smile. When it's her real smile, her eyes sparkle and her face lights up.

It feels like I've known her forever, we click on every level. We have the same taste in music, *Empire Records* is our favourite movie, we both love beer; especially craft beers. Oddly, we like white wine in summer, and red wine in winter; I've never met anyone who drinks and likes wine like this. But most of all, we agree wholeheartedly that the best way to spend a Sunday afternoon, is down at the local pub having a few brewski's with friends.

Even though what Clint did was horrible and horrific, it bought us closer together. The last six weeks have been tough, not only for her but for me too. I'll never forget how I felt when I ran into Sarah at the college the day she was attacked. If hearts could break, I swear mine broke into a million tiny pieces that day.

When I walked into her hospital room the day after, and I saw her beautiful face, bruised and swollen, my heart skipped a beat and started to race erratically. I swear it was going to beat out of my chest. It was in that moment that I realised, I was falling for Mackenzie Merlot.

After visiting her at the hospital, I broke down and cried when I got home. Relief flooded through my body that she was safe and okay, but all the emotion I was holding in came rushing out.

Keeping my feelings for Kenz hidden was tough. I didn't want to scare her; she'd been through enough as it was. Kenz had just been to hell and back, she didn't need me to make it harder, even though she made my cock hard, constantly. I'd get hard seeing her smile, seeing her laughing. Actually, I get hard whenever I think about her. And when she sips her coffee, that is the ultimate hard on.

Kenz has no idea how sexy she is, and that only increases her sexiness.

Selfishly, I bought her coffee all the time, just so I could hear her moan. Hearing that was enough to make me smile, plus it gave me an excuse to see her. Hearing her moan was stored in my spank bank for use later... when I was alone. Don't judge me, you'd totally do it too if you heard her.

One Saturday, when I was at the coffee shop near Kenz's place, I bumped into Sarah, who had the same idea. Adding another coffee for Sarah to the order, we waited together. She turned to face me, staring me in the eyes she leant forward, pointed directly at me and warned, "You better not hurt her, buddy," She poked me in the chest. "She is not only my best friend, but she's also like a sister to me. If you hurt her, I will hunt you down, and you will feel pain like you have never felt before."

Looking back at her, right in her eyes, I replied. "Sarah, I would never do anything to intentionally hurt Kenz. She is the most amazingly beautiful person, inside and out, that I have ever met. If I get a chance with her, I assure you that I will never do anything to jeopardize that or her. It will be my life's mission, to give her the happily ever after that she deserves."

Sarah looked at me dumbfounded. "Um, wow, that totally was not what I was expecting you to say, but I'm very glad that we are on the same page, and that you will look after my friend when you get your chance."

Our order is called, Sarah collected it and walked out. I stood there, staring at her retreating form in shock. Her reply was totally out of left field and it knocked me off kilter. I was sure she was going to warn me off, tell me to stay in the friend zone. Walking out to my car, I smiled to myself when I realised that she said when and not if. My heart did a little flutter at that tidbit of information.

———

Kenz and I see each other just about every day, and most weekends we hang out, either at her place or mine. This weekend she suggested we go out for lunch. Reaching for my phone, I tell her I'll call Sarah to meet us and she hesitantly says, "No, just us. If that's okay?"

Smiling at her, I reply, "Yeah sure. That's fine." Inside I'm mentally high fiving myself, yelling fuck yeah and doing my happy dance; yes I have a happy dance. I try to act all cool, but my heart is bursting with happiness right now. I'm pretty sure she knows that I'm falling for her, just like I'm pretty sure she's falling for me too.

Kenz and I have our first date, unofficially of course, and it could not have been more perfect. We go to Just Catch and get fish-n-chips, then head to the pier and watch the sunset.

We sit down at the pier for hours, chatting and laughing. It isn't until we realise it's dark out that we pack up and head back to her apartment. I pull up at her place, and after seeing her inside safely, I drive home. The drive home is a blur, but I do know that I've never felt so happy to be on a non-date before.

———

Two weeks before Kenzie's graduation, I finally grow a pair and I officially ask her to be my girlfriend. It's a Saturday afternoon and we are sitting on her couch, watching some chick crap, when I ask. My heart is pounding, my palms sweaty. I look over at her and I decide that it is now or never. It isn't very romantic, I'm too nervous for romance, I just blurt it out. "Kenzie, will you be my girlfriend?" The silence after I ask is deafening, I feel like I'm going to throw up, but when I see her face is lit up like the Rockefeller Center Christmas tree, I know she is going to say yes.

Smiling, she immediately says, "Jordan, I'd love to be your girlfriend".

Best seven words ever to have been spoken.

Before my brain has a chance to register that she actually said yes, she leans over and kisses me. I'm telling you, this kiss is the kiss of all kisses. It feels like fireworks are exploding within my body, and when she runs her fingers through my hair and pulls me closer to deepen the kiss; I nearly come in my pants like a horny fifteen-year-old.

Pulling back from the best kiss ever, she looks deep into my soul and whispers, "Hi, boyfriend."

Smiling, I lean forward, placing a gentle kiss on her nose before drawing back, I run my finger slowly down her now healed cheek and whisper, "Hi, girlfriend."

She gives me a megawatt smile, before kissing me again. My cock begins to twitch. She climbs over and straddles my lap, my cock is now pressing painfully against my fly but I wouldn't change a thing. We make out on her couch, like horny teenagers on a Saturday night at the drive-in. We are interrupted by the sound of the kitchen door slamming shut, and Sarah yelling, "I've come to clean ze pool!" Sarah and Josh walk into the lounge room, Josh laughing at her cheesiness.

Kenz and I freeze, we turn our heads to see both Sarah and Josh standing there open-mouthed. In unison we both say, "Hey, guys," We both burst out laughing; we constantly do the speaking in unison thing.

Sarah smiles, turns to Josh, slaps him on the chest,

and says, "Cough up, buddy, told you they'd be together before Kenz graduated." Josh shakes his head, reaches into his wallet and hands over one hundred bucks.

He looks to us both and says, "Seriously, guys, you couldn't have held off a little longer?"

With that statement we all burst our laughing.

Kenz climbs off my lap and steps into the kitchen and grabs four beers out of the fridge. She leans in to Sarah and says, "Did you seriously bet on me again?"

"Yep, and at the rate I'm going I'll soon be able to buy my very own vineyard."

"I think I should get a cut of these winnings, after all it's due to me you keep winning."

"Keep dreaming Kenz. I won fair and square."

Sarah grabs a beer from Kenz and then Kenz passes one to Josh and me. The girl's head down the hall into Kenzie's room to get ready to go out to dinner. Josh sits down and we catch the last of the footy game on TV while we wait.

Half an hour later, they both emerge and my heart stops. Kenzie is wearing a sexy as hell purple dress that accentuates her curves and these killer heels that make her already sexy legs look even sexier. Managing to stand up, I walk over to her. "Wow, you look stunning."

Sarah squeals, "Fuck, yes, she does. My girl is smokin hawt!"

She turns towards Josh, clears her throat while doing a spin. Josh rolls his eyes. "Sarah, you also look hot." He wraps his arms around her and dips her upside down. She squeals, and when he places her back on her feet, he kisses her senseless.

While they are making out, I gently grab Kenz around her waist, hugging her closer to me. Lowering my head, I gently place my mouth against her soft luscious lips. Her tongue slipping inside my mouth, our tongues twisting together passionately before resting our foreheads together, gazing into each other's eyes.

Breaking our moment, Josh slaps me on the back. "Come on, you two, lovebirds, I'm starving."

Kenz pulls away and grabs her purse off the breakfast bar, I grab my keys and wallet, and we all head to Dragon Garden; for the first of many official double date nights.

———

Sarah and Josh drop us back at Kenzie's place after dinner. We offer for them to come in for a nightcap, but they decline, thankfully. I want some alone time with my girlfriend. *Man, I love saying that Kenzie is my girlfriend.* As they drive off, I grab Kenzie's hand and entwine our fingers together as we head inside. Kenzie is taking her shoes off, so I grab a couple of beers from the fridge and we sit on the couch chatting, just like we used to.

A few hours later, I get up to leave, and Kenzie reaches out grabbing my wrist. She looks up at me and hesitantly says, "Please stay."

"Are you sure?"

She stands up and lifts her purple dress over her head; she is standing there like a goddess in a black lacy strapless bra and matching lacy boyleg undies.

"I guess you are sure then."

She steps towards me giggling, before wrapping her

arms around my neck, nuzzling her way to my ear and whispers, "I've never been more sure of anything in my life, Jordan."

Placing my hands under her ass, I lift her up and she wraps her legs around my waist and kisses me. I carry her down the hall into her bedroom, gently setting her down next to the bed. Reaching out, she slowly untucks my navy dress shirt. One by one, she carefully undoes the buttons, the anticipation is killing me. Once the buttons are all undone, she rakes her fingers up my stomach and pushes the shirt off my shoulders and down my arms. She then turns her attention to the button and fly of my jeans, but her fingers are shaking. Her breathing is labored. Placing my hand over hers, I undo the button and fly; she places her hands inside the waistband and pushes them down along with my boxer briefs. Stepping out of them, I stand there in front of her fully naked. My dick is rock hard and standing to attention.

Stepping towards her, I wrap my arms around her silky soft shoulders and I pull her into me, our lips colliding. She slightly opens her mouth, and I take the chance to slip my tongue in. I gently nip her lip as I pull back. Looking into her eyes, I see they are ablaze with lust and desire, and it makes me harder knowing she wants this as much as I do. Kissing down her neck and along her collarbone, I unclasp her bra and it falls to the floor.

When I see her breasts for the first time, I near come right there. She has the most amazing tits I've ever seen; they are the perfect size for my palm. Her pert pink nipples are erect and hard, I can't wait to suck them. Gently massaging them, I softly tug her nipples, rolling them between my thumb and finger, before bending down and taking one into my mouth, gently suckling and nibbling the taut peaks.

She pushes away; I panic, thinking that she doesn't want this anymore but she bends down and quickly removes her undies. We are both now fully naked, the air between us thick with erotic lust. Glancing down her beautiful body, I see her bare smooth pussy is glistening already. Stepping forward, I gently place my hands on her cheeks, "Are you sure about this Kenz?"

She looks deep into my eyes. "Yes, Jordan, I'm sure. You make me feel safe and I've never felt that before. I want you to make love to me." That's all the reassurance I need, I lean forward and kiss her, pulling her closer to me; I escalate our kiss. Reaching down I rub my finger around her clit, she is soaking wet. We both moan into our kiss, as I continue to circle her clit with my finger, she begins to grind her pussy on my hand.

Easing her back gently, I lay her on the bed. Once we are both lying down, I kiss my way down her chest. Licking from her belly button to the top of her mound; when I reach her clit I take it into my mouth and suck. Her back arches off the bed and she moans, shoving her pussy further into my face. Inserting a finger, I suck on her clit harder. She moans as I lick down her slit, flicking my tongue into her tight hole, before licking back up to her clit. I gently bite her swollen nub as I insert another finger. Arching her back as I hook my finger around to find her G-spot, her movement, effectively shoving her pussy further onto my face.

She reaches out and tugs on my hair, while I continue

to suck and nip on her clit, I feel her walls clenching around my fingers. I hear her whimper, "I'm coming." She tugs harder on my hair as I thrust my tongue deeper into her pussy, my tongue and fingers pumping in and out, faster and faster until I feel her explode all over my fingers and tongue. I suck all of her glorious juices, as she comes down from her orgasmic high.

When I feel her relax, I work my way back up her amazing body. Looking into her glorious green eyes, I say, "Hi, girlfriend."

She giggles and tugs me in for another kiss. I swear each kiss is more electric than the last. Breathlessly, she pulls back, "Hi, boyfriend."

Before I register what she's doing, she wraps her hand around my dick and pushes me onto my back. Stroking my cock as she works her way down my chest. When she reaches my cock, she licks the tip while continuing to pump up and down my shaft with her hand. She hollows her cheeks and takes my cock deep into her mouth and sucks. "Fuck me, Kenz, ohm yeah, suck me harder." She keeps pumping and sucking. I feel myself about to come when I lift her up. "Kenz, as much as that is fuckin' amazing, when I come with you for the first time, I want to be buried balls deep inside of you."

Giggling, she slowly kisses her way back up to my mouth. I grab her face and slam my lips against hers. She reaches into her nightstand, grabs a condom, and straddles me, ripping it open with her teeth before slowly rolling it over my thick, throbbing cock. Getting up on her knees, she slowly lowers herself onto me, her eyes rolling back in delight, as she seats herself completely on my cock.

Watching her ride my cock is the hottest thing I have ever seen. We move into a sensual and evocative rhythm, our bodies aligning together. Closing my eyes to savour the moment, I groan with desire, opening my eyes, I see Kenz squeezing her tits and tugging on her nipples. She moans and I feel her muscles tighten on my cock. She explodes around me and screams my name as she rides out her orgasm, letting out one final moan as she grinds her hips on my cock. With a guttural grunt, I release my seed deep inside of her and we ride the final waves of our orgasm together.

Kenz collapses onto my chest, we are both breathless, our hearts frantically beating. After a few minutes, she lifts off me; I remove the condom and place it in the bin in the corner. Lying back down, she snuggles into my side and throws her leg over me. We lay there in each other's arms, subconsciously, I rub my hand up and down her arm; I'm so content right now. *The world could end, and I'd die a very happy man*, I laugh at that thought.

Kenz lifts her head to look at me. "What's so funny?"

"I was just thinking that I could die right now and I'd be okay with that. Kenz, that was the most intense sex that I've ever had. You are amazing Mackenzie Merlot. I'm so glad that you came crashing into my life."

Her smile grows and her cheeks turn a deeper shade of pink, enhancing her post orgasmic glow. "Jordan, you're amazing and I'm ever so glad I bumped into you, too."

Leaning over, I kiss her. Pulling back, I stare into her

eyes, I'm lost in a sea of green and I smile. She returns my smile and my heart skips a beat. "Kenz, you are the most beautiful person I have ever met and your after orgasm glow is sexy as."

She reaches up, grabs my face and kisses me. I roll us over, so I'm between her legs; my cock is already hard when she starts to rub her pussy against me. Grabbing another condom, we make love again before falling asleep, in each other's arms.

16

KENZIE

Graduation comes around quickly, and after struggling to catch up, I pull some long nights and big weekends and I manage to complete all that I missed. Officially, I graduate with the rest of my class in October, minus one person of course.

Clint is still safely locked away, not able to hurt me or anyone again. I used to check in weekly with the Department of Corrections to ensure he is still locked away, but I haven't checked in with them or thought about him in a long time. I'm ever so grateful that he's locked away, it allows me to get on with my life but most of all, I'm not letting him win.

Graduation day is hectic but amazing at the same time. Mum and Skye travel down for it and stay with me for the weekend. I finally tell them that Jordan and I are dating. "Finally," they both say in unison. I'm glad they approve and are happy for me; looking back, I wish I had listened to everyone's concerns regarding Clint. Maybe then he wouldn't have assaulted me.

Before the ceremony I'm super nervous, I'm scared that I'll trip on my gown and fall flat on my face. To be on the safe side, I decide to wear black ballerina flats, with my Nine West black three-quarter pants and a fuchsia silk sleeveless top. After several different hairstyle trials, I decide on a simple and chic, low bun. Looking at myself in the mirror, I look and feel sophisticated, I feel like a graduate.

The ceremony goes off without a hitch and I don't trip when I walk up onto the stage to collect my diploma. When my name is called, Mum, Skye, and Jordan are all shouting with glee; it's quite embarrassing but I can't help but smile. I've not felt this happy, or relaxed in forever, it's very refreshing. Kenzie is finally back.

Once the ceremony is over Mum and Skye take me out for a celebration dinner, just the three of us. It is nice to be just us girls again, I realise how much I miss them. They bought me a beautiful gold and white gold watch as a graduation present; I cry happy tears when they give it to me.

After dinner Jordan meets up with us for drinks. We head to the casino, and as Skye is under eighteen, she heads back to my apartment. Jordan, Mum and I end up doing karaoke and drinking margaritas until three in the morning. Man, do we all have horrible hangovers the next morning.

Waking up early the following day, I decide to do some laundry while I wait for the coffee to brew. Mum and Skye are still sleeping, so I quietly grab the basket and head down to the laundry, which is located in the garage. Walking through the kitchen, I open the back door and there is a package sitting on the top step, addressed to me.

It's a beautiful eggplant purple box with a shimmery silver bow. I immediately smile and think it's from someone close, as it's my favourite colour. When I open it up its full of sunflowers, I smile and think they are from Jordan...unbeknownst to me, they're not from him.

The weekend with Mum and Skye flies by. I wish they could stay longer but they have to get back in time for Skye to be at school on Monday, as she has her end of year finals. It's hard to believe my baby sister will be in her last year of high school next year. Just before lunch on Sunday, I wave Mum and Skye off, and this time I cry happy tears when they leave.

Jordan wraps his arms around my waist, and we stand there, enjoying being in each other's arms. It isn't until Sarah and Josh pull up that our trance is broken. Sarah knew I'd be a little upset with them leaving, so they decided to pop over and whisk us away for a relaxing beach day.

This impromptu beach trip is just what I need, Sarah knows me too well. We all have a great afternoon and it definitely takes my mind off missing Mum and Skye. As usual, I proceed to get extremely sunburnt and my face looks like a Goddamn ninja turtle from my sunglass tan. Who knew that expired sunscreen did not work? I didn't, but I do now, ouch.

———

After everything that happened and working super hard

to graduate on time, I decided I wasn't going to get a job until the new year. A little 'me' time was called for. However, the universe had other ideas, and two weeks after graduation I was offered an amazing job at the local tourism board. Turns out Michele knew someone there, and when she heard they were looking for someone she suggested me. I felt pretty honoured to have her recommend me.

As fate would have it, this job didn't start until January so I still got to have a few months off before entering the workforce. Early in the new year, I start working at the tourism board. It was an amazing position and I loved going into work each day. It really was my dream job.

———

Just before Easter, Jordan and I officially move in together, we are pretty much living together anyway. When we made it official we decided to get a new place, somewhere that was ours and had no memories. My apartment has memories of Clint and I don't want those memories tarnishing the relationship that Jordan and I have. Some nights, those memories haunt me but a fresh start with Jordan is what we both need. He agreed when I told him why I wanted us to get a new place and the house hunting began. Even though moving in together is a big step, I have no qualms about it at all.

I'm excited for this next adventure and I'm so glad to be taking that step with Jordan.

We found an amazing cottage with everything that

we wanted and it was pretty much in the middle of my work and Jordan's university. After graduating college, Jordan decided to continue his studies. He now wants to own his own bar, not just manage one for someone else. Luckily, his diploma from Stratton College managed to cut eighteen months off his bachelor course.

I cannot wait to move into our cottage, I fell in love with the kitchen as soon as I saw it, it's amazeballs, I don't care about anything else. I wanted this cottage for the kitchen alone. It has chocolate granite bench tops, honey coloured timber cabinets, a built in coffee machine, thirty-two bottle wine fridge and a stainless dishwasher. It also has the most gorgeous verandah that leads onto a massive entertainment area. Our little cottage is perfect and exactly what I had in mind.

The first thing I bought, just for us was a kwila timber Jack and Jill setting with green cushions for the front verandah. It will be the perfect place to sit and have my morning coffee or a quiet wine/beer with Jordan, at the end of the day.

Jordan's only stipulation was the house had to have a shed, or beer cave, as I like to tease him, so he can start brewing his beers on a bigger scale. He has become fanatical about brewing beer recently. I've never met someone so passionate about beer, or life in general.. His passion and heart are two of the many many things I love about him.

It's finally moving day and the last box has been unpacked. We are sitting on the verandah enjoying a beer, and organising a house warming party, Mike's idea of course. Even though I sometimes want to gaffe tape his mouth shut and throw him off the pier, with a ball and chain wrapped around his ankles to keep him there, Mike is harmless and I love him to pieces. He is always there for Jordan and me, and we really appreciate it.

Jordan told Mike he needs three weeks to get the beers brewed and ready for the party, to which Mike agreed as he is Jordan's number one beer fan. It's really nice to see him passionate about something other than my safety.

CLINT

No... no ... no ... no! Why is she moving in with twat boy? When my cousin came to visit me today and told me the devastating news, I lost it.

How can she do this to me? To us?

She is mines; her and I are meant to be together.

Why is it all going wrong?

I've left her flowers; doesn't she know that I love her? That we are meant to be together?

I need to up my game.

Soon, Sweetcheeks, soon you will be mines.

KENZIE

IT'S THE DAY OF OUR HOUSEWARMING, AND I'M IN the kitchen making sausage rolls, Thai chicken balls that I can never get to actually look like balls, home made dips including, mum's super yummy cheese log, and my famous brownies. Jordan walks in, and he wraps his arms around my waist, nuzzling my ear as he pulls me in tighter. "Do you know how sexy you look, right now?"

Turning around, I wrap my arms around him and he bursts out laughing. I look at him confused. "What's so funny?"

"You have brownie mixture smeared all over your face, it kinda looks like shit."

Without even thinking, I dip my finger into the mixture and I smear it down the side of his face whispering, "Now you have shit on your face, too."

"Oh it's on like Donkey Kong, woman." Jordan chases after me, with the brownie bowl in his arms; I manage to sidestep him, running around the bench, so that I am now standing across from him. He places the bowl back on the bench, I lean over and dip my finger in. Slowly I lift my finger to my mouth and suck the mixture off, while letting out an exaggerated moan. Jordan stops and stares at me, his eyes immediately heat with desire.

We both step around the bench towards each other, our lips colliding in a passionate kiss. He pulls back and dips his finger into the bowl. As he lifts it up towards his mouth, I lean forward and suck the mixture off his finger and moan. Angling towards him, I slowly lick the mixture off his face that I smeared there earlier and look into his eyes. "Mmhmm, that tastes amazeballs," I huskily whisper.

I suck his cheek and lick along his jawline, groaning as I go, slowly kissing my way up to his lips. Coaxing his lips open with my tongue, I slip mine in and out of his mouth. Leaning up onto my tippy toes, I wrap my arms around his neck and pull him closer, deepening our kiss. Sighing into his mouth, my pussy tightens when I feel his cock pressing into my stomach.

Taking a step back I slip the straps of my sundress down so I am standing there only in my blue silk undies. Looking deep into Jordan's eyes, I dip my finger into the mixture again and smear it across my breasts. "Oops," I seductively say.

Jordan steps towards me, lowering his head, he licks across my collarbone and down my breastbone. Sucking the mixture off my skin before taking my nipple into his mouth. It immediately pebbles and with his other hand he massages the other breast. He alternates between the two, my body tingling all over. I cry out in pleasure as he gently bites my nipple; the pain quickly replaced with ecstasy as he sucks my nipple harder.

Dunking my finger into the mixture again, I smear it down his neck. Bending forward, while he keeps massaging my breasts, I lick and suck the batter off him. I work my way down his abs and lower onto my knees; I undo his button and make quick work of his zipper. His cock springs free when I lower his boxer briefs, moving forward I lick the pre-cum glistening on the tip of his erect penis. I push his shorts and boxer briefs down to his ankles and he steps out, kicking them to the side. I begin to massage his balls while, I suck him further into my mouth, hollowing my cheeks I take him deeper down my throat, just like I did the first time we made love.

"Fuck, Kenz, your mouth is amazing."

That's the added encouragement I need, I start bobbing my head faster, working up and down his thick shaft. Feeling his balls tighten in my hand, I know he's close. Seconds later, I feel the first creamy spurt of his cum hit the back of my throat. I suck every last drop from him and I lick any that spilt. Wiping the side of my mouth with my finger I look up into Jordan's eyes and then suck my finger. "Mmhmm."

Standing up, I draw him closer and kiss him deeply. Jordan lifts me up and I wrap my legs around his waist. He pushes aside the mixing bowl and lowers me onto the edge of the island bench and quickly removes my undies. Leaning over, he dips his finger into the mixture, smearing it over my stomach and the top of my mound.

Jordan proceeds to suck it off me, while massaging my breasts. Rolling my nipples between his forefinger and thumb. I lean back on my elbows, closing my eyes and I lose myself in the pleasure overtaking my body.

He licks down my stomach to the top of my mound, his tongue darting out, flicking my clit. When his tongue hits my clit a second time, it sends a bolt of electricity to my pussy and I feel myself instantly get wetter. I moan and lie down on the bench, as he takes my clit into his mouth and sucks harder. His tongue laps my slit, sliding in and out, before sucking and nibbling on my clit once again. Clenching his head between my thighs, I never want this feeling to end, I let out a loud moan and run my fingers through Jordan's hair. With one final flick of his tongue on my clit, I'm coming. My body buzzing from head to toe, as wave after wave of pleasure rushes over my entire being. He sucks every last drop of my orgasm from my body.

Once my orgasm has finished, he pulls me closer to the edge of the bench and guides his throbbing cock into my pussy. Wrapping my legs around his waist, grasping him closer to me; he slowly pulls out and slams back into me, again and again. We pick up a frenzied sensual rhythm, our mouths hungrily devouring each other as he continues to pound into me. Without warning he stops, lowers my legs, and tells me to turn around. Quickly, I spin around and grab the edge of the bench. He enters me from behind with such force that my orgasm immediately starts to build.

Arching my back, I reach my hand up to cup his cheek, turning my head to kiss him. Jordan reaches around and starts to rub my clit. I can feel my climax intensifying. Reaching down with my other hand, I help

Jordan massage my clit; our fingers working together, rubbing my swollen nub in circles, skimming our fingernails across my sensitive core. Before long, I'm exploding around his cock, my whole body shuddering due to the force of the climax. While I'm riding out my release, I feel Jordan still before he detonates inside of me.

We stand there, with our arms wrapped around each other, panting, gazing into each other's eyes over my shoulder. Jordan is the first to speak, "Fuck, I love your brownies," and we both laugh.

He spins me around and kisses me, this is the kiss of all kisses. I can feel it deep in my soul. In this exact moment I know that I love Jordan with all my heart. Mid-kiss he pulls away, "Fuck, we didn't use a franga."

Without hesitating, I reply. "I'm due next week, we should be fine, and if not, we will deal with it. I love you, Jordan." Realising that this is the first time that I have said it to him, I don't panic. I'm happy that I said it and I don't regret those three words. Grabbing his face with both of my hands and I look deep into his eyes. "Jordan, you and I can overcome and do anything, as long as we are together." I say it again, "I love you."

"I love you too, Kenz."

We stare into each other's eyes, Jordan leans down and kisses me again, but this kiss feels different somehow. I think because it's a kiss of love and not just lust. Pushing back, I smile. "Ummm, we better go have a shower and get cleaned up, and then I need to finish cooking. Our guests will be here soon."

"Yeah, I guess we got a little sidetracked. Come on;

let's have a shower. To be earth conscious, and all that shit, I think we should have a shower together."

"Yes, cause we are so earth conscious," I sarcastically reply with a laugh.

Grabbing my hand, he leads us into the bathroom, but us saying the 'L' word has unleashed something inside of us. We make love on the bathroom floor ... and again in the shower together, being all earth conscious about the amount of water we use.

An hour later, I'm putting the last brownie batch in the oven, and have just set the timer when Sarah and Josh arrive. Josh pokes his head in to say hey and then heads to the backyard where Jordan and Mike are setting up the tables.

Sarah stays and helps me get the rest of the food organised. Once everything is ready, we take the food, rest of the drinks, and cutlery outside. We have just finished setting up when everyone starts to arrive.

Jordan's beer is flowing and it tastes amazing. I haven't seen him this happy in a long time. Actually, I haven't been this happy in a long time. Everyone has a fantabolous night, and Jordan's beers are a hit, as are my brownies.

It's just after midnight, and only Mike, Sarah, Josh, Jordan and I are left. We are lounging in the living room when Mike pulls out a bottle of tequila...that's when things start to get really messy. Jordan hides as he and tequila don't mix very well, kind of like oil and water. I remember one messy night in first term after exams; all the Stratton College students were at the Dirty Duck celebrating. Someone decided to start a game of higher or lower with tequila as the prize; I use the term prize loosely. Poor Jordan sucked at that game. I have never seen someone so sick before. Thinking about that night, I start to snort laugh and everyone looks at me. "Jordan, remember that evening in college at the Dirty Duck, after first term exams and we were playing higher or lower?"

He shudders. "How can I forget, worst night of my life." Everyone laughs. "And I have not touched tequila since and it's not gonna happen tonight either." He gives me a kiss goodnight. "Night everyone, thanks for coming and all your help." He then walks down the hall to our bedroom.

"You're such a pussy," Mike teases and slaps Jordan on the back as he walks past. He grabs the bottle, turns to us with the biggest smile on his face, "Let's play, assholes."

We start playing higher or lower, the card game from hell. You pray for the card to be higher than the previous one and nine times out of ten, luck is not on your side.

The next morning when, my mouth feels like the bottom of a dirty ashtray, and I feel like I have been hit by a bus and then reversed over, twice, I wish I had hidden like Jordan. Ugh! Why do I do this to myself?

Worst. Hangover. Ever.

19

KENZIE

JORDAN HAS BEEN MY ROCK, MY HERO, THE ONE I turn too when it feels like everything is crashing down on me. He is my savior and I want to do something for him, something to show how much I appreciate all that he has done for me. I've arranged for us to go to Europe and attend the opening weekend of the Oktoberfest. The idea came about when I won a $2000 travel voucher.

Originally I had planned for Mike and Jordan to go, but Mike had just gotten a new job and was unable to attend, so I stepped in, such a shame that was. Plus, when I think about it, Mike would have totally gotten them both arrested, so it was probably better that Jordan and I went. I didn't tell Jordan what we were doing, or where we were going. All I told him is that were flying to Europe for a tour, and everything is arranged. As soon as Jordan realises we are flying into Munich, he puts two and two together and figures out we are off to the Oktoberfest.

We arrive at the hostel and I immediately question my decision. "Oh My God, Jordan. What have I done?"

He looks at me confused. "What's up, Kenz?"

"Dude, this place looks like the one from that creepy *Hostel* movie, I don't think I can stay here."

Laughing, he replies. "You are too funny, Kenz, this place will be fine BUT if we get inside and you're still creeped out, I'll find us somewhere else to stay."

"Jordan, it's the opening weekend of the Oktoberfest, nothing will be available." Taking a deep breath, I add, "Guess I just have to put on my big girl undies and go with it."

"Personally, I prefer you with no undies but if it means we can stay then by all mean, grandma undie it up."

Punching him in the arm as I walk past, I lug my suitcase up the stairs and head inside. Thankfully when we get inside it loses it's creepy vibe and any fear I have vanishes. "Oh, thank God!" I whisper to Jordan.

He laughs, "Man I love you and your over active imagination. Let's get checked in and enjoy ourselves."

While Jordan checks us in, I look around. It's a pretty retro hostel; black and white checked flooring, neutral walls, which are covered in pictures, musical instruments and artwork, ranging from historic photos from around Munich, to old school record covers, and a few classic black and white film posters. The ceiling is littered with thousands of tiny fairy lights, I'd love to just lie back and stare at them. It would be like lying under the stars.

We meet the tour group in the basement of the hostel at 5:00 p.m. as per our itinerary, where we get our shirts and all the information that we need to know for the weekend. We all then head to this awesome outdoor beer garden, which is about a ten minute walk from the hostel.

This beer garden is magical. There are long rows of picnic tables with red and white checked tablecloths, little wooden crates filled with cutlery and condiments sit in the center. At one end of the garden there is a L-shaped timber bar with wooden barstools along one side of the L, the other side is a standing only service area. Through the rafters there are thousands of fairy lights hanging down.

We spend the afternoon, and well into the evening, drinking steins of beer and getting to know the rest of the group. After drinking five too many steins, Jordan and I stumble back to the hostel and pass out.

———

Today is the opening day of the Oktoberfest. The sun is shining and there's excitement in the air; Munich is buzzing. Bright and early Jordan and I are up, surprisingly not hung-over; *I love German beer*. After getting a coffee, we make our way to the Oktoberfest grounds, which is a short fifteen-minute walk from the hostel. Even though it doesn't officially open till 12:00 p.m., we need to be there at 9:00 a.m. in order to get into the Hofbrau Haus beer hall that the tour guides say is the best.

When we arrive, we get the typical touristy photo under the Oktoberfest rainbow entry, similar to the one in the hostel, and we make our way to the Hofbrau house and line up. The gates to the beer hall open at 10:00 a.m. and when they open, it's a free-for-all. Luckily we are with a tour group and get unofficial priority once inside. While we wait for the first keg to be tapped at noon, we eat German pretzels and drink Coke in steins.

The band keeps playing *Ruby Ruby Ruby* by Kaiser Chiefs, and when they do, everyone goes mental and sings at the top of their lungs. If it's this much fun when no alcohol is being consumed, I can only imagine what it will be like when the beer is flowing.

The first beers arrive just after 12:00 p.m., our waitress, Helga, can carry twelve steins at once; she's a rock star. I struggle to lift my stein, let alone carry twelve and dodge drunken fest goers at the same time. The day progresses and Jordan and I get extremely drunk and have a beertabolous time.

I'm so glad that I decided to surprise Jordan with this trip, and I'm really happy that Mike couldn't come; sorry not sorry, Mike. By 9:00 p.m., we are all beer'd out and we head back to the hostel. We shower and fall into bed, ready to do it all again tomorrow.

The next morning is a bit of a struggle, but apart from a queasy tummy, I feel fine. After a greasy brekky and a big ass coffee, Jordan and I walk back to the fest with the others. We start day two, or three if you count the day we arrived, in an outdoor beer garden. Once again the sun is shining and there is not a cloud in the sky. This beer garden is similar to the one from the first night, timber tables and bench seats, adorned with red and white checkered tablecloths and mini timber kegs filled with cutlery, serviettes and condiments. Hanging along the fence are wooden planter boxes with amazing red, white and pink peonies.

Sitting in the sun, drinking beer with the man of my dreams, I'm deliriously happy. This is what dreams are made of. Hours later, it's pretty hot and perfect outdoor drinking weather. Jordan looks to me and slurs, "Kenz, I'm gonna make beer just as good as this, and we are going to open a brewery. Yep, you and me are gonna open a brewery, and we is going to become the beer king and queen of Queensland, move over XXXX there's a new Queensland beer coming for you."

I look over and laugh, "Whatever you say, dude, have another beer."

He places his hands on my shoulders, squeezes and looks directly into my eyes, "No, Kenz, I'm serious. We *are* going to open a brewery and we're going to make amazing beers and live hoppily ever after."

Along with the rest of the group, I laugh at him. "Did you seriously just say hoppily ever after?"

"I sure did, Kenz, and I'm serious. Babe, we are going to open a brewery, I can feel it in my bones."

I look over at him and smile; I know that if Jordan wants to open a brewery that it will definitely happen … one day.

20

JORDAN

SERIOUSLY, I CAN'T BELIEVE THAT KENZ SURPRISED me with a trip to Europe and the opening of the Oktober-fest. Boy, am I glad that she bumped into me on the first day of college. If I had my time over, I would have asked her out sooner. That way she would have never hooked up with Clint and maybe I could have prevented her from getting assaulted and hurt by that asshole.

The Oktoberfest was so much more amazing than I ever thought it would be. I know Kenz thinks I'm joking about opening a brewery, but after saying that on the second day; I can't stop thinking about it. I decide that I'll chat to Kenz on the plane ride home and see if she'd like to embark on this venture with me.

After a rough cab ride from the hostel to the airport, we check in and decided to get some brekky while we wait for our flight. Kenz can only stomach a coffee, but I get the works: bacon, eggs, sausage, mushrooms, tomatoes, toast, and a big ass coffee. Her face turns a little green when my food arrives, and she takes off running to the bathrooms. *Poor baby,* I think to myself, before diving in and devouring my brekky.

She comes back ten minutes later and has a terrified look on her face. "Kenz, babe, what's wrong?"

"So, umm, yeah. I was sick and when I flushed, the toilet backed up and it overflowed, and I kinda vomited some more." Spitting my coffee out, I can't help it and I burst out laughing. Kenz doesn't look too impressed with my laughter. "I'm sorry, babe, but that is so friggin funny, I can't wait to tell Mike."

When Kenz sees me laughing, she starts to laugh as well. One minute she is mortified and the next, she's pissing herself laughing and snorting, in the middle of the Munich airport.

Man, I love this woman.

Our flight is called and we make out way to the gate. We get seated and the flight takes off, I turn in my seat and look at Kenz. "Hey, babe, you know how I said I want to open a brewery?"

"Yeah." She looks at me curiously.

"Well, I really want to do it, I can't stop thinking about it. In my mind I can see it now, all my brewing equipment behind glass walls so you can see everything that goes into making your beer, an awesome bar along one side. Tables and booths around the place, I seriously can't wait to start this. I've got it all worked out and I've only been thinking about it for thirty-six hours. I know which building in town I want. I have an idea for the layout, including a kitchen that serves kick ass food, and in honor of the Oktoberfest, and the creation of this dream, an outdoor beer garden, complete with timber bench seats, planter boxes, and flowers. Maybe I'll plant a sunflower garden in honor of you. "

Pausing, I add, "I want you and I to do this together. I know you enjoy helping me brew and you have a keen eye for everything. I can make the beers and you can manage the rest."

"Ooh my God, you seriously are serious about this."

"Deadly serious, Kenz. I think between the two of us we could make this happen and it will be amazing. Together, we can make beautiful beers and live hoppily ever after."

"Actually, if I'm honest, I haven't been able to stop thinking about it either. I'd love nothing more than to do this with you, Jor."

"Are you shitting me?"

"I'm serious, Jordan, I think this will be incredible. You and I can make beers and live hoppily ever after, as you would say. Besides, we will be adding a wine bar once the brewery is up and running and I can stock all my fav wines. Its win/win in my eyes."

"You seriously are awesome, Kenzie Merlot. I'm so glad you smashed into me eighteen months ago."

"Naw, you are too kind, Jordan McRoberts."

Kenz puts on her headphones and watches a movie. I, on the other hand, have a million and one ideas running through my mind. Before I can do this, I need to finish my course, so I can dedicate all my time to this venture.

21

KENZIE

AFTER WE RETURN FROM THE OKTOBERFEST, JORDAN and I are stronger than ever. This is the happiest I've been in my entire life. Jordan concentrates on finishing his degree, perfecting his already amazeballs beers, and setting up our brewery. He's so determined; I have never seen him like this before, and it's a total turn on watching him.

Sometimes I feel like I hardly see him during the week. He has increased the number of subjects he's doing each term, so he can finish his course quicker. However on the weekends, we both spend time together in the shed perfecting the beers. Much to my surprise, I'm really enjoying the behind the scene beer creation process. I mean, I like drinking beer but I never thought I would enjoy making it. My only wish is be that it smelled better while its fermenting—the hops and mash are disgusting, and when I comes to cleaning, ugh, I gag and dry retch every time.

Jordan finishes his course in record time and graduates in the top two percent of his class. I was so proud to see him walk across that stage and collect his degree. His graduation present from his parents is a two-week holiday in Mexico. They booked us into this amazing, all-inclusive adult-only resort in Cabo San Lucas. It has its own 2.5km private beach, five restaurants and bars, a spa, and a golf course. We treat ourselves and upgrade to an oceanfront suite with a butler, yes, our own personal butler. The room has a private balcony with unobstructed ocean views, and when we head to the beach we have our own dedicated cabana, also with our very own butler—this place seriously is heaven.

For the first three days, we laze by the pool or swim in the ocean; it's pure bliss. The sea is an amazing blue colour and the sand is so fine and white; I've never seen anything like it. Jordan teases me as I love sitting on the shoreline, digging my feet into the sand, and then I lie back and stare up at the sky. Whether it's sunrise, sunset, or the middle of the day its perfect and ohh so peaceful.

On day five, I send Jordan off on a deep sea fishing trip, and I spend the day in our cabana reading and drinking margaritas. At one point, I doze off because I wake up with Jesus, our cabana butler, tapping my leg. He's holding a silver box with a purple bow; reminding me of the one I received at graduation. He places the package on the end of the cabana and walks away.

Smiling, I think Jordan has sent me something special since I sent him off fishing for the day. I quickly sit up, untie the bow, and quickly lift the lid off. Looking inside I see that it is full of yellow daisies. It's similar to the one I received after graduation, again there is no note but something doesn't feel right this time around.

I keep an eye out for when Jesus returns with my margarita, I want to ask him about the package. I see him approach the cabana, and after he has placed my margarita down, I ask, "Jesus, who delivered my package?"

"I'm not sure *Señorita*. Someone from reception asked where you were and I offered to bring it to you. Is everything all right?"

"Yeah, I was just curious, that's all."

I pass the box to him and ask if he can deliver it to our room. With a smile he takes the package from me. Picking up my margarita I take a huge sip and moan. Jesus sure knows how to make a killer margarita.

After I finish my cocktail, I signal to Jesus for another, and I also order two shots of tequila. That eerie feeling I had earlier is back, I need to settle my imagination and tequila will fix that...I hope.

Jesus delivers my drinks and after sinking my shots, one after the other, I start to feel relaxed. Looking to my left between the flapping cabana materials, I see Jordan walking towards me. My heart flutters, he's wearing his favourite Billabong boardies and no shirt. I clench my thighs to ease the tingly feeling developing in my girly bits.

His aviator Ray-Ban's cover his eyes and he has the most amazing smile on his face, I'm guessing fishing went well. Our eyes lock, I jump up and race over to him. Wrapping my arms around him, I hug him tight. Him being here is just what I need. Closing my eyes I savor this moment. I rest my head on his chest, the beating of his heart calming me further.

"Well hello to you, Kenz." Pulling back he notices my uneasiness. "What's wrong?"

"I'm probably being silly, but I got a package while you were fishing. I thought it was from you but I'm not so sure anymore."

"What was in the package?"

"It was a box of daises, similar to the sunflower package you sent me after graduation."

Shaking his head, he replies, "Kenz, I didn't send you a package after graduation."

"What?" I shriek, garnering the attention of a few other guests.

"Kenz, I didn't send you flowers after graduation. The only present from me was the dinner I took you to."

"Then if you didn't send them, who did?"

"I don't know baby, maybe we need to check in with corrections and make sure that Clint is still locked away."

"That's a good idea, I'll text Mum and ask her to call. Actually, I'll text Sarah, I don't want to worry Mum. She's been through enough."

I have just finished texting Sarah when Jesus arrives with a Modelo for Jordan, and another margarita for me; seriously he is the best bar guy ever.

Jordan leads me back to our cabana and we snuggle, enjoying our drinks and watching the sunset over the ocean. The sunset tonight is remarkable; each day's sunset is more beautiful than the previous one. The colours are so vivid; oranges, pinks, purples, and yellows all meshing together.

The sun has just set and we are still snuggling in our cabana. I look over and see Jesus and another guy walking towards us with dinner. Jordan sits up and says, "So, I had a great fishing day, and the chef has prepared a feast for us with my catch."

We dine in our cabana on fresh Mahi Mahi, Bonita, prawns, salad, and chips. It is one of the best meals I've ever had. Jesus comes and clears our plates, returning with churros for dessert.

He returns a few moments later with two tumblers of tequila, which apparently goes amazingly well with churros. I snort laugh as he places the tumblers down, Jordan thanks him and he heads off. Being the ever so nice girlfriend that I am, I grab Jordan's tumbler and have a sip. It is seriously the best tasting tequila ever and I moan. Jordan looks at me and I say, "We should grab a bottle to take home for Mike, and by Mike, I mean me."

Jordan laughs and I manage to convince him to try the tequila. He hesitantly takes a sip, after swallowing, he looks to me and says, "After drinking that, I think I might like tequila." With his seal of approval, we ask Jesus to bring us a bottle. I see him smile in approval because Jordan has refused every tequila he has bought over to us to try so far. I, on the other hand, have knocked back every single one offered, and I have loved every one of them.

After dessert, Sarah texts me back to say that Clint is still locked up, and that he has not had any visitors except his cousin and lawyer; however she did say that he will soon be up for parole due to good behavior. I feel relieved to know he is still locked up, scared that he is up for parole and anxious about the flowers. I try and relax with Jordan, but the flowers weigh heavily on my mind. Jordan and I spend the rest of the night in our cabana drinking tequila and relaxing.

Jordan puts me at ease, telling me it was probably delivered to me by mistake; after all there was no card so it could have been for anyone. That makes me feel a little better, so I relax and enjoy the rest of the evening.

With the amount of tequila I consume, I soon forget about my anonymous gift and enjoy my time unwinding, with the man of my dreams.

The next two days we spend at the resort lazing about. Jordan and I even manage a round of golf. Well, I would not call what I did golf but we had a blast together.

I convinced Jordan to go to a local tequileria that Jesus recommended to us. This place had over three hundred different tequilas on offer, I had died and gone to tequila heaven. We tried a few, but between us we didn't even come close to trying them all. We both tasted one that was velvety smooth on your tongue, and easily slide down your throat, leaving you warm and fuzzy on the inside. We bought a bottle to take back home, but this will be one that we hide from Mike. We did however find one that would be perfect for him.

———

A week after we arrived, Jordan arranged a spa afternoon for me; while I was being pampered, he was going to play a round of golf. He was acting strange as I was leaving, but I was too excited for the bliss that I was about to enjoy to really take notice. Leaning down, I gave him a kiss and headed off to the spa.

I'm booked in for a Spa Indulgence Package, which includes a body wrap, facial, massage, and a glass of bubbles. I also added on a spa manicure and a glam pedicure.

Three hours later, I emerge feeling chillaxed and amazing. My skin is as soft as a baby's bum, and I have pretty toe and fingernails to go with it. Bright fuchsia pink for my toes and fairy floss pink for my fingers. *The ladies back home need to come here for training*, I think to myself on the way back to our room. As I pass the sports bar, I look at the time and decide to stop in and enjoy a glass of bubbly before heading back.

After two glasses of bubbly, and a chat with Miguel, the bar tender, I look at my watch and guess that Jordan should be finished by now. Waving goodbye to Miguel, I head back to the room. I start thinking about what we will do tonight. Since I'm super relaxed from my spa afternoon, I'm thinking room service on the balcony and more bubbly sounds perfect.

On my way back to the room, I see a private table being set up in the Oceanfront Bar, and I make a mental note to ask Jordan if we can do that one night before we leave; it looks so romantic.

Arriving at our room, I open the door and my mouth drops open in shock. There are tea light candles everywhere and a rose petal path leading into the bedroom. On the bed, there is an amazing pink chiffon strapless dress and silver wedge strappy sandals in a box next to it. On top of the box is a note in Jordan's handwriting. As I read the note from Jordan, tears well in my eyes, and my face breaks out in the biggest smile. This is the most romantic thing anyone has done for me.

> MY GORGEOUS KENZ,
> I HAVE ARRANGED A SECRET SURPRISE FOR YOU THIS EVENING, COMPLETE WITH CLOTHES AND SHOES. YOUR MAKE-UP ARTIST WILL ARRIVE AT 5.30PM AND I WILL PICK YOU UP AT 6.15PM FOR A NIGHT TO REMEMBER.
> THERE IS A BOTTLE OF BUBBLY IN THE BATH-ROOM WAITING FOR YOU, ENJOY AND I WILL SEE YOU SOON GORGEOUS.
> ALL MY LOVE,
> JORDAN XOXOX

There is a knock on the door and I rush over; it's Rosa-Maria from the spa, she did my nails. Smiling at her, I step aside so she and her trolley can come in.

She works her magic, and twenty minutes later I look stunning, if I do say so myself. I have smoky eyes, rosy but subtle cheeks, and my lips look amazing. My hair is in a low bun that looks awesome. She then helps me slip on my dress and I put my shoes on, while she packs up her stuff.

I stand up just as she walks out of the bathroom and she looks over at me, with a smile she says, "*Te ves Hermosa.*" She laughs at my confused look, I don't speak Spanish, so I have no idea what she said but it sounded beautiful. Walking over to me, she places her hand lovingly on my cheek. "You look beautiful."

As I am not one for compliments I blush. She nods at me before grabbing her things and leaving. Looking at the clock I see I still have ten minutes until Jordan arrives, so I pour myself another glass of bubbly. With my glass full, I head out onto the patio and watch the sun start to set while I wait. The sky is already filled with amazing colours, I can't wait to see the sunset tonight.

22

JORDAN

Kenz just left for the spa, she thinks I'm playing golf but I'm not. Secretly I'm setting up the most epic proposal in the history of proposals, I hope. Before she left, I was so nervous; I felt like I was going to vomit, but I don't think she picked up on it. Heading to the Oceanfront Bar, I meet up with Alejandro; he and I have been covertly speaking since we arrived to get this all arranged. Kenz and I don't keep secrets from each other, and I hate keeping this one, but I know that it will all be worth it in the long run.

Arriving at the Oceanfront Bar, I see that all the couches and lounges have been moved to the side, and there is a lone table in the middle, set for two. Smiling, I think to myself, *it looks amazing already; I can only imagine how it's going to look at sunset with all of the fire pits lit.*

I walk over to Alejandro, "Dude, this looks amazing, thank you for everything."

"Your welcome, *Senior*. The flowers will be delivered

just before you arrive, as it's still quite hot, and I would hate for them to wilt. Everything we have arranged for your soon-to be-fiancée is happening as we speak. I must tell you, you are a lucky man, *Senior*."

Slapping him on the back, I smile. "Tell me about it, Alejandro. I pinch myself everyday that I get to wake up beside Kenz. I want to make this a night she will remember fondly, forever. I'll let you get back to it." Turning, I head towards the bar to grab a beer to calm my nerves. My heart is erratically beating and I'm sweating like a bitch right now.

Miguel looks up from the bar as I walk in, smiling he says, "Here's the man of the hour, you nervous?"

"Not at all, dude, not at all...okay, maybe just a little." We both laugh, "I've been waiting for this day my whole life. I can't wait to see the look on her face. She deserves all the happiness in the world, and I'm the lucky son of a bitch, who will get to wake up next to her everyday, for the rest of my life" I hope. *Shit what if she says no?*

Miguel places a Modelo in front of me. "Thanks dude, I need this to calm my nerves." Taking a sip, I groan in pleasure, "Fuck this is good beer, one day I will make beer, just as good, if not better."

After throwing back two more beers, I feel a sense of calm wash over me. My nerves have changed, from scared to excited. On my way to get change, I spy Kenz, and hide behind a column and watch her. She looks extremely relaxed and so, so, beautiful; my cock twitches at her beauty in the afternoon sunlight.

I'm unbelievably lucky that she fell into my life. She heads towards the Oceanfront Bar and I start to panic.

Then I see her detour towards the sports bar where I just was. *Lucky I left when I did.*

After changing into beige linen slacks and a charcoal grey button-up shirt, I head back to the sports bar for another calming beer, my nerves have reappeared with a vengeance. It's amazing how beer can calm me. I finish my beer and look at my watch. "It's show time, Miguel, wish me luck."

He puts down the cocktail shaker he was wiping, and shakes my hand, saying, *"Buena suerte,* Jordan." Looking at him confused, he laughs and says, "Good luck, Jordan".

I nod my head, "Thanks," I nervously reply, before rushing off to meet my girl.

23

CLINT

THE PAROLE HEARING GOES IN MY FAVOUR, AND I'M let out early for good behavior. It was so easy to trick those fuckers. Luckily my cousin has taken me in, without her I would be screwed. You can always count on family to help you in a time of need, just like I was there when she needed me. We have each other's back when it counts.

My cousin managed to get the address of where she moved, I've been watching Sweetcheeks from a distance. It has been so hard staying away but I need to wait, we will together again soon. I'm currently outside her house, I can't stay away. It's been too long since I have seen her, so I pop over for a visit. Standing on her back patio, I'm looking into her and asshats house. It doesn't look like anyone is home, and it doesn't look like anyone has been here for a while. Being ever so nice, I wanted to drop off a package for Mackenzie, but I decide that I'll deliver the package when I know she is home.

I really hope my Sweetcheeks is okay.

Starting to worry, I look through the French doors and see a photo of her on the fridge. She is smiling at me, I forgot how beautiful she really is, my cock hardens when I think about her. Unzipping my cargo shorts, I walk over to the green timber lounger, where I have photos of her sunbaking topless; I sit down and take my throbbing cock out. Thinking about her beautiful tits, my cock hardens, it's now rock hard, it could slice through steel. Licking my palm, I rub it over the head, closing my eyes. I grip it tight and imagine that it's Mackenzie's hand and not mine. Clenching my shaft, I pump faster and faster, squeezing tighter with each stroke. With my eyes still closed, I visualize her beautiful green eyes staring up at me as she pumps my cock faster and faster, flicking her tongue out before taking me deep into her throat.

Rolling to my side, I lean over and can just see her picture on the fridge. Her beautiful face is smiling back at me. Increasing my strokes, they become quicker and more aggressive, before I know it, I'm coming all over my hand and the lounger.

As I put my cock back inside my cargos, I smile and picture her, lying here topless again. My cock twitches as I think about my Sweetcheeks naked, lying here in the future. Now that I have marked my territory, we will be that much closer until we can be together again.

After I leave her place, I meet up with my cousin and we head to a bar for a few drinks. There is a blonde checking me out. It's been a while since I have sunk myself balls deep in pussy and I think she will do. I stalk over to her and its too easy, she's heading out back with me before I've even bought her a drink.

Grabbing her roughly, I slam her against the brick wall near the industrial bins and shove my tongue deep into her mouth. She kisses me back before she bites my lip, drawing blood. The metallic taste turns me on, and I plunge my tongue back into her mouth, roughly kissing her before spinning her around so she's facing the building. Lifting her non-existent skirt over her hips, I rip her red g-banger off and slam myself balls deep into her tight hole. She grinds her ass further into me, so I continue to pound into her. I wrap my hands around her throat, squeezing it, shutting off her air way. The panic radiates off her body and it's such a turn on. I keep slamming into her, squeezing tighter and tighter with each thrust. She starts scratching at my hands and it makes me squeeze tighter. "Ohh, Sweetcheeks, I've missed this," I growl as I continue to plow into her. I feel her body start to slacken just as I pull out and release my load all over her ass.

Letting go of her, she stumbles away, turns around and slaps me hard across the cheek, "You fucking prick, you were choking me."

"Yeah, and?"

"You are one messed up asshole." She pushes her skirt back down, tears flowing down her cheeks. "Stay the fuck away from me, asshole."

"With pleasure, you were a lousy lay anyway."

She storms off and I head back into the bar where I have another drink with my cousin before we head home.

24

KENZIE

Swallowing the last of my bubbly, there's a knock at the door. My heart rate increases and nerves settle in; I'd recognise that knock anywhere, its Jordan. Placing my empty glass on the wooden TV cabinet, I make my way to the door; with each step my nervousness increases but I'm sure that this will be a night to remember.

Opening the door, I see Jordan standing there in a charcoal grey shirt and beige linen pants; the muscles between my thighs immediately tighten when I see him. Raking my eyes up and down his svelte body, I smile. Looking up I see he has a smug smile on his face. "You like something you see?" he cockily says, raising his eyebrows seductively before winking.

Staring into his eyes, I shrug my shoulders and innocently reply, "Meh, I've seen better." We both burst out laughing.

It's Jordan's turn to look me up and down, and I can't

help but notice some movement in his pants. I can't help but cheekily say, "Like what you see?"

He stares into my eyes and I can feel his gaze deep within my soul. "Fuck yes. My God, Kenz, you are stunning."

Wrapping his arms around my waist, he leans down and kisses me, his tongue grazing across my lips, before pushing in. Our tongues do the tango, fighting for dominance. I moan into his mouth as he deepens our kiss and draws me in closer. He pulls back and rests his forehead against mine, panting, "We better get going, otherwise I won't be held accountable for what I do to you. I knew this dress would look stunning on you, Kenz, but fuck me dead, you are gorgeous."

The smile on my increases at his comment. "Thanks, you don't look to bad either, handsome. So, what have you got planned for tonight?"

He pats the side of his nose. "It's all a surprise, baby, now come with me. Tonight will be a night you will never forget." He winks at me, grabs my hand, interlaces our fingers and we head towards to beach. My nerves kick up a notch as we head off and happiness courses through my veins with each step we take.

Jordan leads me towards the Oceanfront Bar where they were setting up earlier. In the middle is a single table set for two, beside the table is a bucket of bubbly and an amazing bouquet of sunflowers.

When I see the sunflowers, I realise that this is for me. I stop midstep and take it all in. There are several fire pits lit and the flames flicker, their shadows dancing on the sandstone paving, creating a romantic atmosphere.

The serenity is enhanced by the sound of the waves crashing onto the beach below. A cool breeze is blowing, wafting the scent of the ocean and kitchen towards us. I'm in awe of the scene set out in front of me.

As we walk towards the table, our waiter, Alejandro, approaches with two flutes of bubbly. He hands the glasses to us with a smile and slight nod of his head, "*Senior, Señorita*," before turning and walking away.

Jordan grabs hold of my hand and we head to the edge of the bar area and gaze out at the sunset over the ocean. The sky is burnt orange, filled with many shades of red. The fiery orb of the sun is slowly sinking into the horizon; leaving in its wake a midnight blue sky filled with millions of tiny shimmering stars; it's spectacular.

"Jordan, that was the most magnificent sunset I've ever seen. I don't think I've ever seen such vivid colours or so many stars." I say in amazement, looking up into the night sky. "It was stunning, Jordan."

Looking over I see Jordan staring at me. "Yes, you are stunning."

My cheeks heat and I feel my neck breaking out in my nervous rash. I lower my head in embarrassment, my heart is beating so loud within my ears. Jordan takes my bubbly and places it on the stonewall next to us. Turning back, he grabs both of my hands in his, his thumb rubbing back and forth, I can feel him shaking. I gaze into his eyes and the moonlight shining from behind me makes them sparkle. Any and all thoughts disappear, I'm lost in Jordan.

Jordan clears his throat and takes a deep breath. "Kenz, you came crashing into my life, literally, and I was mesmerized by your emerald green eyes and the red wine coloured top that you were wearing. You were, and still are, the sexiest person I have ever met, you constantly take my breath away and you are just as beautiful on the inside. From that day on, I went out of my way to see you whenever I could. I know it was a dick move considering you were with him, but I just had to be near you. When I got my chance, I was over the moon. I do wish I got my chance without all the shit that went with it, but it led us to this point right here. You have brought such joy into my life, Kenz. I can't imagine my life without you in it."

Excitement builds when I realise what's about to happen. My heart rate increases, my palms become sweaty, I feel sick with nerves and excitement and I'm pretty sure, I stop breathing.

Letting go of one of my hands, Jordan reveals a hand-crafted timber box with two love hearts engraved on the top. Still holding my right hand, he lowers down on one knee. "Kenzie Louise Merlot, will you do me the honour of becoming my wife?"

Through tears I look down at Jordan, I look around and it's just the two of us under the moonlit sky. I'm so nervous and floored; I ask the stupidest question ever. "Is that for me?"

Jordan laughs, "It sure is, baby. There is no one else I want to spend the rest of my life with. Kenz, baby, will you marry me?"

Pulling my hand free, I cover my mouth, and with a smile I yell, "Yes, yes, Jordan McRoberts, I will marry you!" Jordan opens the box to reveal a stunning gold and white gold engagement ring. It has one central diamond and on either side encased in white gold are six tiny diamonds, three on each side. He slips the ring onto my finger and stands up. Wrapping his arm around my waist, I wrap mine around his neck and we have our first kiss, as a newly engaged couple.

Lifting me up, he spins us around, our lips meshing together in one of the most romantic kisses of my life. He places me back down and stares into my eyes. "You have made me the happiest man alive."

He turns around and shouts into the night sky, "Kenzie Merlot just agreed to marry me, I am the happiest man on Earth!!! WooHoo!!"

He turns back to me and places his hands on either side of my face, pulling me in for another kiss. This one is full of passion; I place my arms tightly around his neck and deepen our kiss, just as fireworks go off in the distance. Out to sea, we can see a boat on the horizon and the fireworks are coming from there. Jordan spins me around, and we watch the fireworks show, with our arms wrapped around each.

When the fireworks finish, Jordan leads me over to the set table and signals Alejandro to bring the meals. We sit down and enjoy an amazing three-course feast.

After Alejandro clears away our dessert plates, he brings another bottle of bubbly, places it in the ice bucket, and then moves it next to one of the wicker lounge chairs by a fire pit.

Jordan stands up and puts his hand out to help me up. I place my left hand in his and my engagement ring flickers in the moonlight; I smile and wiggle my finger in the moon's radiance. We make our way over to the lounge, where we snuggle together by the fire, not saying a word, just enjoying each other's company, the bubbly, and the serenity. Blissfully dozing off to sleep in Jordan's arms, I wake up when he lifts me and is carrying me back to our suite.

We arrive at our room and Jordan tenderly places me on the bed, removes each of my shoes, stands up and stares down at me; his eyes are full of desire and I'd say mine are the same. Positioning myself up onto my knees, I smile as I wrap my arms around his neck. Kissing and nipping along his jaw line and up to his mouth, I gently tug at his bottom lip before crushing my mouth to his. Our tongues do the tango but this time Jordan wraps his arms around my waist, crushing me flush against his chest, intensifying our kiss. He kneels onto the bed, and gently eases me back so he is lying on top of me. Not once do we break our kiss, our lips sealed together. I run my fingers up the back of his head and back down his shoulder blades, gripping onto his tight perfect ass, pulling him closer to me.

Our kiss builds up, as the muscles between my legs clench, I drag him closer to me, moaning into his mouth, loosing myself in this perfect moment. Jordan gazes down at me, his eyes ablaze with lust, I whisper, "Make love to me, fiancé."

Jordan smiles. "As you wish, fiancée."

He quickly removes his shirt, stands up, and removes his pants and boxer briefs, in one swift motion. I lay there, staring at my sexy fiancé, wondering how I got so lucky to be engaged to this fine specimen standing naked in front of me. My eyes, roam over his body before

landing on his impressive erection. I lick my lips in anticipation; he reaches his hand out for me and pulls me until
I'm sitting up.

Grabbing the hem of my dress, he gently and ever so
slowly slides it over my head, discarding it to the pile with
the rest of his clothes; leaving me in my bra and undies.
He gently pushes me back onto the bed and crawls his
way back up my body. Placing kisses gingerly up my legs
and across my stomach, sadly bypassing my pussy. He
arrives at my breasts and begins to rub me through my
purple strapless bra. My nipples peak immediately,
reaching behind I unclasp my bra. Jordan flicks it to the
side and takes my erect nipple into his mouth and begins
to massage the other.

Pleasure cascades through my body, as I start to grind
myself against his leg, my wetness seeps thru my undies,
coating his leg. Jordan alternates between my breasts, and
I can feel myself getting wetter and wetter. Tugging on
his hair to get his attention, he kisses his way up my neck
towards my ear, nibbling on my earlobe, I giggle. He
kisses along my jawline much like I did earlier and then
up to my mouth. Opening up, I let him in and he kisses
me deeply.

We kiss like this for a few moments before I spread
my legs, inviting him in. Smiling as I feel his hard throbbing cock at my entrance, he gently rubs my sex from top
to bottom, the friction from the satin intensifying. He
shreds my undies and gradually slips the tip of his rock
hard cock into my wet folds, before withdrawing all the
way back out. I cry out in frustration as he continues to
tease me.

Finally he enters me.

"Ohh, Jordan."

He gently thrusts in and out of me, I wrap my legs around him as we fall into a passionate rhythm. Reaching down, I grab Jordan's ass, digging my fingers in, our rhythm quickening. I start to feel that magical tingling sensation develop deep in my belly. Before I know it, I'm tumbling into my orgasm, fireworks exploding, my whole body quaking; the hairs on my head prickling as my orgasm continues to erupt through my body. As I'm coming back to earth, I feel Jordan exploding inside of me, his body trembling with ecstasy as he releases his seed.

He pulls out and collapses next to me. We are both breathless from the most intense sex we have ever had. We roll onto our sides, and stare into each other's eyes. No words are said but the air is electrified. Love radiates uncontrollably between us. Reaching out, I grab Jordan's hand and I entwine our fingers together, leaning forward I gently kiss his knuckles. Pulling our clasped hands towards me, I tuck our hands between my breasts. We fall asleep gazing at one another with our hands held close to my heart.

———

The sun is shining through the shutters the next morning, and I wake up to Jordan lifting my leg over his shoulder and his head between my legs. Nipping and sucking at my clit. Smiling, I arch my back, pushing my pussy closer to him. He sucks harder and licks down my slit, inserting his tongue into my wet passage, darting his tongue in and out and occasionally sucking on his way out. He inserts one finger and then another, all while rubbing my clit with his thumb. It doesn't take long for the tingly feeling to appear in my belly. I come with such force; I grip the sheets tightly, turning my knuckles white, as pleasure courses through me. I scream out his name as my orgasm reaches its peak.

Lifting his head, he wipes the side of his lips. "Mmhmm, breakfast of champions." He lays back down next me and I take the opportunity to straddle his hips. I grind my drenched pussy onto Jordan's growing cock. Leaning over, I drag my breasts up his chest and kiss him. Tasting myself on him, makes me wetter.

Lifting up onto my knees, I gently lower myself onto his pulsating cock. Arching my back I take him deeper, as thrust and I ride him. Reaching down, I start rubbing my clit with one hand as I massage my tits with the other, pulling and tugging on my nipples. Closing my eyes, I feel my orgasm building. My head falls back and Jordan nudges my hand out of the way. He uses his thumb on my already swollen clit. I whimper in delight as my orgasm continues to build. Jordan reaches up with this other hand and grabs my nipple between his thumb and fore-finger, squeezing tight before massaging my breast with his palm. The pain is quickly replaced with pleasure, and I begin to ride him faster and faster.

Feeling Jordan's cock harden within me, I clench my pussy tighter riding him quicker and quicker. Within moments, together we tumble over into the orgasmic abyss.

Climbing off of him, we lie next to each other, breathless, our chests rapidly rising and falling as we try and catch our breath. Smiling, I look over at Jordan. "Morning, fiancé, you can wake me up like that anytime."

He rolls onto his side to look at me, "Morning, fiancée, I will happily wake you like that everyday for the rest of your life." He leans over and kisses my cheek.

"Don't make promises you can't keep, fiancé"

A few hours later, I wake up alone and see Jordan sitting on our verandah in a robe sipping coffee; grabbing the other robe, I head out and join him. When I open the slider, I'm hit with the amazing smell that is coffee and fresh salty ocean air. Leaning over, I kiss Jordan's shoulder, and then his cheek before I walk around and sit on the other timber lounger.

Smiling at me, he leans over and pours me a coffee. As I take my coffee from his outstretched hand, I smile. Taking a sip, I groan.

Jordan grins. "Fuck, I will never tire from hearing you moan like that. I remember the first time we had coffee at Java Lava, I near came in my pants I hearing you moan like that."

Laughing at the memory, I also smile, it's one memory of Jordan that stands out in my mind too. That day I was so upset and in an instant Jordan made me feel safe and relaxed. Even though it all went to shit later that day. But again, Jordan was there for me when I was recovering, I don't think I would be sitting here if it weren't for him.

Looking up, I see Jordan staring at me. "Thank you for making me the happiest girl in the world, Jordan.

Yesterday was just perfect, like beyond my wildest dreams perfect. I love you, almost as much as I love coffee."

"Your welcome, Kenz, and I love you almost as much as I love beer." He winks at me, "You saying yes has made me the happiest man in the universe." He stands up and sits on the end of my lounger, before kissing me fervently, pulling back to rest his forehead against mine. He then kisses the tip of my nose. "So, fiancée, what should we do today?"

I love hearing him say fiancée and it's only been twelve hours; what am I going to be like then he calls me wife? "Well, fiancé, how about we head to our cabana and have a lazy pool day? Actually, lets sit at the swim up bar and get super rotten drunk. Then we can come back here and have super drunk fiancée sex in the bathtub, I've been dying to do that since we got here. We can ask the bar dude to get our butler dude to fill up the tub, just before we are ready to come back. What do you say fiancé?" *I love saying fiancé just as much as hearing Jordan say it.*

Jordan rests his chin on his fingers and taps his lip as if deeply thinking about what I just suggested. "Well, fiancée, I think that is the second best idea you've ever had."

Looking inquisitively at him. "Second best?" I question.

"The first was when you agreed to marry me last night," he says matter-of-factly.

"Dude, that was a no brainier. You could have taken me to Maccas and I still would have said yes, but I do absolutely love the way you proposed to me. I can't wait to tell Sarah all about it." As I get up to get changed, I wonder when Josh is going to propose her?

Half an hour later we are both changed and ready to go. Jordan is wearing teal Billabong boardies, and I have a patterned orange and beige tankini that shows off my girls nicely, with a solid orange bikini bottom with ties of the same pattern as the top.

After placing our stuff in our cabana, we dive into the pool and the water is amazing, so refreshing. We swim over to the Aqua Bar and it's none other than our favourite bartender, Miguel, on duty today. He looks at us and smiles. "It's the newly engaged love birds, congrats, *Señor y Señorita*." He shakes Jordan's hand and leans over to kiss my cheek, as I flash my hand towards him to show off my ring.

"What can I get you, *Señorita*?"

Looking at the cocktail menu I say, "Miguel, can I please get one of your amazeball margaritas." Looking up I add, "And Jordan will have a Mo..." Before I finish, Miguel is placing a Modelo in front of Jordan; I shake my head.

"What?" Jordan asks as I raise my eyebrows at him. "What can I say? Miguel is awesome at his job and knows what I like."

Five minutes later, Miguel places the biggest margarita I have ever seen in front of me, and I cannot help but smile. Taking a sip I close my eyes, savour the taste and moan. It is seriously the best margarita I have ever had. I look over towards Miguel and shout, "Thank you, Miguel, this is freakin' amazeballs!" He nods and smiles before he starts serving another couple.

Jordan and I spend the rest of the day swimming and drinking beer and margaritas. It's so relaxing and the most chilled-out holiday I have ever had. I cannot ever remember being this happy and relaxed. *Thank you Mr. and Mrs. McRoberts for this amazing trip.*

We spend the next few days how we started our holiday, either lazing by the pool or swimming in the ocean. Before we leave, we finally manage to christen the tub and I have one of the most intense, electrifying, mind-blowing orgasms of my life in there. I even have the bruises to show for it.

This has been one amazing trip. Not just because I got engaged, but it was spent with my soul mate Jordan. Never have I been this happy before, I am literally on cloud nine right now and nothing could change that...or so I thought.

25

KENZIE

...7 months later

OUR WEDDING IS ONLY SEVEN WEEKS AWAY AND I'M over the moon excited. Everything is organised for a small intimate wedding with just our immediate family and close friends. The ceremony will be at the rotunda on top of Mount Coo-tha, with the reception hosted at the Summit Restaurant. We have about twenty-five guests in total, I think, and so far everything is going to plan. There may have been one or two bridezilla moments, so I think I am doing extremely well.

Clint was released seven months ago from prison; surprisingly it doesn't bother me. Even with him free, I feel safe and happy. Thankfully, I haven't seen or heard from him. I can finally put the nightmare that is Clint MacNicholson behind me and keep moving forward with my life.

Currently I'm on cloud nine and could not be happier. In seven weeks I'm marrying the man of my dreams and today, at work, I was promoted to team leader. When we returned from Cabo I thought I was happy but at the moment, I am ecstatically happy and nothing can bring me down.

Hopping off the bus, I walk down the street to our house, as usual, and in my peripheral vision I see a yellow car pull up beside me. All of a sudden, the hairs on the back of my neck stand on end, fear building inside me. Before I have a chance to look around, a cloth is placed over my face and everything goes black.

26

CLINT

Fᴜᴄᴋ! I ʟᴇꜰᴛ ɪᴛ ᴛᴏᴏ ʟᴏɴɢ. Sᴡᴇᴇᴛᴄʜᴇᴇᴋs ɪs engaged to that wanker.

I can't fucking believe it.

She is mines not his!

I need to make my move but she's always with him or with that skank ho slut, Sarah. I'll get my chance and then Sweetcheeks and I will be together forever.

Finally, she is alone.

I'd just left another flower package on her doorstep, and as I was driving down the street I look up and see her. Her golden hair blowing in the breeze as she steps off the bus and I know that it's finally time to put my plan in motion.

This is my chance.

Thank you fate.

Driving past her, I pull over and park. I open the boot and soak a rag to make my move. I'm ever so thankful that I had all of this ready and waiting in my car.

Sneaking up behind her, I wrap my arms around her

waist and shove the cloth in her face. She goes limp quickly and I catch her as she falls, cradling her in my arms. *My beautiful Sweetcheeks.*

Taking a deep breath, I breathe her in; her scent is remarkable. Having her in my arms again is wonderful, and my cock agrees. He hardens in my jeans, it hasn't been this hard in a long time.

My beautiful Sweetcheeks is back in my arms...I cannot wait to sink myself inside her.

Quickly, I throw her in the boot before climbing into the driver's seat, and I race away to our cabin. We arrive a short time later and it's just as I left it when I came here a few weeks ago. Looking around, I smile; our love nest is perfect.

I cannot wait to be with Sweetcheeks forever.

27

KENZIE

When I come to, its dark and then I realise that I'm in the boot of a car. Fear takes hold and I kick and scream. We drive for what feels like hours, but in reality it was only about thirty minutes. We eventually screech to a halt. I hold my breath and anxiously wait for the boot to open. When it does, the sunlight is blinding. It takes a few moments for my sight to come into focus and I see Clint's evil face staring back at me. "Your awake Sweetcheeks, welcome back to our happily ever after."

Grabbing me by my upper arms, he roughly wrenches me out of the boot of a canary yellow SUV of some sort, dropping me on the ground before he slams it shut. I scream at the top of my lungs. He slaps me hard across the face, I see stars from the force. He pulls me up by my hair and drags me towards the cabin, again I scream. When he hits me again, I black out.

This time when I wake, I find myself handcuffed to a rusty metal single bed, which was once white with pink little flowers, similar to Sarah's when we were growing up. The mattress is ratty and torn in spots; springs poke through, digging into my back. There's a white wooden dresser by a door, with a full-length mirror that has seen better days, it has a jagged crack down the center. I presume there's either a wardrobe or ensuite bathroom behind the door. There's also a small side table next to the bed, similar in design to the dresser.

The window has been painted black, casting the room into darkness. The only light is from a dim bulb hanging down from the ceiling. I've no idea what colour the walls are since they are covered in a light sheen of dust. I'd guess they are a buttery yellow. The room is absolutely disgusting, the musty smell nauseating, and I'm scared shitless.

My chest tightens; I struggle to breathe, my body shaking, and sweating, as the attack sets in. I close my eyes, trying to calm myself down. Telling myself, "breathe in, breathe out." Taking a final deep breath, I calm myself down, keeping the attack at bay...for now.

Opening my eyes again, I take another look around the room and notice that one wall is covered in photographs; photos of me. There are pictures of me at work, me lying topless in the backyard, Sarah and I at the gym, Jordan and I at the beach; any photo with Jordan in it has his face scratched out. There are even photo's from my graduation; it seems that while he was locked up, he had someone watching me.

From the corner of my eye, I notice Clint sitting in the corner in a wicker chair. Staring at me. He doesn't say a word, he just silently stares at me. I can feel the anger radiating off him. I start to panic and wrench on the cuffs, but as I thrash about they get tighter and tighter. As the panic escalates, I start to cry.

He looks at me and smiles, it's the creepiest smile you can image, I cringe as his eyes roam over my body. "Mackenzie, baby, now we can be together forever. No one will come between us. I have everything we need here. We will never have to leave again. It will be you and I, forever."

I stare at him in shock, I cannot possibly be hearing him correctly. Finding my voice I manage to squeak out, "Wh...what d...do you m...mean fff...forever?"

"Mackenzie, Sweetcheeks, baby, we are meant to be together and you and I now will be. We are the modern day Romeo and Juliet."

Before I have a chance to reply, he jumps on top of me. Gyrating his hips into me, grunting and groaning; his cock hardening against me. He continues to dry hump me, each thrust becoming rougher, and rougher.

"Mackenzie, feel how hard you make me?" He licks up my cheek, "No other girl has ever made me this hard. Your sweet pussy was made for me. I am never leaving you."

He kneels up, unzips his fly, and his pulsating hard cock springs free. He begins stroking himself and then he lifts up my work skirt, rips off my undies, and forces himself inside me. I scream in pain, it burns. I scream and he punches me in the face. He continues to thrusts in and out of me. Harder and harder, deeper and deeper. He continues to thrust over and over. The burn is unbearable, I feel like I'm being split in half.

Just when I think that I can't take anymore, he pulls

out and sprays his cum all over me. With a sickening smile, he stares down at me. He reaches out to wipe my tears away, I shake my head to avoid his touch. He grips my chin, leans down and tries to kiss me. I thrash not wanting him to touch me. This pisses him off again and he slaps me hard, right near where he punched me. I can feel my face start to swell. With the crack of his palm against my cheek again, my head flies to the side. I keep it there staring at the yellowing wall...into nothingness.

With a grunt, he stands up, puts his cock away, zips up his pants, and walks out of the room, slamming the door behind him. Leaving me alone with my own thoughts. I begin to cry again. I pray that someone will find me, and soon. This is so much worse than when he attacked me at my apartment, I have never been this scared in my entire life.

Returning moments later, I notice a sharp knife in his hand. My eyes widen in fear as he begins to cut my black pencil skirt down the middle, pulling it from beneath me, he tosses it onto the timber floor. Placing the knife on the side table, he rips open my worktop; buttons fly everywhere. Picking up the knife, he cuts my teal green bra between my breasts, nicking my skin. I scream out in pain when he digs the knife in.

He slaps my left cheek. "Shut it, bitch," he growls.

He picks up my undies he tore off of me, scrunches them up in his fist and sniffs them. Breathing in deeply. "Beautiful," he whispers, licking his lips while he looks down at me with an evil grin, I notice the bulge in his jeans starting to grow. Shutting my eyes, I hope that when I open them again that this will all be a horrible life-like dream. Opening them, I deflate when I see him standing above me.

He's staring down at me, his hand stroking his cock through his jeans. He unzips his black denim jeans, works them down his legs, exposing his purple throbbing cock. He slams him cock inside of me before I have a chance to comprehend what's about to happen.

Screaming out in pain, I start to cry. Once again, it feels like I'm being split in two. He repeatedly pounds into me, the tears flowing down my cheeks, I whimper and scream louder as the pain becomes intolerable. Drawing his fist back, he punches me in the face, as he continues to thrust into me.

"Shut the fuck up, bitch." He growls as I lay there and let him violate my body.

———

Over the next few days he rapes me over and over, but he never comes inside of me. He always pulls out at the last minute, spraying his cum on my body. I lose count at how many times he rapes me. I begin to wish for death; I'm don't know how much more of this I can survive.

My body aches. My face is throbbing, and between my legs is torn to pieces. There is dried cum on my body and blood between my thighs. Bite marks adorns my body. He told me he was marking me as his. "You are mines." He repeated over and over and he bit and marked my skin.

I've given up screaming, I realise we must be somewhere pretty remote.

No one has come to rescue me yet.

I don't know how much longer I can go on.

I'm ready to give up.

I feel like I have been here forever, but it's only been seven days, I think. Time is ticking by so slowly. Everything is starting to blur together. I continue to wish for death but fate is a cruel bitch. I'm still alive, broken, but alive.

I'm shocked awake when I feel something roughly being shoved into my ass, followed by a long thin silver dildo into my pussy. When he turns the one in my pussy on, I groan, but when he turns the one in my ass on, I scream out in pain. My ass has never been touched before and the pain is horrendous. It feels like I'm being ripped open from the inside. I start to sob again. He plucks the one in my pussy out and quickly shoves his cock back into me with such force that my teeth pierce my tongue. I can feel the metallic taste from the blood in my mouth and I start to cry, my sobs wrack through my body.

He slaps me across the face and between clenched teeth he spits, "Stop crying, bitch, you had this coming." He keeps thrusting harder, faster and deeper; just before he comes he pulls out and squirts his load all over my chest and chin. He bends down licking the cum off me, roughly rubbing what's left into my skin. Once he's finished licking and rubbing me clean, he starts slapping my face, over and over; eventually I pass out from the pain.

The next morning, Clint comes back into the room with a contented look on his face; immediately I'm fearful for my life. He places a tray with orange juice and a sandwich onto the bed. That's when I notice the carving knife. I start to panic; why does he need a carving knife for a sandwich? My heart starts to race and my breathing becomes shallow.

It's in this moment that something deep inside of me clicks; I decide I want to live and that today I will escape; even if it's the last thing I ever do. If I want to get out of here alive I need to pretend to be the Juliet to his Romeo.

God, I hope I can do this.

Looking towards him I smile and whisper, "Clint, baby."

"Don't call me baby, you lying whore. I saw you having coffee with that twat, right after you ripped my heart out. How long have you been screwing him, huh?" He is yelling now, seething with rage, "Where do I fit into this scenario, huh?" Between clenched teeth he hisses "You. Are. Mines."

I'm dumbfounded by what he is saying. "Clint," I plead, "I'm not screwing him, or anyone else for that matter, Jordan and I are just friends."

He clenches his jaw and glares at me. "Don't say that fucker's name." He looks towards the window before looking back at me. "I know you two are friends who fuck. What's that called? Yeah, fuck buddies."

"No!" I scream. "Clint, I swear." As the panic sets in, I start to cry again. I sniffle, "You are the only one I want to be with."

"Bullshit, you little slut. You're just using me to bide your time. Bitches like you always do."

At this point I have no idea what's going to happen but I need to do something quickly; otherwise I will be here forever. Clint sits on the side of the bed and looks down at me. He almost looks sad and I think this is my chance. I try and lift my hand to reach him, to sooth him but my hands are still bound. I take a deep breath and in my sweetest voice possible I whisper, "Do you think you can unlatch or loosen the cuff, please?" I look at him pleading, I try and lift my hand, but it barely moves. "Please, Clint, I need to make this up to you. I...I need to fix us." I whisper before quickly adding, "I made a mistake breaking up with you, please, please forgive me? Let me fix this, baby, let me fix us."

He looks away before turning back to me and rubbing his hand down the side of my face. I try really hard not to flinch. "Do you really mean that?"

I tilt my head into his palm. "Of course I do baby." Inside I'm saying to myself, *"You wish you fucking freak."*

Again I plead with him, "Can you please uncuff my hands, so we can be together again?" Glancing up at him I bat my eyelids, hoping like hell that I don't look like I'm having a fit.

Dropping his hand from my cheek, he stands up. My heart sinks, but he pulls out a little brass key. He reaches across me and uncuffs both of my hands. I slowly sit up, rubbing my wrists. He bends down and cuts off the cable ties, holding my ankles together. I sit there staring at the floor, he sits down next to me and rubs my leg. Shivering from his touch, he assumes I'm cold. He takes off his shirt and slips it over my head; at least I'm not naked anymore.

Looking towards him, I take a deep breath and quietly murmur, "Thank you!" Leaning over, I pretend that I'm about to kiss him, but instead, I lunge for the knife on the tray. Grabbing the knife, I swing with every-thing that I have left. I manage to slash his face, and with all my might, I shove him off the bed. I swing back my leg, kick him in the stomach, turn and run.

I make it out the front door and down the rickety wooden stairs. I run like I've never run before. Huffing and puffing, I don't stop. I just keep running. My body is aching, but the adrenalin coursing through my veins keeps me going. I have no idea where I get the energy or the confidence from, but somehow I make it to the main road.

After what feels like an eternity, I finally see a car. I turn around, waving my arms, yelling and screaming for them to stop. My waving becomes erratic, my arms flinging around above my head like a mad person. The SUV stops and a middle-aged gentleman gets out. He walks over to me and I collapse into his arms with relief and begin to sob. He calls triple zero and hold me tight, rubbing my arms reassuringly.

"My name's Trevor darling." He sooths after hanging up, "Help is on the way." I thank the powers above, Trevor is definitely my guardian angel.

The police and ambulance arrive at the same time. Trevor lifts me onto the stretcher and the ambo looks me over. He can't see any major injuries, but he is concerned that my cheekbone might be fractured. Due to the amount of swelling he cannot tell for sure. Again he tells me that I'm very lucky as none of my injuries are life threatening.

Before we leave, the police ask me questions regarding what happened. I tell them what I remember and after I give my statement. Just as they are closing the ambulance doors, the officer returns and tells me that that a missing person's report was filed, and they have someone contacting my family now. As the doors slam shut, I start crying at the thought of seeing everyone again. I never thought I'd see them again, the emotions overtake me and the ambo gives me something to calm down and I drift off into a peaceful abyss thinking of Jordan and my family.

28

JORDAN

KENZ JUST CALLED TO TELL ME SHE WAS PROMOTED today, I'm so proud of her. I'm also glad that my trip to Melbourne has been cancelled. I really don't feel like going to meet these investors; my head just isn't in it at the moment. All I can think about is our wedding and making Kenz, Mrs. Jordan McRoberts.

Stopping atthe bottle-o around the corner, I pick up a bottle of GH Mumm to surprise Kenz and celebrate her promotion; another reason I'm glad that my trip is postponed. As I'm driving up our street, I see Kenzie's monstrosity of a purse and her jacket on the footpath. Pulling over, I stop and pick them up; immediately that sick feeling from earlier is back, with a vengeance.

Quickly racing back to my car, I haul ass to our house but no one is home. There is a bunch of sunflowers sitting at the front door, but this time there is a card, its signed 'Love, C,' my heart immediately drops.

I know that Clint has taken her.

I've failed my beautiful Kenz when I promised to protect her.

Grabbing my phone I call the police immediately. They send someone over, but it takes the officers an hour to get to our place. They tell me that Clint didn't check in with his parole officer yesterday and with the flowers signed 'Love, C' they also think that he has taken Kenz. The assholes also ask if it could be a case of cold feet as we are getting married soon. I lose it with the officer, "My ass she has cold feet. She's just as excited as I am for us to get married." He apologises and says he had to ask; they need to cover all bases. They leave and tell me they'll be in touch when they have news.

Standing in the kitchen, I yell, "Fuuuuck!" I stare at the pic of Kenz and I on the fridge, I say, "Fuck this, I know Clint has you baby, I will save you."

Snatching up my phone, I call Margaret and let her know what has happened. She tells me that she and Skye are on their way. I tell them to drive safely and I'll see them soon.

Next, I call Mike and tell him what's happened, and he tells me he will be over as soon as possible. Mike gets here ten minutes later, racing in the front door. "Dude, what the fuck is going on?" He takes a seat on the chaise, staring at me.

Taking a deep breath, I fill him in on everything. "I've failed her again, Mike. What if I lose her? I can't live without her."

"Kenz is one tough chick, if anyone can beat this, it's our girl."

Mike quickly stand ups and says, "Let's go for a drive

and see if we can find her. I don't know where to look but we can't just sit around and do nothing."

"Sounds like a plan, Mike." Standing up, I grab my keys but Mike stops me.

"Okay, let's go but asshat, I'm driving. You're too worked up and we need to get there safely, for our girl."

I knew I could count on Mike.

Mike and I drive around for hours but we don't find her; I wasn't holding out any hope that we would. By time we get back to our place, Margaret and Skye are waiting on the front steps. I wrap my arms around Margaret as she cries. I feel broken and lost right now, I can only imagine how Margaret must feel.

———

The next seven days are pure torture.

I can't eat.

I can't sleep.

I just keep thinking about Kenz, hoping and praying she is safe.

When we get the call to say she's been found and alive, we are all so relieved. We race to the hospital to wait for Kenzie to arrive. When I see her, my heart breaks into a million tiny shards.

The girl lying in front of me is broken, physically and mentally.

She's fragile.

She's lost.

And there's nothing I can do to help ease her burdens.

29

KENZIE

I'VE JUST GOTTEN SETTLED IN MY ROOM WHEN THERE is a knock at the door, the officer from today is here. He informs me that the police searched the area, and they found the cabin but Clint was nowhere to be found. They will keep searching and looking for him but at this stage there is no trace of him. It's like he vanished into thin air, if it weren't for my injuries you'd think I made this up.

A warrant for Clint's arrest has been issued, and his parole terminated. They assure me that they are doing everything they can to find him and that an officer will be stations outside my room until Clint has been apprehended.

The next morning, Clint is arrested when he tried to visit me at the hospital. As soon as I heard he was here, I lost it. I was crying and screaming, fear coursing through my body. They had to sedate me to calm me down.

Later that day, the officer returned by to let me know

that Clint was formally charged with parole violation, assault causing grievously bodily harm, criminal sexual conduct, violating a restraining order and kidnapping. He is to be remanded in custody as he is delusional and they fear he will be a menace to society; and me. I sigh in relief knowing he is locked up again.

I'm kept in hospital for ten days due to the extent of my injuries and mental state. My left cheekbone is fractured, I also have two broken ribs, four cracked ribs, five stitches to the laceration between my breasts and my lower intestine is torn from the anal penetration. Due to the savageness of the rape, there is also a high probability that I will never conceive a child.

I've hardly spoken a word to anyone. I pretend to sleep most of the time, and when I'm alone, I sob. I'm numb, broken beyond repair and even though someone is always around, I feel alone.

When I'm released, I crawl into myself, and stay locked in our bedroom, only venturing out when I need the toilet. I only shower, eat, or drink when Mum, Jordan or Sarah make me. The rest of the time, I just lie in bed and stare at the ceiling.

I'm not sleeping. Every time I close my eyes, I see his face. When I do fall asleep, I wake up screaming from horrible nightmares. Every time I close my eyes, I relive it all over again. Someone always races in to soothe me, but I cannot stand to be touched at the moment, so it takes a while to calm me down.

It's been two weeks since I was released from hospital, and I haven't left the house. Whenever I get near the front door, I start to panic and run back to our room. My fear is heightened when corrections called to let me know that due to Clint's mental state, the doctors feel he is unfit for trial. He is to be remanded in custody indefinitely at a psychiatric hospital.

As soon as I hang up, I have a complete break down. I scream. I cry. I let out all my frustrations. Mum and Jordan, just stand there and watch, helpless to help me. Once I'm finished, I race back to our bedroom and I'm so exhausted, I cry myself to sleep.

———

I see his face when I close my eyes.

I see his face when my eyes are open.

I see him everywhere, I can't go out in public.

I'm broken.

I'm scared.

I'm lost.

I decide to take an indefinite leave of absence from work; it's not fair to my coworkers. My boss, Karl, is awesome about it, and he tells me that my job will be waiting for me when I'm ready again. *I'm not sure I will ever be ready again.*

Two weeks later, and four weeks after the incident, I move out of Jordan's and my bedroom and I lock myself in our spare room. It isn't fair for him to be on eggshells in his own room. Each and every time I look at him, I feel guilty. I try to explain how I feel but he doesn't understand, no one understands. Every Tom, Dick, and Harry tells me that I'm not to blame and that they love me, but

I am to blame for this and love won't fix this...nothing will.

I wish they would just treat me like they did before all of this happened. They all look at me with pity and that makes me feel inferior. Internally I keep screaming at myself for letting this happen again.

Again?

How could this happen to me again?

I've let down Jordan, I can no longer give him a child.

I've let down Mum, I can no longer give her grand-children.

I've let down myself.

I've let everyone down.

I'm worthless.

I'm nothing but a waste of space.

This time it's much harder to deal with it. This time the attack was much more brutal. How stupid I am to get attacked again? And by the same person? Being attacked once is bad enough, but to be attacked twice by the same monster makes me weak and unworthy.

I just want to be me again.

Thankfully, Jordan gives me the space I need, but I can see it's taking a toll on him. The only good thing to come from this mess is Jordan spends all his time in his beer/man cave, perfecting his recipes. I guess that's the silver lining to all of this.

A few weeks later, I'm in the toilet when Mike arrives, I overhear him and Jordan talking in the kitchen. Jordan says, "I don't think she is getting any better Mike, if anything she is pulling away even further."

"Give her time, dude. I can't fucking imagine what

she is going through right now. To be attacked once is terrible, but twice and the second time being so much more brutal; I know if it were me, I wouldn't be the same. She just needs time, Jordan." Pausing, he looks at me and adds, "Just remember, Kenz is strong. She will get through this."

"I know she is strong, and I know she will get though this but I'm not sure how much more I can take." I gasp at hearing this, and they both turn and look at me standing in the hall with tears streaming down my face. Turning, I run back to my room and lock the door.

Jordan races down the hall, he tries the handle but thankfully I locked it. I can't look at him right now. He keeps rattling the doorknob and when it doesn't budge, he starts knocking and banging on the door. "Kenz, I didn't mean it like that. It's not what you think, please let me in."

Ripping open the door with tears pouring down my face, I stare at him. The floodgates have opened and there's no stopping them now. "How am I meant to take not sure how much more I can take? Huh? Tell me? Tell me?" I yell, beating my fists against his chest; my tears are uncontrollable by this point. "It's killing me, Jordan, I feel so weak, so useless, so...so..." But I can't talk anymore; the tears have taken over. My whole body is shaking as I collapse into Jordan's arms. He wraps them tightly around me and for the first time since the attack, I feel safe in his arms.

We sink down to the floor in the hallway and we sit there in each other's arms while I cry into his chest. He doesn't say anything, he just keeps whispering. "Shhhh, let it out, baby." Occasionally, he kisses my head, reassuring me that he is still here for me.

After crying for what feels like days, I look up at Jordan. "Why can't people see that I'm strong? I survived this once before, I can survive this again, I just need time Jor." Pulling away, I stare at him, and add, "I refuse to let him ruin my life, because if I do, then he wins and I will not let him win."

Jordan doesn't say anything, he leans forward, kisses my forehead and whispers, "You are the strongest person I know, Kenz. You will survive this and I'll be right there with you, every step of the way."

We snuggle into each other further and Jordan starts to rub my back in circles, just like Sarah does when I'm upset. When I realise what he is doing for the first time in weeks, I laugh. Jordan pulls back and looks at me, "What's so funny, Kenz?"

"You're rubbing my back exactly how Sarah does to soothe me when I'm upset. It's not really funny, but it is, if that makes sense."

Jordan lets out a throaty laugh, leans down and kisses my forehead just like he used to. *It's starting to feel like old times.* We sit in the hall together, not saying a thing, both sitting there quietly supporting each other. Glancing up I notice that it's now dark outside, and that Mike is no longer here.

Jordan is still rubbing my back and he hasn't stopped since we ended up sitting here. "This is nice," I whisper. I push away and look up at him. I gaze into his eyes. All I see is love; no pity, no remorse, just love. Smiling at him I say, "I think I need to make an appointment to see Jeannie. I can't do this to you or me anymore. I want to be me again."

"I'll call her in the morning for you, Kenz, but for now I want to take my fiancée to bed." Tensing in his arms, I start to panic. He draws back and looks lovingly into my eyes. "To sleep, but first you need a shower."

Reaching up, I wrap my arms around his neck for a cuddle. "I like that plan," I whisper, as I hold him tighter. Feeling better after my meltdown, I smile against Jordan's chest.

I AM strong and I WILL survive this.

We stand up and Jordan leads me into the bathroom. Jordan takes his shirt off and starts to unbutton his jeans. I freeze. "Umm, Jor, I'm not ready to shower with anyone yet, baby steps." A look of hurt flashes across his beautiful face but he quickly smiles. "No worries Kenz, I'll go lock up the shed and be right back." He grabs his shirt from the hamper and walks out.

As I climb into the shower, I start to cry again. I stand under the steaming hot water and let it all out. Wishing I could just wash away all my fears. *If only it was that easy.*

After my shower, I put on my grey trackies and Kings jersey and head to the kitchen. Jordan is on the phone, he looks up at me when he hears me coming into the kitchen, and his face lights up just like it used to. He quickly finishes his conversation and hangs up. "Hey, baby, feel better after your shower?"

Jumping up onto the island bench I look over at him. "Yeah, I do, actually. I um, um, I want to apologise for everything."

He leans on the bench opposite me. "Kenz, you don't need to apologise for anything, if anything I should be apologizing to you." I look over and see sadness in Jordan's eyes, "Once again I didn't protect you. I promised your mum that I would always protect you when I asked her permission to propose." Looking up at me, he smiles sadly, before adding, "But most of all I failed you, I promised to do so, when you agreed to marry me, and I didn't live up to that promise. I've failed you both."

I look at him inquisitively, "You asked Mum's permission?"

"Yeah, it's the right thing to do," he replies, as if I asked him to pass the chips.

Again I find myself smiling, a genuine smile not the fake plastered on one I have been wearing recently. Looking over at him with such love in my heart I say, "You are amazing, Jordan McRoberts, how did I get so lucky?"

"Well your clumsy ass kept bumping into me, so I thought for my safety I should ask you out." He looks up at me with a sneaky grin.

"Hardy har har, asshat."

As I sit here with Jordan, I realise that for the first time in weeks I'm not scared and I can't help but smile at that revelation.

Jumping off the bench, I walk over to where him and I wrap my arms around his waist, resting my head on his shoulder just like I used to. I breathe him in and sigh, "I'm sorry for pushing you away, Jordan. I'm sorry for letting you down."

He tilts my head up and looks me in the eyes. "How did you let me down, Kenz?"

"By letting him take me, I'm a failure." Lowering my head again, that happy euphoric feeling is quickly disappearing. The fear and weakness sneaking back in.

"Kenz, look at me."

Lifting my head, I look up and I see nothing but love in his eyes. "I'm only going to say this once, you are not a failure. It's not your fault that some psycho asshole douchcanoe fuckwit did unspeakable things. You are not to blame, you hear me?" I nod, and I snuggle back into the comfort of his arms, but deep down; I know I'm to blame.

Pulling away I say, "Can we snuggle on the couch and watch *That 70's Show?*"

"We can watch whatever you want, Kenz, but I refuse to watch that Kardashian crap." Laughing I grab his hand and we head to the lounge room. We snuggle together on the couch and watch *That 70's Show* for a few hours, just like old times.

Later that night, for the first time in weeks, I fall asleep, peacefully in Jordan's arms. I sleep the night through and no bad dreams plague me.

The next day, Jordan and I call Jeannie, and she makes room for me on her schedule. We meet with her, and just like last time; she makes me see that I did nothing wrong, and that I am strong. I am a survivor and I will get through this; again.

After we get home Jordan heads to his beer cave and I take a relaxing bubble bath. While soaking, I shake my head in frustration at myself, I really I wish I had been back to see her earlier. She helped me the first time, and after just one session I feel so much better already. I really am lucky to have such amazing people on my team.

For the first time in weeks, I feel free, liberated, and not scared. Yesterday's meltdown was exactly what I needed.

30

JORDAN

Last night snuggling and watching *That 70's Show* with Kenz was amazing. I was starting to feel like I was losing her, but after her hallway breakdown, I think we are back on track.

When I realised she had heard my conversation with Mike, I felt like a piece of shit. While I meant what I said, I never wanted her to hear it. I was just venting. There's no way in hell I would ever abandon her. Kenz is my everything. I would do anything for her, anything.

Today though, I can see that it was the jolt Kenz needed. As much as it pained me to see her breakdown like that, it was the push she needed to start her recovery. I'd been pestering her to go and see Jeannie, but no one tells Kenz what to do; she's quite stubborn. I'm glad she decided to go back and see her therapist. She worked wonders the first time around, and after just one session, I can see that this time will be just the same.

After her appointment, I suggest that we stop at the Java Lava for a coffee, but I see the hesitation in Kenzie's eyes, so I don't even wait for her answer and we head straight home.

We get home and she heads upstairs to have a bath and read one of her dirty books. Leaving her alone, I head to the beer shed and start working on a new pale ale. The last one wasn't quite right, so this time, I use a different hops. I hope and pray to the beer God's that it works.

Once all the new ingredients are in the wort tun, I turn off the lights, lock up, and head back upstairs. Just as I get upstairs, Kenz is coming down the hall, still rubbing cream into her arms. She looks up at me. "Hey, baby, how'd you go?"

Smiling back at her, I say, "All good, got the new pale down, and I hope to God it tastes better than the last one. Do you wanna watch *That 70's Show* before bed?"

"Actually, I think I'd like to watch *The Walking Dead*, if that's okay? I'm also going to open a bottle of wine, would you like a glass?"

"I'd love one and *Walking Dead* sounds great."

Kenz opens a bottle of white and I grab the wine bucket and two glasses. Then we snuggle on the couch, drinking wine and watching *Walking Dead*.

Smiling, I realise, that things are starting to feel normal again and that we will be okay and we will get through this.

31

KENZIE

...6 months later

OUR WEDDING DAY IS THE BEST DAY OF MY LIFE, AND the wedding night is one I will not forget anytime soon. Jordan and I are married on Hayman Island with our closest friends in attendance. It's just Jordan and I, Sarah and Josh, and Mike and his latest floozy, De-Niece.

The day is absolutely perfect.

Our parents were upset not to be included, but as I explained, I don't want a big fuss anymore. We each had our special one-on-one time with them for specific wedding related things.

Mum and I had a lovely girls' day out the day I found my wedding dress, complete with pampering at the local day spa.

Jordan and his dad went golfing together one day, where his dad passed on the secret to a happy marriage. Apparently, Jordan just needs to remember two very important phrases, "Yes dear," and "You're right."

The morning of our wedding, Sarah and I get ready in her suite. Jordan and I had to give up our room, as Mike and Sarah have a surprise for us; if Sarah wasn't involved I would be scared. Who knows what Mike would get up to on his own? Actually, leaving those two to their own devices IS super scary.

I'm in the bathroom and yell out to Sarah to give me a hand with my dress. My dress is a Collette Dinnigan original; it's made from beautiful French lace with cap sleeves, a low V-back with scalloped lace edging and three layers of silk lining. It comes with a gorgeous detachable belt that has small pearl and bead detail. Leaving my hair down, I curl it and wear the tiara that Mum wore when she married Dad.

It's ten to three, so Sarah and I make our way down to the beach. When I reach to the archway, *Pachelbel: Canon in D Major* starts to play, that's my cue. Taking a deep breath, I start walking towards Jordan. I even manage to stumble when my foot gets caught on my dress. I look up and everyone is laughing, tripping on my wedding day is so me.

Glancing up, I look towards Jordan and get lost in his emerald green eyes. It's in this moment that I know that this is it for me; there are no butterflies in my tummy; this is where I'm meant to be. I've never been happier, and I'm pretty sure the smile that is currently on Jordan's face, is a mirror image of mine.

It's a quick ceremony, and before I know it the celebrant is pronouncing us husband and wife. Jordan dips me and we have our first kiss as Mr. and Mrs. McRoberts; it's sensual, erotic, and it left me breathless. It's the second best kiss of my life. The best being my first kiss with Jordan after our first official date.

As we sign the registry, *Nothing Else Matters* by Metallica starts to play. Mike yells, "Fuck Yeah!" We all laugh, trust Mike to swear at a pivotal moment on our special day.

After the ceremony, we pose for a few photos and then we head to the restaurant for a relaxed reception. They place us at a table in the back of the restaurant. The table is laced with sunflowers and tea light candles; it's absolutely breathtaking.

The bubbles are flowing and the food is to die for. After dinner Mike asks everyone to follow him; we are walking down a pathway that is lined with tea light candles. As we get closer to the beach, *Lanterns* by Birds of Tokyo starts playing. When we step onto the beach, we look up and there are hundreds of paper lanterns floating in the sky. On the sand is a big love heart, lined with candles, with J and K etched in the center.

Looking over to Mike, I see him smiling. I'm pretty sure that the smile I have on my face is just as big as his. Letting go of Jordan's hand, I walk over to Mike and give him a hug. No words are said but none are needed in this moment. After the incident, Mike and I have a newfound relationship. It's one I will treasure forever, and this gift has left me speechless. It's so enchanting, something right out of a fairytale.

The next song to play is, *Everything I Do (I Do It For You)* by Bryan Adams. Jordan asks me to dance, placing my hand in his we walk to our heart. We stand in the middle and lose ourselves to the music. I look over and see that Sarah and Josh, and Mike and De-Niece, are also dancing. We dance for several songs, drink the bubbly, and enjoy the night together.

Leaving the beach, we head to out room. When we arrive, Jordan lifts me up and carries me over the threshold; I can't help but giggle. He places me down just inside the door, and I place a quick kiss on my husband's lips. *I love saying husband.* We turn around and there are, what feels like, thousands of tea light candles flickering and sunflower petals strewn on the floor, making a pathway to the bed.

Turning to Jordan, I see he is staring at me. "Mackenzie McRoberts nee Merlot, you are the most beautiful bride I have ever seen. This dress is absolutely stunning, and I cannot wait to see it on the floor."

Blushing at what he says, I look up into my husband's eyes and in a low sultry voice I whisper, "Well, what are you waiting for, husband?"

"Absolutely nothing, wife."

He pushes me up against the back of the door and kisses me senseless. This kiss is now the most romantic kiss of my life; it leaves me lightheaded and my lips are tingling when Jordan pulls away. I wrap my arms around his neck and I drag him in closer. I lift one leg up and wrap it around his thighs, his hands roams up my leg and over my garter. I shiver in delight as his hands inch higher up my thigh. He groans into my mouth when his fingers reach my undies and feels how wet they are.

He rubs my slit through the silk of my undies; I moan

and rub myself on his hand. Lowering my leg, I spin around, lifting my hair, and without prompting, he carefully undoes the clip at the top. He places feather light kisses across my shoulder blade as he lowers the zip. Carefully, I lower the straps down my arms, wriggling my ass, my dress falls down, the lace and silk pillowing out at my feet. Turning around, I face my husband in nothing but my tiara, silk undies, silver heels, and a beaming smile. Jordan's eyes roam over my body; I have never felt sexier in my entire life. "Fuck me, Mrs. McRoberts, you are fucking beautiful."

Carefully stepping out of my dress, I step towards my husband, "You, my husband, have far too many clothes on for me to really appreciate you." As I reach him, I rip open his dress shirt. Pearl buttons fly everywhere, and I make quick work of removing his shirt. Reaching forward, I undo his belt and lower his fly. Slipping my hand inside for a quick squeeze before I push down his pants and boxer briefs in one swift motion.

Kneeling down, I take his thick throbbing cock in my mouth. Licking from tip to base and back up again, while squeezing the base of his cock; I hollow my cheeks and take him deeper into my mouth. With my other hand, I massage his balls while I bob my head up and down, sucking and licking his pulsating cock. His balls tighten in my hand and I feel his cock tense. Just before he comes, he lifts me up by my shoulders and kisses me deeply. He pulls back and cradles my face is his palm. "Kenz, the first time I come with you as husband and wife will not be in your mouth, it will be together as one."

Leaning forward I kiss him again; I drape my arms

around his neck and raise my leg, wrapping it around his waist. He grabs my ass and lifts me up. I wrap both legs around his waist, digging my heels into his ass. Our kisses becoming frenzied as he walks us over to the bed. He gently lays me down on the mattress and hooks his fingers into the sides of my undies and slowly works them down my legs.

Grabbing my ankle, and ever so slowly, he kisses his way along my calf, up my thigh and across the top of my mound. I think he's going to suck on my clit, but he pulls back and spreads my legs wider. He bends down and finally licks my slit. Starting at the bottom, taking his sweet time, he slides his tongue to the top, before sucking on my swollen nub. My back arches off the bed as he twirls his tongue around and around, sucking, licking and gently nibbling my clit. Gripping the sheets, I throw my head back in ecstasy as my orgasm starts to build. Arching my back further, I thrust and grind my pussy onto his face. He licks down, spreading me open wider as he slips in a finger. Pulling out his fingers, he smears my wetness all over my pulsating pussy.

His tongue darting in and out of my pussy is mind-blowing. He inserts two fingers and finds that magical spot deep inside. As I run my hands over his head, I gently massage his scalp, tugging on his hair; the tingling in my pussy intensifies. I'm writhing in ecstasy when he inserts a third finger and sucks on my clit. Gently blowing on my sensitive nub, as his fingers scissor in and out of me. I scream Jordan's name when he sucks on my clit, as my orgasm detonates, it's like fireworks going off on Australia Day. My body vibrates from head to toe, as my orgasm takes over my soul; it's the most amazing feeling, ever.

As I am coming back down to earth Jordan kisses and licks his way up my stomach, over my nipples, up my neck, and along my jawbone. Gently nipping my earlobe before he eases back to look at me; I see nothing but lust and hunger in his eyes. Closing his eyes, he leans forward to kiss me, and that kiss takes my breath away. I can taste myself on his lips and it ignites a fire deep in my belly once again.

Wrapping arms around his neck, I bring him closer to me and I guide his cock between my legs. He gently eases into me, before pulling out and slamming back in. I lift my hips to give him better access and spread my legs further apart. I have never felt Jordan so deep inside of me; I moan into his mouth and kiss him deeper. Meeting him thrust for thrust, Jordan reaches between us and rubs my clit as I tighten my legs around his waist. My pussy muscles clench his cock tighter, as we tumble over the edge, and orgasm together, for the first time as husband and wife.

Jordan rolls off me and I snuggle into his side. We lie together, both catching our breath. I run my fingers over his chest and nipples, back and forth until I feel his nipples harden. Rolling onto my side, I rest my head on my palm and I look into his beautiful green eyes. "Wow, Mr. McRoberts, that was just...wow."

"You're not wrong there, Mrs. McRoberts."

He reaches out to brush a tendril of hair behind my ear and whispers, "I love you, wife," before kissing the tip of my nose.

"I love you too, husband." Leaning over, I kiss him. Shuffling towards him, I deepen the kiss, pushing up so I'm straddling him. Rocking my hips, I feel his cock growing beneath me as I continue to grind my pelvis onto him.

He sits us up, wrapping his arms around me as I wind my legs around his waist. He bends down to take my breast into his mouth, alternating between sucking my nipple and massaging my breast, while twisting and tugging my other nipple between his thumb and forefinger; which he knows I love.

Pulling up I gently lower myself onto his hardening cock; I push him back so he is lying down and I ride him. Throwing my head back as that tingling sensation starts to creep all over my body, I keep riding him, rocking my hips faster and faster. Arching my back, I reach down to rub my clit while playing with my own nipples. "Kenz, that is so hot." Rubbing and circling my finger faster; the sensation on my clit becomes overwhelming and my orgasm quickly ruptures through my body. At the same time, I feel Jordan's balls tighten, and he releases himself inside of me for the second time tonight.

Collapsing onto Jordan, I lie there for a few moments before I roll off onto my back. Jordan leans over and kisses my cheek and whispers, "Good night, Mackenzie McRoberts," but I'm already fast asleep.

The next morning, I wake up to Jordan's cock pushing between my ass crack and him nibbling my neck. Grinding my ass into his cock, I throw my leg over his hip and guide his cock into my pussy. His hand snakes around and he starts to tweak my nipples. Letting out a contented sigh, I turn my head to kiss him. He starts thrusting into me quicker, and I reach down and rub my clit, sending myself over the edge. I keep thrusting and Jordan soon releases inside of me.

Rolling over to face my new husband, I give him a kiss on the cheek. "Good morning, husband, that was a wonderful way to wake up."

"Good morning, wife, I'm happy to wake you up that way for the rest of your life."

"Mmhmm, I won't say not to that." I snuggle into him and soon we both fall asleep wrapped in each other's arms.

After a horrible start to the year, Jordan has managed to turn it around and into one that I will never forget.

I am Mrs. Jordan McRoberts. I'm blissfully happy and safe...for now.

KENZIE

...18 months later

Today is the day that we finally move in to the old Queenslander we renovated and I'm sooo excited. We stripped the house back to bare frame, removed a wall, added internal stairs, and started from scratch. Repainting the outside a deep brown with reddy-brown surrounds, we added beautiful French doors that lead out to an extended verandah, which runs the length of the house. There are timber stairs that lead directly to the beer shed and a paved undercover entertaining area which leads out to the grassed backyard and inside to the family room, laundry and internal stairs.

Jordan insisted on putting a shed in straight away and I'm glad we did. Having an ice-cold beer at the end of the day after renovating, especially in the summer when it was hotter than hell, was beertabolous. I'm pretty sure this is why the renovation took so long as he'd tinker with his beers rather than renovate but Jordan really knows how to make a great beer, so I'll allow it.

Now that the reno is complete, Jordan and I can concentrate on our next dream, opening our brewery, Malt Me. If it had not been for my attack, Malt Me would be up and running by now.

With the last piece of furniture coming through the door, we are officially moved in; thank firetruck for that. I've come a long way in the last two years. For a while there I was lost, but I have the support of my family and friends; but most of all I have Jordan. He is my rock. I honestly don't think I would have survived this the second time, if it were not for him.

The only major DIY injury I sustained was severe blisters on my hands from removing the glued lino-on-lino that was in the old kitchen; ohh and a broken ankle when I was taking empty paint tins to the bin. That was twelve weeks that I never want to go through again. The only good thing about my broken ankle was all the reading I could do.

Jordan and Mike have just hooked up the stereo system, and I head down to the shed and pour three beers. Coming up the back stairs, I walk in as Mike and Jordan are laughing their asses off. I can't help but smile, it's nice to see him relaxed, for a change.

Handing them their beers, I raise my mug and say, "A toast, to finally moving in."

Jordan adds, "Cheers to that. I guarantee you, we are never doing that again, tell me again why I let you convince us to do this?"

"Well, it looked easy on The Block, ohh, and you love me."

Mike clears his throat and says, "As long as you keep brewing stuff like this, asshat, I'll hang around. This is the bomb dude."

Quickly I jump up and yell, "Jordan, never make this one again if it means we get rid of Mike!" I wink at him as I walk into the kitchen to grab us some snacks. It feels good to finally relax and enjoy our house.

I'm bending down in the pantry, to get out the platter, when Jordan walks over and places his arms around me, "I love you, Kenzie McRoberts. I can't wait to christen every room in this house."

Mike interrupts, "Hello, I'm still here."

"There's the door, don't let it hit you on the way out!" I shout as I wriggle out of Jordan's arms and step to the fridge to get the cheese, olives, and salami's. After placing it all on the platter, we head to the side verandah and sit at the high-top table with timber-backed chairs and super comfy chocolate brown cushions, which match the window surrounds.

Jordan heads down to the shed to top up our beers. We hang out for a few hours, relaxing and just being us.

"I'll catch you later guys, and Kenzie, it's good to see you still smiling."

Jumping off my chair, I give Mike a big bear hug, and whisper, "Thanks for everything, Mike, you have not only helped me but you've been there for Jor when I couldn't be. I'll never be able to repay you for that."

"You can pay me in beer," he whispers, I can't help but laugh.

Mike heads inside to get his phone and keys, and on the way out, he yells, "Later, assholes!" before slamming the front door. Just as Jordan and I both yell in unison, "Don't slam the door!"

———

Jordan takes the pizza boxes out to the bins after dinner, and I relax on my uber comfy, charcoal grey suede corner lounge with chaise at one end, and recliner at the other. I look around at all that we've done to this place, and I smile. We, well Jordan, has done a brilliant job.

Jordan walks back in and his smile is just as big as mine. "It's so great to see you smile, I love seeing you smile." He leans over the back of the couch and pecks on the forehead. "We finally finished this place and I couldn't be happier."

Looking up at him I say, "It's all thanks to you, baby."

He jumps over the back of the couch and pushes me down. He lies on top of me before crashing his mouth to mine. Our tongues fighting it out as my girly bits begin to tingle. Jordan pulls back and looks deep into my eyes. "Now, about christening this place." He leans down, I close my eyes and he places a kiss, just under my ear. "I" **kiss** "think" **kiss** "we" **kiss** "should" **kiss** "start" **kiss** "right" **kiss** "here" **kiss**.

Opening my eyes, I look into his mesmerising green ones; before I can reply, his mouth is on mine again. Any coherent thoughts I have evaporate, and I lose myself in Jordan. Wrapping my legs around him, I intensify our kiss when I feel his hands slide under my magenta singlet and cup my breasts. My nipples immediately pebble, and he pushes my shirt up further and sucks on my nipples through my lacy bra. *This man knows exactly how to pleasure my tits.* I moan at the sensation escalating between my thighs. With his other hand, he wriggles my shirt over my head and slides my shorts down.

Lying on the couch in just my bra and undies, his eyes wander over my body and darken with lust. He quickly removes his shirt and then crushes his lips against mine once again. I start to wriggle under him and rub my hands up and down his back, eventually cupping his ass, squeezing and guiding him closer to me. Sliding my hands around, I work his button free. In one go, I get his boxer briefs and cargos down far enough that I use my feet to push them down the rest of the way and nudge them off completely. Reaching down, I cup his balls and grip his shaft, stroking him from base to tip, while rubbing myself on his leg.

He manages to undo my bra, while I shimming out of it, he pulls my undies down my legs. He slowly crawls back up my body and in one swift motion, he fills me completely. Pulling back out before slamming back in. I bend my knee, allowing him to get deeper. We move into a steady rhythm and before I know it, I'm plummeting over the edge as my orgasm bursts through me. I feel Jordan's body tense and I know he isn't too far away. A few thrusts later, Jordan shatters as his orgasm takes hold.

We lie there in each other's arms before I say, "Jor, you're squishing me. Let's take this to the bathroom to clean up, and if you're up for it, old man, maybe round two."

He lifts up and looks into my eyes. "Old man? Really?"

We both giggle; he helps me up and wraps me in a bear hug, before throwing me over his shoulder like a caveman, slapping my ass, and carrying me into the bathroom. We christen the bathroom twice, before falling into our newly built bed, courtesy of my man. We christen our bed and bedroom before we fall asleep, wrapped in each other's arms, blissfully happy.

It was a perfect evening for the first night in our house.

TRAITOR

Look at how happy that bitch is? She so does not deserve to be happy; her breaking her ankle was karma of the best kind. Clint lost his shit when I told him that she broke her ankle, but not as much as when I told him that she was married.

To this day, I don't know what Clint sees in her. She must have a magical, hypnotic pussy or something. I just don't see it. For Clint's sake, I hope that when this is all said and done that he's happy with this bitch.

After what this bitch has done, my cousin deserves happiness. If being with her makes him happy, then I'll help him anyway I can, that's what family does for each other. He was there for me when I needed him and now it's my turn to return the favour. That's what family does for each other.

The local florist is going to love me with all the sunflowers that I'll be delivering on Clint's behalf. It's time to put his final plan in motion

JORDAN

Thank God, we have finally finished renovating and are now completely moved in. It's great to see Kenz happy and relaxed, it's been a while since I've seen her this content. Finally, I have my girl back and I couldn't be happier. If I had known renovating, looking after Kenz, and getting Malt Me off the ground would have been so tough, I wouldn't have let her convince me to do this.

I must admit, it is pretty awesome to see all our hard work and effort pay off; we have a magnificent and unique house. Kenz did an amazing job picking colours and coordinating everything, that woman continues to amaze me.

Looking at the shiny polished floors, I'm glad she convinced me to sand and polish the floorboards; they look gorgeous and really add character to the house. Her squeal when we lifted the old carpet up to find the black-butt boards underneath, in amazing condition was priceless; she was like a kid in a candy store. Only a few had to be repaired, but as Kenz reminds me, it's a forty-year-old house and they give it charm and charisma; as does the half V-Jay walls with feature belt rail, Colonial skirting and cornice, and plantation shutters. I'm so glad I managed to convince Kenz to put them in, they really are amazing.

I'm relieved today is over, because I hate moving. I cannot thank Mike enough for helping us move today. It was also nice to have a few chillaxed beers with him before chilling with Kenz.

We decided on pizza for dinner, as neither of us could be assed cooking. After a day of moving furniture, beer and pizza was definitely called for.

After having my way with her on the couch, and again in the shower we fall into bed absolutely exhausted. She falls asleep immediately and I lie there staring at her. Kenz is amazing; she has been though so much yet she's so strong.

I will never get my fill of this woman. She is my life. I will do anything to protect her and give her the happily ever after that she deserves.

35

KENZIE

THE NEXT MORNING, JORDAN COOKS ME HIS FAMOUS bacon and creamy scrambled eggs on my new stove. Yes, he christened my stove before I did. However, Jordan's eggs are to die for; like *Masterchef* winning good, so I was happy to allow him to christen my stove.

After breakfast, we both head down to the shed to set up the new kegging and bottling system. We only set up the brewers and filtering system while renovating, as we needed the space for renovating materials.

Ducking back upstairs I grab my surprise for Jordan. He has worked his ass off to get this house finished, and he has been my rock. Now that it's completed, it's time for Jordan to be in the spotlight, for a change.

Skipping back into the shed, Jordan has his back to me as he places a canister on the top shelf. I wrap my arms around his waist and say, "Babe, don't get mad but I did something."

Jordan turns around, wraps his arms around my waist

and eyes me questioningly. "I know that you said when the house was done we'd concentrate on getting this all up and running but..." He tries to interrupt me, as usual, I place my finger over his lips to shush him. "And that's why I did this..." I hand him the package and watch him as he registers what it is

"Is that what I think it is?"

"It sure is, baby, it's our registration for the four day Black Gold Premium brewing course at the Coleuses Brewing Company in Melbourne, including flights and accommodation. I also got us two House of Red Bull tickets for the F1 on Saturday and Sunday. If we are lucky, we will be able to meet Colton Daniels."

"Seriously?"

"Seriously, we fly out Sunday lunchtime."

"Oh My God, Kenz, this is the best surprise ever, even better than the Oktoberfest surprise. As much as I was looking forward to having some downtime, this is seriously...I'm speechless, this is amazing. I love you so very muchly, woman."

"I know. I am pretty awesome." I wink at him. "So... wanna christen your beer cave?" I look seductively at him.

"Are you trying to be sexy again? You look like your having a fit," he laughs.

"Screw you, asshole." Walking past him I look back over my shoulder and seductively murmur, "Well, I guess you don't wanna see what I got online from Victoria's Secret then."

Before I can make my getaway, Jordan picks me up,

and I'm on my back on the black pleather couch. He is nipping and nuzzling my shoulder, while his hands are rubbing me ever so seductively in all the right spots. "You mentioned something about Victoria's Secret?"

I look up and his eyes are full of heat, and a pulsing begins between my thighs. My breathing is short and fast, my heart racing. "Maybe, why don't we swap positions and I might show you...if you're lucky."

Before I know it, I'm on my feet, and Jordan is sitting down, staring intently at me; his eyes filled with desire and lust. Taking a step back, I lift up the hem of my emerald green, halter sundress, but I drop it back down. Hearing Jordan exhale in frustration, I reach behind and undo the tie at my neck. My dress falls to the floor, and I am standing before him in a pale pink strapless bra with black trimming and matching boy legs.

Jordan rakes his eyes over my entire body; I have never felt so sexy in my life. "Fuck me, you're gorgeous. Come here, woman, so I can worship your body."

Swinging my hips from side to side, I walk back over to the couch and straddle him. My mouth is on his before he has a chance to reply. Pulling him closer; I escalate our kiss as I wrap my arms around his neck. Rubbing myself on his growing cock, I feel it hardening by the minute. His hands graze up my sides, cupping my breasts and squeezing, before moving around my back. He swiftly works my bra free, exposing my tits to the air, my nipples immediately pebble. I let it fall away without breaking contact, our tongues melding together to become one.

Jordan lets out a moan, "Kenz, if you don't stop, I'm gonna blow my load." Standing up, I slide my undies down, while Jordan quickly strips out of his cargos and boxer briefs.

Straddling him again, I rub myself over the end of his thick pulsating shaft, "Please, Kenz, fuck me now," he whispers, so I lower myself over him, rubbing the end of his cock on my drenched pussy. Slowly I slide down his length, taking his hard cock deep inside me.

Jordan pinches my left nipple and takes the right into his mouth and sucks. I throw my head back as the pleasure courses through my body. My pace quickens and I lean forward to kiss him. Our kisses become aggressive and frenzied. "Jor, I'm gonna come are you with me?" I don't wait for his reply as my orgasm flows through me, my entire body tingling. I feel Jordan's body tense and together, we ride out our orgasms.

We sit with our foreheads touching, our breaths slowly returning to normal. "Seriously, Kenz, are you trying to kill me? Four times last night and just now. If I'd known finishing the house would have unleashed this side of you, I'd have finished it a year ago."

Laughing, I give him a passionate kiss before standing on shaky legs and getting dressed. "Jordan, you just bring out my inner devil...remember when we first started dating? Well, I think that your lil' sex kitten is back."

Jordan shakes his head and says, "Well, yeay for me." We both laugh. He stands up and we finish getting dressed. Once clothed, he kisses my forehead and we continue to unpack and set up the remaining brew gear.

A few hours later, I look over and Jordan is leaning against the stainless steel bench that houses all the brew ingredients and he is smiling. He must feel me looking at him as he looks towards me, and smiles. "Kenzie, thank you for everything. You seriously are awesome. Thank you so very muchly for smashing into me on the first day of college."

Winking at him, I reply, "That smash was my pleasure."

36

JORDAN

Okay, so I thought I knew a fair bit about beer and brewing, but I actually know jack shit. This course has opened my eyes up, I am now confident about moving forward with our brewpub. I seriously cannot thank Kenz enough for this. After this course, I am certain that between the two of us, we now know everything that we need in order to open and successfully run Malt Me.

The F1's are phenomenal, they are best two days ever and it's the greatest way to end the week. Hearing the roar of the engines, as they as they buzz past you in excess of two hundred kilometers an hour, is indescribable. It's deafening. It's thrilling. It's Goddamn awesome. These driver's really are talented; to drive at the speeds that they do and on such a tight course, wow, just amazing. Watching them on TV does not do them justice; up close and personal is so much better. We even manage to meet Colton Daniels, getting photos and an autograph, which is a super highlight for Kenz and me.

On the plane home, I tell Kenz that I'd love to get my

hands on the co-op just out of town, but the old fart who owns it has already turned me down once, maybe this time will be different. *Please, beer God's, help a guy out.*

I'm on such a high right now; I can't wait to get back into my cave.

37

KENZIE

We are having a tasting at our place this weekend; it will be amongst our closest friends. We will be asking them to rate the names and see what they think of the beers. Jordan has just ducked out to pick up the food from the caterer, and I'm doing a final tidy up, getting everything ready for tonight. I'm nervous and excited for Jordan.

I've just stepped out of the shower, and I'm standing in the kitchen, wrapped in a bath sheet, having a glass of water when all of a sudden all the hairs on the back of my neck stand on end, like someone is watching me. Looking around I can't see anyone, I tell myself I'm being paranoid, I'm the only one here.

As quickly as the feeling appears, it disappears just as quick, so I head back into our bedroom to finish getting ready. I put on my favourite ass-hugging jeans and an emerald V-neck singlet, slipping on my sparkly thongs to complete my outfit. After applying my lipstick and one final check in the mirror, I head down to the shed to make sure everything is set.

As I'm walking down the stairs, a navy blue car slows down as it passes our place and the creepy feeling from earlier is back. A car horn beeps and they quickly take off. Jordan then comes zooming into the driveway. Getting out of the car, he looks up at me, standing on the stairs and smiles. "Hey, sexy lady."

Smiling back, I race down the stairs, run up to him, jumping into his arms, wrapping my legs around his waist; I envelope him in a hug, just having him near makes me feel safe. Placing me back on the ground, he lifts my chin and quietly asks, "What's up, Kenz?"

Taking a deep breath, I tell him about the feeling inside and the blue car just now. He doesn't have an answer for the chills but he says, "Most people slow down to have a look at the house. For so long, we've been 'the house that will never finish.' Naturally, people are intrigued now that it's complete. I'm sure it was nothing and they were just sticky-beaking. You called and checked with the hospital last week and Clint is still safely locked away."

I'm sure he's right. "Yeah, you're right babe. Thanks for reassuring me." Helping unload, I grab a few bags from the boot and head down to where the fun tonight will happen.

As soon as I've finished arranging the cheese platter, Mike rocks up with De-Niece. There is something about her that irks me. The way she looks at me all the time is really off putting. Plastering on a fake smile, I say, "Hey guys." I quickly rush back upstairs, pretending that I have forgotten something. I secretly hope that Sarah and Josh get here soon. No sooner do I finish that thought and reach the top of the stairs, they pull up. Looking to the skies, I say a silent thank you.

Walking out, I greet Sarah, " Heya. Let me help you there, bitch."

She envelops me in a hug, "Thanks, ho, how've you been? It's been ages since I have seen you."

"I'm doing okay. Had a little freak out earlier, like I did that day you and I went to the movies but Jordan and I came to the conclusion it was someone just looking at the house and my mind overreacting."

"Kenz, you're allowed to freak out. It was a lot to deal with. I can only imagine how you feel but I'm glad you are talking about it and not bottling it up like you usually do." She pauses, "Kenz, you are the strongest person I know."

Wanting to change the subject I say, "To tell you the truth, Sarah, I'm nervous about tonight. I know you guys have played guinea pig before, but tonight it's different. This is the final test run for our Malt Me beers, there is a lot at stake."

"Kenzie, it will be fine. Jordan would not be doing tonight if he weren't one hundred and ten percent sure with the recipes. Hell, you wouldn't even give me a taste test and I'm your sister from another mister. Now, let's get these chairs set up and drink some amazeballs beers."

Just as we have set up the chairs, Jordan comes out with six beers. *What perfect timing.* Passing them out, he toasts, "Cheers everyone, here's to a beertabolous evening"

We all salute and clink mugs. "Cheers!"

Mike takes a sip. "Ahhhh, one of the best brews around. Here's to a beertabolous evening."

All our guinea pigs are seated and Jordan dives right in. He goes into professional beer man mode, explaining each beer. We try six different beers. Jordan describes the different flavours and how mellow and crisp they each are. It's a total turn on seeing him all professional.

We proceed to have a great night, and we score six out of six with the beers. By the end of the night, everyone is absolutely shitfaced. Mike and De-Niece, and Sarah and Josh, decide to crash at our place, as they are in no state to drive, and getting a taxi this time of night is a total bitch.

As usual, everyone else has crashed out and I'm left cleaning up. Finally, the last of the dishes have been loaded and I have just turned the dishwasher on. Not ready for bed just yet, I head downstairs and pour myself a beer. With my beer in hand, I head back upstairs and I sit on the Jack and Jill on the front verandah.

As soon as I sit down, my hairs stand on end again, just like they did earlier in the day. Looking towards the road, I see there is someone standing on the other side of the street, staring at me. I'm absolutely frozen, I can't move. They start to walk across the road, towards the house when Jordan opens the front door. Startling them, they turn and run off.

Jordan looks at me, and he immediately knows something is up. Striding towards me, he squats in front of me, "Kenz, what's wrong?"

Holding my arms, he lovingly rubbing up and down

to bring me back to the present. I'm still frozen and all I can manage to say is, "Clint." He immediately turns around, runs to the street, and looks up and down but no one in the there.

A few moments later, he returns and sits next to me on the Jack and Jill. Standing up, I climb onto his lap and he rubs my back just like I like. Eventually I look into his eyes and the tears begin to flow down my cheeks. "How is he here?" **SOB,** "He should be in hospital." **SOB**

"Kenz, I checked, there's no one out there. You've had a lot to drink and tonight was a big night for us. You're on a high, your exhausted and your seeing things. Trust me, no one out here, except you and I. We'll call the hospital tomorrow to make sure he's still there. Besides, they'd have called us if anything happened. "

I'm too tired to argue. "Okay," I sniff, but I know what I saw and deep down, I know that he's back.

"Kenz, even if he is out there, I will not let him hurt you again. Look at me, Kenz."

Looking up into his eyes, which are currently sparkling in the moonlight, he reassures me, "I love you to the moon and back, and I'll do everything in my power to protect you, but you have to remember you're strong." He leans over and kisses my forehead, "You are the strongest person that I know. You need to tell yourself, 'I'm Mackenzie "Kenzie" McRoberts nee Merlot. I'm strong and hot, and I'm not afraid.' Now, say it, Kenz."

Again I sniff and wipe my nose on Jor's shoulder. "Sorry," I giggle.

"Kenz, say it."

Taking a deep breath I say, "I'm Mackenzie "Kenzie"

McRoberts nee Merlot. I'm strong and hot, and I'm not afraid."

"That's my girl, now let's get you into bed. It's been a long day and I want to fall asleep with my wife in my arms."

"Sounds perfect to me." Jordan slings his arm around my shoulder, pulling me closer. I wrap my arm around his waist and snuggle in.

After locking the doors, we climb into bed together. Jordan pulls me close and whispers, "I love you, Mrs. McRoberts nee Merlot" He then places a kiss on my lips.

"And, I love you too, Mr. McRoberts."

The next morning after everyone has left, Jordan and I call the hospital. They confirm that Clint is still safely locked.

Jordan is relieved but I still have an uneasy feeling.

———

Jordan and I are both a bundle of nerves at the moment. On Thursday, we have a meeting lined up with the cranky ass who owns the co-op. Fingers crossed the stick up his ass has been removed and this time he will sell it to us for a great price.

The meeting with old Mr. Cranky Ass went better than either of us could have hoped for; he passed away, unfortunately, yeay, and left it to his son. Luckily for us, the son has no interest in the co-op and was happy to sell it to us, for a bargain price and with a quick settlement. In ninety days time, subject to us finalising our finance, we will have a building for Malt Me.

Fortunately, I had already started the finance ball rolling and the bank were happy to lend us the money. In ninety days time, we will officially have our premises.

That's when the fun will begin: gutting, designing, rebuilding, and setting everything up on a larger scale for the opening of our dream; Malt Me brewery.

Holy shit, we bought the building for our brewery.

Holy shit, we are starting a brewery.

Holy shit, our dream is coming true.

Holy shit, I'm a real adult now.

———

The next ninety days fly by and as of 2:00 p.m. today, Jordan and I are now the proud owners of the co-op, future home of the Malt Me brewery.

Just as the agent leaves, Mike and De-Niece pull up; I'm glad to see Mike but De-Niece, not so much. It's confusing as to why she is still around. Normally, Mike would have moved on by now, but he seems to be hypnotized by her. *She must have a magical voodoo pussy.*

Mike jumps out of his truck, meets her at the back. They then emerge with a huge balloon bouquet saying CONGRATS, an esky full of beer and wine, another one full of food, and a huge bunch of sunflowers, which I presume are for me.

Running over to Mike, I wrap my arms around him. "Oh My God, Mike, you are awesome." He hands me the flowers and I hug him again.

"Don't thank me, this was De-Niece's idea."

Looking over his shoulder at De-Niece, I'm slightly

confused, she has always being such a bitch to me. Why is she being nice now? She's standing there with her creepy smile; I walk towards her, "Thanks De-Niece. This is totally awesome." I pull her in for a hug, her body is stiff at first, but she eventually relaxes and hugs me back.

Releasing her from the hug she says with a smug smile, "Your welcome, Mackenzie." Emphasising, Mackenzie.

"Please, call me Kenzie. I hate being called Mackenzie."

"I know." She smugly smiles at me.

Shaking my head, I see Sarah's Corolla pull up and grin. She jumps out of her car, yelling "Surprise!" Running over to me, she envelopes me in a huge hug. "Congrats, bitch, I'm so happy for you guys."

With drinks in hand, the five of us stand the in car park of our brewery. Mike makes a toast "Cheers to Malt Me," and we all salute, cheer and celebrate our new venture.

————

The co-op building is just perfect for Malt Me. I'm so happy that we were able to get it. Everything is falling into place.

The following three weeks are freaking crazy and full on. It took two solid weeks of working, sun up till sun down, to gut the inside. Once we had cleared everything out, that's when the fun—and I use that term loosely, very loosely—began.

Now that the building has been gutted, and we finally decided on the inside plans, it's over to our builder. He will work his magic and turn this empty space into something amazing.

Four long exhausting months later, our builder is finished with the construction. It's now up to us to paint, fit out and get everything ready to start production. Once that is complete, we can then open to the public.

———

We arrived early in the morning to get more painting done. Between the two of us, we are plowing through our to-do list, ticking off items left, right, and center. It's all going smoothly, until late in the afternoon, when Jordan has to go meet with the bottle people, there is an issue with the custom bottle caps. As he's walking out the front doors, he shouts, "Back soon, Kenz, I'll stop and get dinner on my way back!"

"Give me a buzz, and I'll let you know what I feel like. You know how hungry I get when I paint, and this place is a gazillion times larger than our Queenslander. Thankfully, here there are no V-Jay walls or belt rail's to paint. I hate V-Jay, it looks amazing, but it's a total bitch to paint. If I can get a good run this arvo, I should get the toilets, bathrooms, and our office done, and maybe even start on the kitchen while your gone."

He laughs, "You are a painting machine, but don't push it. I'll call and see what Picasso wants for dinner when I'm done. Love you, wifey."

I laugh at his Picasso comment, "Love you too hubster."

I've got the iPod plugged in and cranked; I totally love the emotional rollercoaster that is iPod random. I love when it switches from *Take Me To Church* by Hozier to *Shut Your Mouth* by Garbage, before switching to *Never Tear Us Apart* by INXS.

When Sinatra's, *Come Fly With Me* comes on, I put the paintbrush down and start dancing around the office, until I hear a noise in the main room. Heading out, I think it might be Sarah, as she said she might pop out. Walking into the main room, I see a box by the front door.

Smiling, I skip over as I think that Jordan has left something for me; he's always hiding things here and there or I'm getting special deliveries. Crouching down to open the box, I start to get a strange feeling.

Opening the box, I discover a bunch of sunflowers have been shredded and there's a note sitting on top of them.

Tik Tok
Hurry Up

My heart drops.

I'd recognise that message anywhere.

Clint is back.

I race into the office and lock myself inside. With shaking hands, I call Jordan. I'm a sobbing mess when he answers, I can't get the words out. He tells me to wait inside and he'll be here soon.

Twenty minutes later, I hear him call out, "Kenz, baby, where are you?"

I immediately jump up, unlock the door and race out to him. I wrap my arms tightly around him and start to cry again. He holds me while I sob in his arms.

There is a knock at the door, we turn around to see two uniformed officers standing there. "Good afternoon, I'm Officer Hamilton and this is my partner, Officer Kincaid."

Jordan walks over to meet them. "Thanks for coming so quickly. Kenz was pretty shaken when she called me so I immediately called you guys. I called the hospital but they wouldn't tell me anything."

"You did the right thing calling us. After I spoke with you Mr. McRoberts, I called the hospital too. Clint was taken to The Royal with suspected appendicitis. That's why they couldn't tell you anything."

I stammer, "Hhhh...he's out?"

"No, he is safely back at the facility now. It was just a case of food poisoning, but it does look like he managed to get access to a phone and arrange your package. All his privileges have been revoked."

I go into shock, their words not registering. I feel like all the progress I have made is crumbling around me. Closing my eyes, I take a deep breath and say Jordan's mantra for me, "I'm Mackenzie "Kenzie" McRoberts nee Merlot. I'm strong and hot, and I'm not afraid."

Jordan finishes up with the officers, locks up and drives us home. He runs me a bath and leaves me alone to process it all.

After my bath, I find him in the lounge room, on the

couch watching *Top Gear*. He mutes the TV, grabs my hand, and pulls me down onto his lap. "How you doing, baby?"

"I'm not sure to tell you the truth. When I saw that package, my heart dropped. When the officers said he was out, I nearly lost it. I'm glad he's locked back up but all my fears are coming flooding back. What if next time he escapes?"

"I can't answer that, Kenz, but after chatting with the officers today, I have faith that he will stay locked away and that you'll be safe. I'm not going to let anything happen to you."

"I love you, Jordan. Thank you for being my rock."

"No need to thank me, Kenz. I love you too. Do you want to watch this or go to bed?"

"I'm going to go to bed. You stay and watch, I'll be fine."

Standing up, I kiss him on the cheek and head to bed.

The next week is tough emotionally. I make an appointment to see Jeannie. Talking with her helps, as does my daily call to the facility to make sure Clint is indeed still locked away.

———

The following weekend, I'm back at Malt Me painting and Jordan is still dealing with the bottle cap drama from the previous week. I'm finishing up the office window architrave when my phone starts to play Jordan's tone, *Nothing Else Matters* by Metallica. "Hey, husband."

"Kenz, I'm so glad to hear your voice. These bottle

caps have been a nightmare. I'm going to look for another supplier. I don't want to work with this asshole anymore. Enough of my issues, how'd you get on, Picasso?"

"Hardy har har. I've done the toilets, bathrooms, and our office is just about finished. I've just got to do the kitchen and then that's the painting done."

"You're a rock star, babe. What did you want for dinner?"

"I'd kill for a burrito and Modelo from Guzman. Since I'm nearly done here, why don't I call it a day? We can meet at home and head there together, have a night out, just you and I?"

"You read my mind, Kenz. I'll see you at home soon."

"It's a date, I just need to finish the frame and clean these brushes, and then I'll head home. See you soon for date night...you might even get lucky, if you play your beers right."

"I see your beer jokes are still just as lame, and by the way there's no might about it. Love you."

"Whatevs, I'm hilarious. Love you too, Jor, see you soon."

Once the frame is finished, I quickly wash the brushes and pack them away. Before leaving, I make sure all the windows and doors are locked, I jump into my car and text Jordan to let him know I'm leaving.

ME – *Just leaving Malt Me now XO*

Before I'm out of the car park, my phone beeps.

JORDAN – *I just got out of the shower, looking forward to date nite. Drive safely, I love you XO*

ME – *I always drive safely I'm not you Love
you more*

———

Walking in the front door, I yell in my best Lucy voice, "Honey, I'm home!" From the back of the house I hear Jordan laughing. After taking off my shoes, I head down the hall to our bedroom. Pushing the door open, I see there are thousands, well maybe not thousands, but a crap load of candles lit and a huge bunch of sunflowers on the dresser. I gasp, Jordan thinks it's because of the surprise, but I see the sunflowers, and kind of freeze.

Jordan walks over to me, wraps his arm around my waist, and places a sensual kiss on my lips. Before long, the kiss turns heated and I have all but forgotten about the sunflowers. Pulling back, I look into his eyes, which look amazing with the flicker of the candles reflecting in them. "Hi," I manage to say.

"Hey, yourself, have I told you how sexy you look? Especially when you have paint sloshes all over you."

"Not recently, but I'm not opposed to hearing it."

"You, my dear, are the sexiest." He kisses my neck. "Most amazing." He nibbles my ear. "Hottest woman on this earth, and I am going to worship every inch of your body. Now strip and get on the bed."

Grabbing the hem of my shirt, I slowly raise it over my head, and then I shimmy out of my shorts. I'm left standing in my plain white bra and undies. Jordan is sitting on the end of our bed, in just his dress pants. If the look in his eyes is anything to go by, I'm going to be panting his name very soon.

"Fuck me, Kenz, you are beautiful."

"You're just saying that in hopes of getting lucky." Walking over to him, I push him back onto the bed and straddle his hips. Leaning down, I place feather light kisses over his pecs, up his neck, and I take his earlobe into my mouth and gently bite down. While rubbing myself on his leg, I feel his cock growing beneath me. I pepper kisses along his jaw and make my way to his mouth, I gently coax his lips apart and slip my tongue inside. Before I know it, he's kissing me back; I don't know where his mouth begins and my mouth ends.

Lifting up onto my knees, I pull back, spin around, and I slowly make my way down his abs; while I arch my back and straddle his face. He reaches up and gently caresses my ass before pulling my pussy to his face. He pushes my undies to the side and his tongue attacks my slit, licking and sucking like it's a melting ice cream on a hot summer day. Moaning, I lower his zipper and grab his shaft with my hand, freeing it from the confines of his boxer briefs. Gently stroking him up and down, a bead of precum quickly builds on the tip. I lick and suck the head before taking his cock into my mouth. He slides a finger into my soaking wet pussy as I suck him deeper into my mouth. I lick down his shaft to his balls before sucking one into my warm welcoming mouth. As I pull back, I reach my hand down to gently massage his scrotum.

Hearing Jordan moan turns me on, so I pucker my cheeks and take him deeper down my throat. His balls tighten, just as I feel my orgasm starting to build, sucking him harder as my climax reaches boiling point. The first spurt of hot salty cum hits the back of my throat just as my orgasm bursts forth. Writhing in pure bliss, my climax continues to surge through me; I continue to suck him until I've milked him dry.

Rolling off Jordan, we lie next to each other, hearts racing, breathing labored, blissfully happy. Once our heart rates have returned to normal, and our breathing settles, I stand up, pull my undies down, unhook my bra and flick it at him. Turning around I say, "I'm gonna get a shower and then we can go."

Before I take a step, Jordan grabs me around my waist, throws me onto the bed and straddles me. "I don't think so, wifey, I want to be buried balls deep inside of you and have you screaming my name at the top of your lungs before we go anywhere." His mouth is on mine before I get a chance to reply.

With our tongues melding together; I start rubbing my already throbbing pussy on his leg. The friction hitting that magical spot, so I shamelessly rub faster. I start to feel my orgasm building when Jordan pulls away. He licks down my neck, across my shoulder blade and down to my breasts. He takes my nipple in his mouth and sucks, while pinching and rolling the other between his thumb and forefinger before swapping to the other breast. He licks and kisses his way down to my pussy. He caresses my clit with his thumb and my hips start to buck, then he rubs a finger up and down my slit before slipping it inside. Still massaging my clit with his thumb, he whispers, "You're so wet, baby."

"Mmhmm" is all I can manage, as I'm lost to the

euphoria building inside. Reaching out, I massage and twist my nipples as Jordan adds another finger. Then I feel his mouth sucking my clit. "Fuuuuck, I love your mouth." I feel the fireworks explode. I tumble over the edge screaming his name, as I climax for the second time this evening.

I'm lying here sated, when Jordan begins to kiss, lick, and nibble his way back up my body. Tugging on his hair, I urge him to move quicker. I pull him towards me and kiss him deeply. Our tongues gently caress each other's. Both our juices mix together, creating an intoxicating blend, which turns me on even more. Before I have time to register, he enters me in one swift motion. We both start rocking back and forth, our hips meeting thrust for thrust, our pace gradually quickening. Lifting my leg over Jordan's shoulder, his cock hits that magical spot. I whisper, "I'm close."

He reaches down to rub circles on my clit. "Come for me baby." After a few more thrusts we both topple over the brink, each murmuring the other's name, as we ride out our orgasm.

I'm still shaking when he lowers my leg and collapses on top of me; we lay here together until our breathing evens out. Lifting my head, I look into his eyes and get lost in a sea of green. All of a sudden I register that Jordan is talking to me. "What?"

With a laugh he replies, "Wow, where did that come from?"

"When I came home and saw all this, I just lost control, sorry."

"Don't ever be sorry for that, feel free to do that

anytime, Kenz. Fuck, that sixty-nine was awesome, it's one for the vault on the nights I'm all alone."

"You weren't so bad yourself," I giggle. "I guess we better get showered. I'm kinda starving now, and I'd kill for a beer."

"How did I get so lucky to get a hottest girl in the world, who also just happens to love beer as much as me?"

"Luck and my clumsiness come to mind."

"And you couldn't resist my ass."

"And all these years later, I still can't resist that perfect tight ass of yours..." Leaning over, I kiss him deeply, losing myself as I kiss the man of my dreams. Before things get too heated, I draw back suddenly. "....and on that note, we better get a move on, cause I don't think Guzman would allow us in dressed, or not dressed, like this, and this lady needs a beer and a burrito."

"You had me at beer, baby."

Climbing off the bed, I put my hand out to help him up. Once we are both standing, I wrap my arm around his neck and kiss him again. "I love you."

"I love you too, Kenz."

We both head into the shower and quickly get washed. I'm adding the finishing touches, when there's a knock at the front door. Mike and De-Niece are here, seeing if we want to head out for a few drinks. I'm just finishing my hair, secretly hoping that Jordan says no, as I'm not in the mood to spend a night with De-Niece; seriously who spells their name like that anyway? When I hear Jordan, "Awesome, Kenz and I were just about to head to Guzman, wanna join us?"

Fuck, I silently scream.

"Sounds great, man." *Fuck,* I silently scream again, so much for a night just us.

I've finished putting my lipstick on and I walk into the lounge. Plastering on a fake smile, I say, "Hey guys."

Mike looks up and whistles, much to De-Niece's disgust. "Looking hawt, Kenz."

Jordan whacks Mike across the back of the head. "Stop ogling my wife, asshat."

De-Niece chimes in, "Mike, you can't say that about Mac...Kenzie."

"Why not? It's true. She looks smokin' hot tonight." Walking over, I kiss Mike on the cheek, while looking directly at De-Niece, and snarkily say, "And you're mighty spunky too tonight, Mike." I wink at him. He envelops me in a hug and swings me around, and I squeal like a giddy schoolgirl.

The taxi arrives a few minutes later and we all hop in. On the way to dinner, I discreetly send an SOS text to Sarah.

ME – *SOS!!! Heading to Guzman with Jor, Mike and you know who, please come*

Just as we are taking our seats, my phone beeps; I grab it thinking it will be Sarah and don't even look at the ID.

UNKNOWN – *You look pretty tonight XO*

Saying to the guys, I'll be right back, I run off the to the toilets. I lock myself in a stall and sit on the lid. My heart is pounding and my breathing is labored. I need to calm down or I'll have a panic attack.

"Breathe in, breathe out." I keep repeating to myself. After a few moments, I calm down. I unlock the cubical and I look at myself in the mirror. I say out loud, "I'm Mackenzie "Kenzie" McRoberts nee Merlot. I'm strong and hot, and I'm not afraid."

My phone beeps again and I freeze, but this time it's Sarah. I sigh in relief, as I slide the screen to read her text.

SARAH – *Just cause I love you Josh and I will come save your sorry ass. I'll have a margarita and it better be waiting for me when I get there*

Before heading back out, I call the hospital and once again, they confirm the Clint is still there. Maybe it was a wrong number. Y*eah it was a wrong number,* I tell myself.

Pulling myself together, I head back out. Jordan has a beer waiting for me and he tells me he's ordered. I tell them Sarah and Josh are on their way. I then head to the bar to order her a double strength margarita and another Modelo bucket for the table.

By time I get back, Sarah and Josh have arrived. Placing the bucket on the table, I give Sarah her drink and a quick peck on the cheek.

Whistling as I sit down, Sarah says, "Your lookin hot tonight, Kenz."

De-Niece rolls her eyes, and in 4.2 seconds flat, Sarah

has managed to make me smile, piss De-Niece off and make me forget about the text.

It's about 2:00 a.m. when we leave; Jordan and I manage to get a cab quickly, which never happens in this town. Leaning over, I start rubbing his crotch in the cab; when we get home as soon as the front door is closed, I jump him.

We start ripping each other's clothes off and we make it as far as the couch. Jordan sits down and I straddle him, this is fast becoming one of my favourite positions; I love our new couch. Rubbing my pussy up and down his shaft as he tweaks, pulls, and sucks my nipples; I throw my head back in delight as I lift up and impale myself on Jordan's hard throbbing cock. Gripping his shoulders, I ride him up and down until we both find our release.

Jordan lifts us up and carries me to bed. He climbs in next to me, and we spoon wrapped up in each other's arms.

We are blissfully unaware that we are being watched.

38

CLINT

I'm so glad that my cousin helped me get out of that place, it took a few weeks to arrange but we finally managed it. The plan she came up with was brilliant. I'm so glad to be seeing my Sweetcheeks in person again.

It has been far too long since I've seen her. Seeing the pictures of her face every time she gets my gifts has been priceless. It's becoming harder and harder watching her from a distance but I need to make my reappearance perfect; she deserves nothing but the best. As much as I wish I could tell her that I'm back, I have to play this carefully. Getting put away again would be pure torture.

I'm watching her hang the washing out and I'm hard as stone. Reaching down, I unzip my fly and wrap my fingers around my cock. I grip and stroke until I blow my load all over the front seat of the car.

Smiling, I can't wait until it's my Sweetcheeks hand doing this and not me.

"Soon, Sweetcheeks, soon, you and I will finally get our forever."

39

KENZIE

The past six weeks have been a mad house, I don't know whether I'm coming or going most days. But it has all been worth it because today is the grand opening of Malt Me. The last eight months since signing the papers for the building have been hectic. But it's all paid of I can't wait to celebrate.

Waking up early, I roll over and no surprise Jordan's side of the bed is stone cold. He must not have been able to sleep, I know exactly where he will be.

While I'm having my morning coffee, there's a knock at the front door. Placing my cup down, I walk over and open the door, but no one is there. Looking down, I freeze when I see a single sunflower with a note attached to it with barbed wire. Shuddering, I bend down and pick it up. A creepy feeling washing over me as I turn the not over and read.

Tik Tok
Hurry Up

Dropping the note and flower on the verandah, my heart rate accelerates and I break out in a cold sweat. I glance up and down the street, but I can't see anyone.

This is really starting to freak me out, I know I need to talk to Jordan about it but today is not the day; I'll tell him tomorrow. I don't want anything ruining today for him.

Heading back inside, I change into my charcoal Cue dress pants and white, sleeveless silk button up shirt, adding a silver bracelet and my Diana Ferrari black ankle boots. Once I'm ready, I head over to Malt Me. On the way, I stop at Java Lava and get us some coffee and muffins.

———

When I arrive, I find Jordan in the brew house tinkering. It's what he does when he's nervous. "Hey, babe, what time did you get here?" I ask, handing him one of the coffees and giving him a quick kiss.

"The sun was just coming up. I couldn't sleep and I didn't want to wake you. I wanted to check and make sure everything is set for today. I just want this to be perfect, Kenz. I never thought this would happen; yet here we are, the grand opening of our brewpub. It all feels surreal."

"I know what you mean, babe. In less than five hours the doors will open and we will sell our first beer to our first paying customer. Today is going to be amazeballs."

If only we knew...

40

KENZIE

It's 11:00 a.m. and the doors to Malt Me are now officially open. You cannot wipe the smile off Jordan's face, or mine for that matter. All our nearest and dearest are here to help us celebrate, as well as the locals, who have been a pillar of support since we lodged the redevelopment application with the council.

We thought there might be some hurdles, but touchwood, everything has been smooth sailing. Jordan and I couldn't be happier.

The kitchen are pushing out the orders and the consensus is that the food is amazing. The beers are flowing and reviews, so far, are all positive. After some convincing, I persuaded Jordan to stock wine too, because not everyone likes beer; shock horror, I know.

I sneak up to the mezzanine level to get a few minutes to myself. I don't think I've stopped smiling since the doors opened; it reminds me of all the smiling on our wedding day. That was the last time I was this excited, nervous, and happy. I'm seriously on cloud nine right now.

I'm looking down at everyone enjoying themselves, and I feel proud, we played a part in their happiness. My eyes gravitate to Jordan, like they always do. He looks just as happy as me. He locks eyes with mine and he heads towards the stairs, racing up them to meet.

He strides across the mezzanine level, lifting me into a hug, spinning us around. When he lowers me down, he places the softest of kisses on my lips, which quickly turns heated. I spin away before it goes any further; after all, as the owners we have to be professional and shit. Jordan heads back down stairs and I stay a little longer; he can sense I need a time-out.

After a few minutes of taking it all in, I do a quick speech, since I have everyone's attention. Managing to thank everyone for coming today and all their support, as usual Jordan pipes in, but I don't mind at all as I could not be happier.

After everyone toasts us, I decide to head back down. I see Jordan smiling and waving for me to come down. Heading towards the stairs I take another look at all that we have achieved, when something by the front doors catches my eye.

I look again and I see Clint standing there, smiling directly at me. He lifts his hand and blows me a kiss. I stumble and before I know it, I'm stumbling down the stairs. I vaguely hear someone yelling, "Kenzie!"

Then it all goes dark....again.

———

When I come around, I'm lying on a stretcher being lifted into an ambulance; my whole body is aching and everything feels foggy. Lifting my hand to my head, I take a deep breath, I hear Jordan but I can't see him; I start to panic. "Jordan, Jordan!" I shout.

"I'm here, baby." Hearing him but still not being able to see him, my panic starts to increase. He pops into my line of vision and the floodgates that I'd been suppressing open. "I'm so sorry, I didn't tell you." I'm sobbing by now and cannot catch my breath. "I'm so sorry, I...I...I didn't want to worry you or ruin today." By now tears and snot running down my face.

Jordan is holding my hand. "Shhhh, don't cry. It's okay, you're okay. Look, they are taking you to the hospital to check you over. You just tumbled down a flight of stairs and bumped your head a few times."

"Don't leave me. I can't do this again."

"Do what?"

"Clint's back." I start sobbing again.

"What?" he bellows.

The ambo interrupts us, "Sorry, guys, we need to get you to the hospital."

"Hang on a sec." He turns to Mike. "Can you wrap up here and meet us at the hospital, please?"

"Sure, man, whatever you need. You look after our girl, I'll get here sorted and meet you there."

Looking at Jordan, I can see all the questions running through his head. Reaching up, I cup his cheek. "I'm so sorry, Jordan, I ruined your special day by keeping this from you."

Jordan takes my hand and squeezes. He hesitantly asks, "Kenz, what else has happened?"

"You know about the flowers. This morning I got a Tik Tok note with another flower. I was going to tell you tomorrow, I didn't want to ruin today."

"Kenz, you should have told me. We need to go to the police; you could have died today. I won't let him hurt you again. I made you that promise, all those years ago, and I still mean it now."

Once again the tears flow down my cheeks, I'm so sick of crying, I've become such a girl lately, crying at the drop of a hat. Clint really has rattled me.

The ambo interrupts us again, "Okay, you need to rest now, your blood pressure is still elevated, which is a concern. We're almost there, but for what it's worth, your husband is right. You could have really hurt yourself today. It sounds like this guy is crazy."

"See, even the ambo agrees with me." Jordan looks at me with raised eyebrows in an 'I told you so' way.

"Fine, I'll go to the police when I am finished here." Jordan smiles and I see him mouth, 'Thanks,' to the ambo.

We pull up at the hospital and I am taken into an exam room. A few moments later, the doctor walks in. He asks me what happened and I tell him. He then checks me over and wants to send me for an MRI scan to make sure everything is okay. I'm still feeling nauseous and keep getting black spots when I try to sit up, but on a good note my blood pressure is back to normal. They wheel me off for the scan and Jordan waits in the room they have moved me into. I tell him to call everyone and let them know I'm okay.

When I get back the police officers from the other week are in my room talking with Jordan. Once I'm settled in bed and comfy, well as comfy as you can be in a hospital bed, all attention is turned to me. "Your husband is telling us that you think you saw Clint MacNicholson today, and you've received another package?"

"Yep," I let the p pop when I reply but I don't expand, as I don't want to relive this again.

The officer looks sternly at me. "Can I ask why you didn't tell anyone?"

Taking a deep breath, I quickly spit out without breathing, "I didn't want to ruin today's opening. I was going to tell him tomorrow. I haven't had any more packages since we last saw you and I've only received the one text."

Jordan jumps up from the chair. "Are you fucking kidding me Kenz? He almost killed you last time, there is no way this fucker is going to decide to just let it go." I roll my eyes and shake my head at his outburst. "Don't you dare roll your eyes at me, Kenz. I almost lost you twice to this asshole, I'm not going to let him succeed this time."

Officer Kincaid leaves the room to take a call, Officer Hamilton interjects, "Mackenzie?"

Interrupting her, I say, "Its Kenzie, I hate being called Mackenzie...Unless I'm in trouble, which it's starting to feel like I am."

"Okay, Kenzie, Jordan is right. His behavior is escalating,"

Officer Kincaid reenters the room, and clears his throat, "That was the facility where Clint was being held. I'm sorry to tell you but Clint escaped two days ago."

"What? How? This can't be happening." Jordan wraps me in his arms and I begin to cry.

"We need you come down to the station so we can discuss your options. I also recommend a restraining order."

Jordan scoffs, "Like a piece of paper will stop him." He turns to me and grabs my hand. "Kenz, please. Take this seriously, I can't lose you. I won't lose you to him again."

"Fine," I huff, "I'll go to the station as soon as I'm out of here."

As soon as I say that, the hot Canadian doctor walks back in. He turns to the officers, "Can I please ask you to step out, I'd like to talk to my patient in private? You are more them welcome to come back in as soon as we are finished."

"Sure, no problem, we were just finishing up. Kenzie and Jordan, here's my card." She hands her card to Jordan, "If there are any issues before you get in to see us, please call me. My after hours number is on there as well. I'll see you both when you come down to the station."

Jordan shakes each officer's hand and both of them exit the room. I really don't like Officer Kincaid; he's an asshat.

The doctor picks up the chart that he placed on the bed trolley and looks up. "So, the scans all came back fine, but we did discover..." I gasp, thinking the worst "...you're pregnant, congratulations."

"Wh...what, pregnant? I can't be," I shake my head in shock. "I was told that the chances of me conceiving were slim to none." Looking over at Jordan, he is just as stunned as I am. After the incident with Clint, the doctors said it was going to be nearly impossible for me to fall pregnant due to the internal damage sustained.

After a few moments of stunned silence, Jordan turns towards me and wraps his arms around my shoulders and envelopes me in the biggest hug.

Releasing me, he bends down near my belly. "Hey, baby, I'm your daddy and this here is your mummy." He winks at me, "She's stubborn as a mule, but she's gonna be the bestest mummy in the whole entire world. You are one lucky lil' dude." He places a kiss on my stomach before looking at me, his face beaming with excitement.

I'd resigned myself to the fact that I was never going to have a baby. I start to cry and for once, I'm crying happy tears. Over the moon, excited, thrilled tears.

The doctor interrupts us, "Sorry to disturb you guys, but due to the fall that you had today, I've asked one of the attending OB's to come down and do an ultrasound to make sure everything is all right with you and the baby. With the history you just gave me, I definitely think it's a good idea. I'll go and see how far away the OB is." Dr. Canadian-McHottie leaves the room.

Jordan grabs my face and his lips crash with mine, the kiss is full of emotion and love. When he pulls away, he rests his forehead on mine. "Kenz, as much as I'm mad at your for keeping this all to yourself, I am over the fucking moon happy right now. I'm so incredibly in love with you." He pauses, "Kenz, we're gonna be parents."

I'm too shocked to speak, I just don't believe it. I wrap

my arms around Jordan and hug the life out of him; that's all I can manage at the moment.

I'm speechless.

I'm stunned.

I'm pregnant.

Holy shit, I'm pregnant.

41

CLINT

Waiting for dickwad to leave so I could drop off another flower for my beautiful Sweetcheeks was torture. I missed seeing her in person but most of all I want today to be special for her. For us, and our reunion.

I'm sitting in my car and I watch her open the front door and receive my gift. Seeing her in her nightie gets me hard, I lower my fly, lick my palm, and start stroking myself. Closing my eyes, I imagine it's her hand yanking and tugging my cock. It doesn't take long for my balls to tighten, and I explode all over a pair undies that I stole from my beautiful angel.

About half an hour later, I see my Sweetcheeks walk out to her car and drive off; she looks absolutely stunning today. Not wanting to be seen yet, I duck down in my seat as she drives past. I follow her to see where she is going. She stops off for coffee at our coffee shop and then she heads to Malt Me.

There are balloons and a big banner out front, stating that today is the grand opening. Parking my car around the corner, I settle in and wait. *Today is a great day for a party,* I think to myself.

ME – *Hey cuz, I'm here. Let's make this a party to never forget. Let me know when shes alone*

TRAITOR – *You got it*

Just after lunch, its go time.

TRAITOR – *She is up on the mezzanine all alone, I will keep asshat busy*

ME – *Thanks cuz*

My cousin is the best.

This task would be so much harder without her help. Walking around the back of the building, I peak through the side window, and feel my cock hardening at the sight of her standing up on the mezzanine level, looking like the angel that she is. She gives a speech, her voice is beautiful. My cock stirs at the sweet sound of her words. She seems happy and that makes me smile, but I think how much happier she will be later; when its just the two of us again.

She starts walking towards the stairs, so I pop into the doorway. She looks right at me. Our eyes connect. Everything but her fades away. I smile and blow her a kiss. Her eyes light up, the look on her face is pure delight. And then it all goes wrong, she trips and falls down the stairs.

My heart stops at seeing her fall. She was so excited to see me she tripped. *See, it's fate that we are meant to be together.*

Looking over, I see my cousin standing near at bar. She's staring at me, while everyone else runs to see if my Sweetcheeks is okay. She tells me to go with a nod of her head. As much as it kills me to leave, I know I have to. Being this close, I cannot let asshat see me.

Sitting in my car, I stare at the entrance and wait to see my Sweetcheeks. They wheel her out and that fuck-stick is beside her. He reaches for her hand, and in anger I dig my nails into my palm, drawing blood. "Don't touch her you asshat," I growl.

As I drive down the street, I say. "Happy opening day fuck-stick."

42

KENZIE

There's a knock on the door and it opens, Jordan and I jump apart, as a petite doctor enters my room. "Sorry to interrupt, I'm Dr. Greene the on-call OB. I understand congratulations are in order."

"Thanks." I manage to squeeze out, nodding my head, still in shock that I'm pregnant.

"Well, let's have a look and you can meet your lil' one." Dr. Greene wheels the ultrasound machine closer. She pushes a few buttons and the machine starts up. Picking up the wand and some gel, she says, "Now this might be a little cold." She squeezes the gel onto my belly, placing the wand against my skin, and the screen flickers. All of a sudden we hear a sound that I never thought I'd hear coming from inside me—*badunk badunk badunk*—it's magical. My eyes immediately fill with tears and I squeeze Jordan's hand. Looking up at him, we are both beaming at what we are hearing.

The doctor points to the screen, and says, "That right

there is your baby, and hiding behind is bub number two."

Both our mouths drop open in shock; with a smirk she says, "Congratulations, you're having twins. I'd say you are about six weeks along and everything looks perfect."

Looking up at Jordan, I smile. My mind is counting back; our babies were conceived on our impromptu Guzman date night. I whisper, "Guzman."

Jordan mumbles, "Guzman, right, so that night was doubly fun." We both laugh.

"Mackenzie..."

I cringe when she calls me Mackenzie "Please, call me Kenzie."

"Okay, Kenzie. I'll give you my card. Since you're having twins, if you have private health insurance, I would recommend that I see you privately." I look at her in shock. "There's nothing to worry about, but carrying twins and with your history, I want to be doubly careful. Don't get me wrong, the public system is just as good." She hands her card to Jordan. "But I think in your case, private will be best."

"Okay, we'll call your office to schedule an appointment. Thank you so much, we really appreciate it."

"Its my pleasure, Kenzie. Now you rest up, and I'll see you in two weeks for your first appointment." Dr. Greene leaves, quietly closing the door behind her. It's now just Jordan, me and the two lil' beans growing inside me.

Dr. Greene returns a few moments later and hands us a print out of our lil munchkins.

It all so surreal, I never thought I would be able to fall pregnant, let alone with twins. I hold the picture tightly to my chest, grabbing Jordan's hand, I pull him in for a kiss and whisper. "Congrats Daddy."

"Congrats Mummy."

Jordan bends down and kisses my belly again.

Holy shit! We're having twins.

43

JORDAN

I've never been so scared, seeing Kenz tumble down the stairs; I swear my heart stopped beating. Racing over to her, I see that she's out cold. I shout. "Someone call an ambulance!" As I drop to my knees next to her.

Behind me, I hear someone reply, but I don't register anything that they say. Holding Kenz in my arms, I try to wake her but she won't come to. "Please, wake up, baby. Please, don't leave me."

The ambulance arrives and the paramedic asks me to step back, I don't want to but I know I have to. Stepping back, they immediately start working on Kenz. They put on a blood pressure cuff and are concerned, her pressure is dangerously high. The second paramedic rushes outside and returns with the stretcher, they lift Kenz onto it and are wheeling her out. As they roll past me, I see her eyes flutter and I breath a sigh of relief.

I follow them outside when I hear Kenz calling out, "Jordan, Jordan!"

I rush to her side. "I'm here, baby."

As soon as she sees me, she starts to cry and my heart breaks for her. I'm confused by what she's saying, the tears pouring down her face. I keep holding her handing, grazing my thumb along the back to sooth her. "Shhhh, don't cry. It's okay, you're okay. Look, they are taking you to the hospital to check you over you. You just tumbled down a flight of stairs and bumped your head a few times."

There is a complete look of fright on her beautiful tear-stained face. She grips my hand tighter, not wanting me to leave. This tumble has really shaken her, she seems confused and then she tells me that Clint's back. I'm taken aback by what I hear and I bellow, "What?"

Kenzie then explains what occurred this morning. I'm angry that she didn't tell me, but I also understand why she didn't. The ambo interrupts us to say it's time to go.

Turning, I ask Mike to lock up for me and to meet us at the hospital. He doesn't hesitate and he runs back inside. He's a trooper; I don't know what I'd do without him.

On the ride to the hospital, Kenz fills me in on the flowers and the text messages. I'm beyond pissed but seeing her strapped to a stretcher and scared; I reign in my fury...for now, I'll let her have it later.

The paramedic tells Kenz that I'm right and I silently thank him.

We see the doctor as soon as we arrive. He admits her immediately and requests a scan due to her fall. We are moved into a private room and just after we're settled, an orderly comes and takes Kenz off for her scan, and I wait in the room.

While I'm waiting, two police officers arrive. I fill them in on what happened today and the bits that Kenz told me. She returns from her scan, and they ask her a few more questions. I start to get angry at what she's telling them.

Why didn't she tell me?

My wife is so stubborn at times.

When they tell us the Clint has escaped, I'm fuming. We have just agreed to come down to the station to make a statement, when the doctor returns and asks them to leave. Once the officers leave, the doctor picks up Kenz's chart. He tells us the one thing that I never thought we would hear. "We did discover your pregnant, congratulations."

Kenzie's grip on my hand tightens, and I stare at him in shock. I can hear Kenz talking to him but nothing is registering. I just keep repeating in my head, *"We're pregnant, we're pregnant."*

Holy fuck, I'm going to be a Dad.

Leaning over, I hug Kenz but I quickly lower myself to her belly, gently placing my hands on her tummy. "Hey, baby, I'm your daddy and this here is your mummy. She's stubborn as a mule, but she is gonna be the bestest mummy in the whole entire world. You are one lucky lil' dude." I softly place a kiss on her stomach before looking up at Kenz.

Her beautiful green eyes are filled with tears, and she has the biggest smile on her face. I rest my forehead on hers, staring into her eyes, still in shock that we are going to be parents.

A few moments later, the baby doctor walks in. Kenz and the doctor chat but I'm in shock, nothing they say registers. Then we hear her say, "Well, let's have a look and you can meet your lil' one."

She picks up this stick, squirts this clear blue gel onto Kenz's belly, pushes a few more buttons and then I hear the most amazing sound I've ever heard—*badunk badunk badunk*—it's a sound I will never forget.

My eyes immediately fill with tears, and I squeeze Kenz's hand. I'm already in love with the lil blob on the screen, even though all I see is black and white static. The doctor points to the screen and says, "That right there is your baby, and hiding behind is bub number two."

I whisper, "Fuck me dead."

Staring at the screen, I'm dumfounded; both our mouths drop open. The doctor looks at us and with a smirk, *cheeky bitch*, "Congratulations, you're having twins."

Holy fuck, we are having twins.

Here we were thinking that we'd never conceive naturally, or even at all and now we're having twins. *I have super sperm*, I can't help but smile.

The doctor and Kenz discuss follow up appointments, and the next thing I know she's leaving the room. She returns a few moments later with the first picture of our munchkins. Kenz grips it tightly to her chest. My heart is bursting with pride at seeing her so happy.

There are so many emotions coursing through my

veins right at this moment: excitement, fear, uncondi-
tional love, apprehension, joy but most of all happiness.
I'm beyond excited to become a dad.

Kenz and I are staring at each other. I notice her
hand gently rubbing her tummy, when we are pulled
from our blissfulness by a commotion in the hall, and
hear, "Kenz, Jordan where are you?" I jump up and
run out.

"Mike, what the hell, dude?" I quietly shout.

"These asshats wouldn't let me through as I'm not
family." He air quotes family. "But that's bullshit, dude,
I'm your brother from another mother, and that means
I'm family."

"Dude, we're in a hospital. You could have just texted
me, and I would have come and got you." I look towards
the nurse and security guard, who is coming up behind
her. "I apologise for my brother, he's a little emotional
about Kenz."

The nurse eyes Mike and says, "One wrong move
and you're out, I don't care that your family." She air
quotes family and storms away.

Mike and I walk back into Kenz's room. He leans
over and hugs Kenz. "Hey, baby girl, how you feeling?"

"Like I fell down a set of stairs and bumped my
head."

"I see your sense of humor wasn't bumped out."

I slap Mike on the back, ready to spill the news when
Kenz interrupts, "Mike, can you be a gem and get me a
Diet Coke please?"

"Sure can, baby girl, you want anything, dickwad?

"I'm good but, dude, keep it down we are in a hospital, and that nurse out there wants your balls on a silver platter."

"Yeah, right, okay. I'll be back with your Diet Coke in a jiffy."

Walking over, I sit on the edge of the bed as soon as Mike leaves, "Why did you interrupt me when I was going to tell Mike the good news?"

"Jor, I don't want to tell anyone, just yet. It's early days, and as it is, I shouldn't have fallen pregnant. I don't want to risk telling people to then have to tell them we're not." A lone tear falls down her face; I reach over and wipe it away. Leaning over, I kiss her forehead.

"We can wait, but I'm just so excited," I say as Mike waltzes back in.

"Oh dude, your excited I'm back, shucks." He hands Kenz her Diet Coke and sits on the end of her bed.

"Thanks, Mike, not just for the Diet Coke but for handling everything back there. We really appreciate it."

"Anything, for you guys, you know that. As I said to Nazi Nurse out there, we are family and family sticks together. We go together like peas and carrots, Cheech and Chong, ham and cheese, lube and..." Kenz puts her hand up to stop him, and I punch him in the arm and shake my head.

"We get it, Mike, trust me we get it. And yes, we are family and we stick together. But anyways, thank you."

44

KENZIE

DR. CANADIAN MCHOTTIE WALKS BACK INTO MY room. "Okay, Kenzie, after conferring with Dr. Greene we've agreed that you no longer need to stay tonight as your blood pressure has returned to normal and all scans came back clear. Here are your discharge papers; you're good to go. Make sure you follow up with Dr. Greene, she really is the best." Mike looks at us apprehensively. We just assured him I'm fine, this will be fun to explain away.

"That's great, thanks, Doc. We will."

He leaves my discharge papers on the bed trolley and walks out. Leaning down, I grab my shoes and put them on and we all head out.

When we get in the car, before we even have our seatbelts on, Mike turns towards me. "Why to you need a follow up with Dr. Purple?"

Laughing, I reply, "It's Dr. Greene and it's just a precaution, Mike. I did just fall down a set of stairs. I'm fine, really." Reaching forward, I squeeze his shoulder in reassurance. He reaches up and squeezes my hand back.

Jordan turns around. "Do you want to go to the police station on the way home or do it tomorrow?"

"Police station?" Mike shakes his head confused, "What's going on? I thought everything was fine?"

With a sigh, I take a deep breath and again in one breath I say, "Clint escaped. I saw him at the opening today, and that's when I tripped and fell down the stairs."

Mike whacks the steering wheel and shouts, "Mother-fucker!" Then he turns towards Jordan and punches him in the arm. "What the fuck, dude, why did you not tell me this?"

Jordan rubs his arm where Mike just hit him. "OUCH, fucker. I didn't know. Miss I Can Handle Anything, in the back there didn't tell anyone. She got a package this morning but didn't want to ruin the opening."

"Look, guys, I'm fine. I'll go see the officers tomorrow, get the restraining order and any other information they have. We can then get back to running the brewpub, whose opening I kind of ruined today." Then I lean back into my seat and close my eyes, I'm shattered.

"You didn't ruin anything and don't think you will be going in anytime soon. You, my wifey, are on bed rest for a few days, you just took a tumble down two flights of stairs and you're..." I raise my eye at him and scowl. "You're, not going in."

"I agree with Jordan, Kenz, you need to rest up."

"Fine, I'll take one day and one day only. Just take me home, Mike."

He looks at me in the rearview mirror and winks. "Do you know how long I've waited to hear you say that, Kenz? You just made my life complete."

This time Jordan punches him in the arm.

"OUCH!"

"Stop flirting with my wife, asshat." Mike pokes his tongue at Jordan and winks at me. "Just take us home."

Mike turns towards Jordan. "Do you know how long I've wait to hear you say that, Jor?" And bat his eyelids at Jordan.

We all burst out laughing. *Man I love Mike.*

Twenty minutes later, Mike drops Jordan and me off, and I climb straight into bed. I fall asleep immediately, subconsciously rubbing my belly.

45

TRAITOR

HOLY FUCK, WE COULD NOT HAVE PLANNED THAT better if we tried. It was so hard not to laugh because the bitch is getting exactly what she deserves.

Clint will be eager to hear how the rest of today goes. Maybe this is what we need to finish this, not sure how much longer I can keep this charade up.

For the life of me, I don't know what he sees her but I owe him my life. If I didn't owe him, there's no way I'd be leading this double life.

A few hours later, I'm hiding out at the hospital and I hear the doctor tell her she's fine, *drama queen*, and wouldn't you know it, she's up the duff. This is gonna be interesting now.

ME – *She's fine but guess what?*

CLINT – *Do tell cuz*

ME – *Your little princess is pregnant, with twins. They released her just a few moments ago*

CLINT – *Great work cuz*

46

KENZIE

THE NEXT MORNING JORDAN DRIVES ME DOWN TO the station. The trip in his Jeep is eerily quiet. Reaching over, I rub his leg. "I'm sorry I didn't say anything Jordan."

I see him glance across at me, it's a mixture of sadness and anger, before returning his eyes to the road, "I'm so angry that you didn't tell me, we don't keep secrets, Kenz. But mostly I'm pissed that he escaped. "

"Me too," I scrunch my face up, "Jor, I'm so sorry I didn't say anything this morning. I didn't want to ruin our special day, guess I ended up ruining it anyway." A lone tear falls down my cheek.

"Please don't cry baby. It's not your fault, it's his. The sooner he's caught, the sooner we can get on with our lives"

"Jordan, you are the one thing that gives me strength," I rub my tummy, "And now I have these lil' ones looking after me as well."

We pull up at the station; Jordan turns towards me

and grabs my hands. "Kenz, I love you more than anything, even beer." We both laugh. "I would do anything to protect you, and now I would do absolutely anything to protect you and our munchkins."

Leaning over, I wrap my arms around his neck and hug him. "I love you Jordan. I promise not to keep anything from you again."

"I love you too, Kenz. Just keep that promise to me, and don't do anything stupid."

"I promise, Jordan. Now let's go in and get this over with."

———

We walk inside, and Jordan tells the officer at the front desk that we are here to see Officer Hamilton or Officer Kincaid. Kincaid seems like a grumpy asshole, who needs the stick up his ass removed, but Hamilton is pretty kick ass; I'd love to be friends with her.

Of course, it's Kincaid that comes out to meet us. He greets us and we head further into the station, he stops outside an interview room and asks us to wait inside. The room is small, cold and void of any ambiance whatsoever. The walls are grey; there's a table in the middle with a single chair on one side and two chairs on the other.

Shivering, I had hoped I would never end up back here, but I was wrong, as usual. The door opens and both Kincaid and Hamilton come in.

Kincaid sits down and Hamilton stands in the corner, leaning against the wall; she crosses her ankles and leans back. She looks over at me and smiles. "How are you doing today, Mackenzie?"

"I'm doing okay, but please, call me Kenzie."

"Right, sorry, Kenzie."

Kincaid looks back at his notes. "Kenzie, you mentioned last night that you thought you were being watched, when did this start?"

"I felt like I was being followed when we moved into our house after we renovated. I knew it wasn't Clint as I kept in contact with the facility to make sure he was still there."

Officer Hamilton asks, "What else has happened?"

"Apart from a few text messages, the sunflowers with a note left at Malt Me and at home yesterday. I hadn't seen him in person, until yesterday."

Officer Kincaid asks, "What did the notes say?"

"Umm, they all said 'tik tok hurry up'. He used to say that to me when we were dating, he was always in a rush to be wherever we were going."

"Okay Mac.. sorry, Kenzie, I think we have everything for now. We'll keep in touch, if you feel threatened or think of anything else please let us know. In the meantime, we have filed another DVO against him." He hands me his card. "Please call me anytime if you have any questions or concerns."

"Thanks, Officers."

Jordan and I stand up and they escort us out.

Not long after we get home Mike walks in, sans De-Niece. *Thank you God.* "Hey guys, how you doing, Kenz?"

Walking over, I give him a hug. "I'm good, Mike,

sorry to scare you yesterday. Thanks for everything, I mean it."

"So it's really true, Mr. Douche-Canoe-Fuckface is back? I was hoping you were pulling my leg." I sheepishly look up and nod. "What the fuck are we going to do?"

"And that there is why I didn't say anything!" I yell, "I don't want you two getting hurt cause of my douche canoe ex. Please let the police handle it."

"Kenz, you're my wife. There is nothing and I mean nothing that I wouldn't do for you. Serious—" Jordan is mid-sentence when I collapse.

He and Mike rush me back to the hospital. They page Dr. Greene, she recommends I stay overnight for observations so they admit me.

Mike and Jordan stay with me all afternoon, the air is thick with animosity and worry. Later that evening, the nurse walks in and sternly says, "Okay boys, visiting hours are over and our patient here needs to rest up. Say your goodbyes, and you can come back tomorrow when visiting hours start again."

Jordan asks, "Can't I stay, please?"

"I'm afraid not, honey. New regulations don't allow it, and as much as you are a sweet, doting husband, I want to keep my job. I'll give you ten more minutes."

Mike leans over and kisses me on the forehead. "Rest up, Kenz, I'll see you when you get home tomorrow."

"Thanks, Mike, I'll see you tomorrow and thanks for everything. Again." He nods his head at me. He looks at Jordan. "I'll wait in the lobby for you, asshat." And with that, he walks out, gently closing the door behind him.

Jordan walks over to the bed, takes my hands, and

gently squeezes them. He looks me in the eye before kissing my forehead. "I really don't want to leave you, Kenz, but rest up, its not just you anymore. Try and get a good night's sleep. We will deal with this tomorrow when we have a clear head. I'm so mad at you right now, but I also love you so very muchly," He leans over and places a soft kiss on my lips, wrapping his arms around me and giving me a tight, warm-hearted cuddle. He whispers, "I love you to the moon and back."

He stands up to leave, as he gets to the door, he turns, smiles and blows me a kiss. After he closes the door, I break down and cry. The tears keep coming and they won't stop. The nurse walks in. "Oh honey." She gives me a hug, which is just what I need. Pretty sure this is above and beyond the call of duty for a nurse, but I'll take it.

Finally, I stop crying and look up. I see her name badge and I say, "Thanks, Tara, that's just what I needed, and thanks for kicking the dynamic duo out. I know they mean well, but..." Then I start to cry again.

"Happy to help, hon. Now I can't give you any of the good stuff due to the babies but do you want anything, or are you okay?"

"I'm fine for now, but I'll buzz you if I need anything."

"No worries. I'll be back to check on you later."

I smile. "Thanks."

As she walks out, she dims the lights and I lie back. I start rubbing my tummy, still stunned that there are two little ones in there. Quietly I whisper, "Mummy loves you guys." I drift off to sleep.

I wake few hours later when Tara is back doing my

obs. "Sorry to wake you hon. I'm just bout finished, you go back to sleep." I'm pretty tired so I nod my head and fall straight back to sleep.

A noise startles me, I open my eyes, and my heart stops beating when I see whose standing above me, Clint. I can't move, I'm frozen with fear. Leaning down, he whispers, "Morning, Sweetcheeks."

Before I have a chance to scream, he places a cloth over my face. I struggle, but everything goes black and for the third time in forty-eight hours darkness engulfs me.

TRAITOR

My phone rings as I'm leaving work. They inform me that Kenz collapsed and they are on their way to the hospital. I make up some excuse about being held up at work but I'll try get there later; *not gonna happen.*

There's a huge smile on my face as I text Clint

ME – *You're precious collapsed and shes back in hospital*

CLINT – *Thanks cuz, looks like I have the perfect opportunity now to finish this once and for all*

ME – *Let me know if you need anything else cuz*

I'm excited as everything is coming together perfectly, I can't wait to see what happens from here. Looks like I'll be out of here sooner rather than later.

CLINT

CAN THIS WEEKEND GET ANY BETTER? FIRST, I HAND delivered a beautiful sunflower to my girl and had the best wank outside her place. Then I managed to ruin the opening of asshats brewery, and to top it off, I find out that my beautiful Sweetcheeks is pregnant.

Now sadly she is in hospital again, but this will allow me access to whisk her away, and we can finally live happily ever after; as a family.

I've been hiding out for a few hours when finally asshat one and asshat two leave. The cute nurse, who I've been flirting with all afternoon, kicks them out. If I have everything understood from my chat with Tara, she'll be finishing at 11:00 p.m. and there will be a shift change. I'll bide my time till then and then I can sneak my Sweetcheeks out, and we can finally all be together.

After what feels like forever, it's time to go get my Sweetcheeks and babies. Sneaking into her room with the wheelchair I stole from some old dude's room, I walk over to her bed and she's stirring. She looks up at me with her beautiful green eyes, and before she can do anything I place a cloth over her face and she drifts back to sleep.

Carefully, I lift her out of bed and place her in the wheelchair, whisking her and our babies away, to start our happily ever after together.

As we enter the car park. I laugh; I so wish I could see asshats face when he realises she's gone. Today is the start of the rest of my life; finally everything I have been through will be worth it.

49

JORDAN

WHEN THE NURSE TELLS ME I HAVE TO LEAVE, I'M gutted. I want to be here to be here with Kenz and the munchkins. As I say goodbye to Kenz, my heart is breaking. She looks so sad, I place a soft kiss on her lips and whisper, "I love you to the moon and back." Then I turn and leave.

As soon as I close the door, I hear her start to cry, it breaks my heart to leave. However, I know Kenz and she needs time to herself. I'll give her this moment, as much as it kills me.

Putting one foot in front of the other, I walk outside and meet up with Mike in the foyer. We both walk to his car in silence, I'm waiting for him to let loose. We get to his car and I smile when I realise he bought the Corvette, this car is sweet. Looking towards him I say, "Thanks, Mike, this is just what I needed to see. Now can I drive?"

"I know, man, and fuck no, you're not driving my baby. Now get in, start from the beginning and tell me what's going on."

I fill Mike in on the recent events as we head back to our place.

"Fuck," he seethes.

"That's not all, dude." Kenz is going to kill me for telling Mike this. "Ummm don't tell Kenz I told you, but we also found out that she's pregnant...with twins."

He snaps his head towards me, mouth gaping wide open in shock. He shakes his head. "Fuck me dead, said foreskin Fred. That's fuckin' amazing, dude. Who knew your lil' swimmers were so awesome?"

I laugh; I can always count on Mike to make me laugh. "You never cease to amaze me with the shit that comes out of your mouth."

"Dude, I amaze myself sometimes, too. Keeps life interesting."

Shaking my head I laugh again, "And that right there is why you are my best mate. Now drive me home, it's been a long ass day. The quicker I get home to bed and sleep, the quicker I can get back to my girl and squids."

Before I know it, we are back at our place. Mike offers to hang around but I say I'm fine and tell him to go and see De-Niece. He gives me a funny look when I mention her name but I shrug it off.

Once Mike leaves, I have a quick shower and jump into bed. Lying on my side, staring out the window I think about Kenz, the babies and Clint; God I hope we can get through this.

Before I know it *Dream On* by Aerosmith is blaring through the alarm clock. Reaching over, I turn it off. I lie there staring at the ceiling thinking about everything once again. Drifting back to sleep, I'm woken later by the sound of my phone ringing. Reaching out, I sleepily answer it, "Hello?"

A stern male voice says, " Is this Jordan McRoberts?"

"Yeah, who's this?"

"It's Officer Kincaid. Can you get to the hospital quickly?"

Instantly I sit up. "Is Kenz okay? The babies?"

"Please come to the hospital and we will tell you."

Gripping my phone tighter I yell, "NO, tell me now!"

"Mrs. McRoberts is missing. It looks like she was taken during the night."

.

50

KENZIE

WHEN I OPEN MY EYES AGAIN, EVERYTHING IS FUZZY. I blink repeatedly and eventually everything comes back into focus. Looking around my heart rate increases, fear courses through my veins when I realise that I'm naked and no longer in hospital. I try to lift my hand but again, I'm tied to a bed, rope wrapped tightly around my wrists and ankles.

Movement at the end of the bed catches my eye. I see Clint is sitting there, also naked. The anger is radiating off him; his eyes are filled with rage, shoulders tight, jaw clenched, and a scowl on his face. He moves and I flinch in terror. This only infuriates him more and my fear reaches fever pitch.

Looking down at me, he smirks. "Good morning, Sweetcheeks." He stands up and tugs on the ropes to make sure my hands, and feet are tightly secured. Darting my eyes around, I want to get an idea of where I am. I start to feel sick when I notice his cock is rock hard.

He looks down at me again and starts to laugh, it's

creepy and grates through me. Reaching down he starts to stroke his cock, looking me directly in the eye, his strokes becoming more rapid. He calmly says, "This here is for you, but not until you have safely delivered our babies."

Groaning, his knuckles turn white as he grips his cock tighter, stroking faster and faster. "I've missed seeing your pretty face up close when I come."

Laughing, he climbs onto the bed next to me, leans over and starts to roughly massage my breasts, violently pulling and twisting my nipples. I scream out in pain, "Please stop, please!"

"There's my feisty little whore, you love it when I do this." He twists my nipple viciously, I'm sure he's going to rip it off. Releasing my nipple, he bends down and sucks on it, biting so viciously that he punctures my skin. I feel the blood dripping down my side. My eyes well with tears, squeezing them tightly shut, I will the tears away.

Against my will my nipples pucker; I hate that my nipples are so sensitive. He grabs his cock and starts rubbing it in between my breasts. Pushing my breasts together, he starts to fuck them, thrusting back and forth while painfully squeezing and pushing them together.

I can't stand to see his face, so I scrunch my eyes closed tighter and imagine I'm anywhere but here.

It's not long until I feel the first spray of cum hit my chin. Shaking my head from side to side, I try to move but I can't. He has me pinned to the bed; he keeps pounding between my breasts until he completely empties his load.

Once he's finished, he leans forward and licks me clean. He laps every last drop of cum, and then licks up my neck; I groan and shudder in disgust. He mistakes this as a pleasurable sound. "Does my, lil' Sweetcheeks like that?"

"Not fucking likely," I spit though clenched teeth.

He licks across my chin and I turn my face away. He roughly grasps my chin so I am looking into his eyes; I scrunch my eyes shut tight and he growls, "Open those baby blues, bitch, I want to see the look in them when I fuck your sweet pussy, over and over again."

Opening my eyes, I hiss, "My eyes are green, asshole."

He slaps my face and I cry. Something snaps inside of me and I completely lose it: thrashing and screaming, kicking my tied legs, as more and more tears pour down my face. "Let me go, argh. You fucking asshole, let me go. I hate your fucking guts!"

Clint stands up, glares down at me, and laughs like a maniac before turning around and walking out.

Leaving me alone.

Naked.

Strapped to the bed...again.

———

My tears have subsided, and I'm lying here staring at the off white ceiling. I notice a spider scamper along. *I wish I could scurry away like him.* Closing my eyes, I pray that they will find me soon, because I don't know if I can survive this again. This time I have the little squids to think about, and then I start to panic; the squids.

The door handle rattling jolts me and I freeze, Clint

pushes the door open and has a sick smile on his face, "Hey, my beautiful Sweetcheeks."

Turning my head, I look to the wall, I refuse to look at him. I pray for death, again. I'm not strong enough to handle anymore. I pray with all that I have that someone will find me soon.

"Cat got your tongue?"

Staring at the wall, I continue to ignore him. I feel the bed dip, he forcefully grips my face and turns my head so I'm looking at him. I close my eyes and he slaps me hard across the face **WHACK**. My cheek stings. He jumps on top of me. I try to move my head so I don't have to look at him, but he digs his fingers in deeper, holding me still. Bending down he licks along my jawbone and bites my lip. Then he shoves his tongue in my mouth and I start to gag. I can feel the bile rising and I can't hold it in. I vomit while his tongue is still in my mouth.

Clint pulls back quickly; he spits at me and back-hands me across the face. **WHACK** "You fucking sick bitch." **WHACK**, "How dare you vomit at me!" **WHACK**

When he's finished hitting me, he proceeds to lick the vomit off my face. I feel his cock hardening against my leg as he's licking me clean, and I start to cry.

Turning my head towards the wall, I cry: uncontrollable sobs overtake my body. Staring at a brown smudge on the wall, I start thinking about the precious cargo that I am carrying, my lil' squids. It's in this moment that I realise I will survive this. Jordan's mantra pops into my head and I keep repeating it; "I'm Mackenzie "Kenzie"

McRoberts nee Merlot. I'm strong and hot, and I'm not afraid."

With that thought, something snaps inside of me and I tell myself to stop crying, pull up my big girl undies, if I was wearing any, and figure this out. Taking a deep breath, I decide that I need to come up with a plan to get out of here. I need to do it quickly, but I'm so exhausted, I doze off to sleep.

———

I wake up with a fright when I feel someone touching me. Hoping that it's Jordan here to rescue me, my eyes flicker open and unfortunately I see Clint. He reaches forward, brushing a few strands of hair off my face. "Sorry to scare you, Sweetcheeks." Pausing, he smiles. "You are so beautiful when you sleep."

Taking a deep breath, I think to myself, *this is it*. Plastering on a fake smile, I put on an Oscar winning performance, and I act like I'm in love with him. Smiling up at him I say with a giggle, "Thanks, I think, but watching me sleep is kinda creepy."

"It's not creepy when it's the person that loves you the most in this world staring at you."

I think to myself, *it's now or never*. "You love me? Still?" I whisper.

"Yes, Sweetcheeks. I've never stopped loving you, and now that you are carrying our babies, I love you even more."

My eyes go wide, how does he know that I'm pregnant? Apart from the doctors and Jordan, no one else knows. Starting to panic, I take a deep breath. Fear isn't good for the babies. *I really need to get out of here, and now.*

He gently caresses my face. "Sweetcheeks, the whole time I was locked away, I imagined this moment right here. Well, without the restraints, and that's why I had to get out of there. My cousin helped smuggle me out, and I've been hiding with her, watching you, and waiting for my chance."

Interrupting him I hesitantly ask, "So why don't you take them off? How can I show you how much you mean to me, if I can't touch you?" I choke this out and am proud of myself, I actually sound convincing.

"You're just saying that." He jumps off the bed and starts pacing.

"No, why would I lie to you? I've had time to think about it and... and I don't want to be anywhere else." I struggle to get the next part out, "The babies and I need you, Clint." Inwardly, I say, *sorry squids, I promise, Mummy will protect you.*

He snaps his head back to me, staring into my eyes, "You mean it?"

"Yyyy...yessss" I stutter.

"First I need to get rid of loverboy to make sure he doesn't ruin it for us again, and then there'll be nothing in our way."

I stare up at him, shocked at his words. "Www...what?"

"You heard me, I'm going to take out loverboy, so we can live happily ever after together in this cabin with our babies."

My mind starts racing and over and over in my head, I repeat, *no...no...no...* I need to think of something and quickly. I didn't anticipate how fucked up Clint now is, he seems to be more cuckoo than last time.

My mind is racing as I try and think of what I used to call him when we were together. "Clint!" I shout. He turns and looks at me, like a lightning strike out of nowhere I remember. "Baby, let's not think of him. He means nothing to me now that I'm here with you. Let's just me and you start over, forget about everyone else."

He reaches down and strokes my face; I lean into his hand and turn my head to place a soft kiss on his palm. Willing myself to cry, "Clint, baby I'm sorry." Miraculously a tear falls. "I'm so, so sorry for everything I put you through." I pretend to sob.

He lays down and squishes me, stroking my hair and whispers, "Shhhh, it's alright, Sweetcheeks. You're here now and that's all that matters."

"Clint, baby, can you please untie me, so you can hold me properly? I need to be in your arms." He lifts himself up and looks down at me. I smile at him and pray to God that he's falling for this. He leans over and loosens the rope. Sighing in relief, I quickly sit up, rubbing my wrists before I wrap my arms around him. I sigh, "It feels so good to be in your arms again, baby, please forgive me for everything."

"Sweetcheeks, I could never stay mad at you." He kisses me, I hold my eyes closed tightly and kiss him back. Pushing back, I rest my forehead against his, closing my eyes, I whisper. "Thank you, Clint." I pull away and look deeply into his eyes; I take a deep breath and kiss him, again. Coaxing his mouth open, I slip my tongue in, sliding it around; I moan in disgust, but he takes it as a pleasurable moan and increases the kiss, crushing me tighter to his body. I feel his heart rate increase. It's in this moment that I know I have him; *my freedom is not far away*.

I pull back and graze my teeth over his bottom lip and sucking. Tenderly, I place my hand on his cheek and with my thumb I rub along has jaw line, "Clint, do you think I could take a shower? I want to make myself beautiful for you." Lowering my head, I look down my body before shyly looking back up at him. "I look like a mess right now."

He lifts my chin and sweetly replies, "Sure, Sweetcheeks, anything for you, but I still think you are the most beautiful woman in the world. I even have new clothes for you," he proudly declares while smiling at me.

"You're so thoughtful, baby." I put my arms around his waist and snuggle into him. I shudder, which makes him hold me in closer to him.

Clint pulls away and bends towards my feet to loosen and remove the ropes. He sees the red marks around my ankles and he gasps in shock. "Sweetcheeks, I'm so sorry that I did this to you. I promise to make it up to you."

Reaching out for him, I gently rub his arm. "You can make it up to me by letting me have a shower."

"Okay, Sweetcheeks. I'll go and get the water hot for you, and I'll come back when it's ready."

Smiling sweetly at him. "Thanks, baby, you're awesome."

He turns around and heads to the bathroom. Taking a deep breath I keep repeating to myself, "I can do this."

———

This shower is the best shower I've ever had. I stand under the showerhead until the water runs cold, not just because it feels great but because I don't want to be near Clint. Just before I get out, I start to doubt that I can do this. Do I have the stomach to do what I need to get out of here? Subconsciously, I rub my stomach and by doing that, it's the reminder I need. I do have the strength I need to survive and I'll do whatever it takes.

As I'm drying my stomach, lost in thought, I don't notice Clint walk into the bathroom. "You are so beautiful, I can't wait to make more babies with you."

I try to hold back the shock on my face, but I obviously do a terrible job, because in that moment Clint looks inquisitively at me, "Are you okay, Mackenzie?"

Sighing, I reply, "Just tired, baby, growing babies is hard work. Do you think we could get something to eat, once I'm dressed?"

Looking to the counter I see a bra, undies, and a purple maxi dress; he remembers that purple is my favourite colour. Smiling as I slide the dress over my head, I walk towards Clint and grab his hand, entwining our fingers together. "Thank you for my beautiful dress, and it's purple, my favourite. You're so thoughtful."

He takes my hand and leads us towards the kitchen. When we reach it, I turn towards Clint and say, "Let me cook you dinner tonight, it's the least I can do for my man." I smile sweetly at him.

He looks sad and whispers, "I don't have anything here, Sweetcheeks."

Eagerly I reply, "Well, let's go into town. I can collect the things the make your favourite, Risotto Napolitana and chocolate self-saucing pudding for dessert. We could even stop and have a coffee while we are out, just like we used to." I smile and anxiously await his reply.

"Okay, Sweetcheeks. Let me grab a shower and then we can go." He kisses me on the cheek before leaving me alone in the kitchen. Holding my breath until I hear the water running and I let out a huge sigh in relief, *I can't believe he is falling for this*.

While he's in the shower, I look around for anything that might help me. Sitting, on the corner of the kitchen counter is his mobile phone; I quickly grab it. Scooting round the edge of the bench, I check to make sure he is still in the shower. Unlocking the screen, I check to make sure the location tracker is turned on and I quickly type a text to Jordan.

CLINT– *help me*

Once it sends, I quickly delete it and hope to hell that Jordan understands what I mean.

Just as I'm sliding his phone back onto the bench, he steps into the room. I quickly turn to face him and with a super fake smile, I say, "Hey, handsome, ready to go shopping?"

"I guess so, I hate shopping."

"Well, why don't you wait in the car while I duck in and get what we need?" I smile, and hope he says yes.

"I'm not letting you out of my sight, Sweetcheeks," he growls.

I guess he still doesn't completely trust me yet, but to keep up the rouse I say, "Okay then, lets go." Clutching his hand, I lead us towards the front door...and my possible freedom.

51

JORDAN

After getting the phone call from Officer Kincaid, I throw on my jeans and a t-shirt and race to the hospital. When I arrive at the hospital, I notice there are four police cars here. Swiftly I park my Jeep and race inside.

Officer Hamilton is standing by the nurses' station and when she sees me running down the hall, she starts walking towards me. I know it's a hospital and I shouldn't be running but I don't give a shit right at this moment, Kenz is gone, again.

I failed to protect her, again.

Slowing down, as I get closer to her, I breathlessly pant, "Any news? Have you found her?" Struggling to breathe I think, *man, I'm unfit.*

"There's no news yet, Jordan, but Kincaid is current looking at the surveillance footage. The nurses last checked on Mackenzie at 11.25 p.m., according to her chart. They went in to do the 5:00 a.m. obs before shift change, and that's when they realised she was missing.

Security did a quick sweep, and when they could not find her, they immediately called us. Once we got here and were brought up to speed, Kincaid called you, while I called in extra help."

Shaking my head, I stare at Officer Hamilton in shock, "How the fuck did this happen?" Leaning against the wall closest to me, I slide down; resting my elbows on my knees, shaking my head mumbling to myself, "Not again, poor Kenz."

A lone tear falls down my face, as soon as I start to think about Kenz and the babies, it sparks something inside of me. I wipe my face and immediately jump up, "Right, what do we do? I need to find my wife and know that her and our squids are okay."

Officer Hamilton firmly says, "You don't do anything. I'm sorry, Jordan, but you cannot be involved in this. We need to do it by the book, so we can get him locked away for a very long time."

"Fuck that!" I shout, "There is no way I'm going to sit around, while some psycho asshole has my wife."

"Jordan, I want to find Kenzie safe as well. Listen to me when I tell you this; you need to go home. Let me do my job. I can't be worrying about you too, Kenzie needs all my focus right now."

Taking a deep breath, I calm myself down. I know she's right but I can't sit around and not do anything. Throwing my hands in the air, I concede, "Okay, fine. I'll go home and wait but you keep me updated on what's happening."

"Jordan, I'll keep you updated, as best as I can. Right

at the moment, I need to concentrate on finding Kenzie, that is my top priority."

Standing up, I say, "Thank you." Turning to walk away, I see

Officer Kincaid coming towards us.

"I've viewed the footage, and it looks like Clint took her around 3:00 a.m. He wheeled her outside and loaded her into a yellow car, at this stage we can't make out the model. I've called the station and I'm getting them to check cameras around here to gauge which direction he went. We should have an idea within the next thirty minutes."

I'm holding my breath, as I listen to Kincaid speak; all I register is that Clint who took her. He was dressed as a doctor, has a yellow car and drove off. As it sinks in that he has her again, I slump down the wall once again, shaking my head in frustration.

Officer Hamilton tells me that they will do everything to get her back safely. I growl, "Don't make promises you can't keep, this guy is deranged. I don't believe for a second that he won't hurt her. Please just find her." With that, I stand up and walk away, before either of them has a chance to reply.

As I wait for the elevator, I repeatedly punch the button to make it get here quicker; eventually it arrives and I jump in. Grabbing my phone from my pocket, I dial Mike, he picks up on the second ring. "What's up, asshat?"

"Kenz is gone. That fucker took her from her hospital bed earlier this morning. The police won't let me help, but I'm not sitting around. That's my wife and babies."

Before I can finish Mike interrupts, "Whatever you need, I'm there, dude. Kenz is family and you know I'd do anything for family." The lift doors open and I race to my car.

"I'm just leaving the hospital, I'll be at your place in ten."

Getting into my car, I throw it into gear and haul ass to Mike's place in record time. When I get there, De-Niece is there too. She jumps up and gives me a hug, but it doesn't feel genuine. "I'm so sorry Jor."

I think it's weird that she calls me Jor, the only person to do that is Kenz, but I shrug it off. "Thanks, D."

Mike walks down the hall. "Okay, asshat, what's the plan?"

Shaking my head, I sigh, I don't know where to begin. I'm lost without Kenz. "To tell you the truth, I have no fucking idea; some husband I am." Standing up, I take a few steps before turning to face Mike. "It's probably a long shot but I'm going to head to where he had her last time. He's unhinged enough that he would do that, fucking sick bastard that he is."

De-Niece yells, "He's not unhinged!"

Turning my head to look towards her, my blood boiling at her reply. "What? Are you fucking kidding me?" I spit. "He has just kidnapped Kenz, for the second fucking time. How is that not unhinged?"

With a confused look on her face, she stammers, "What I mean is he...he...he's in love. If he loves her as much as he seems to, then I don't think he's going to hurt her."

Shaking my head, I reply, "I hope you're right." I look towards Mike. "Okay, let's go."

De-Niece says, "Sorry, I can't go, I have work." Truthfully I don't give a shit about her, but Mike walks over to her and places a gentle kiss on her forehead.

"It's okay, baby, I don't want you anywhere near that fucker anyway. At least if you're at work, I know you'll be safe."

She looks up at him with an odd look on her face. "Okay."

Mike gives her a quick kiss on the lips, and we race towards my car.

"Dude, are you okay to drive?" Mike cautiously asks.

"Yeah, I'm good." Climbing in, I look to Mike and say, "Buckle up asshat, let's go."

We back out of Mike's driveway, and head to the cabin.

Forty minutes later, we arrive at the cabin, but it's deserted. Opening the front door, it doesn't look like anyone has been here in years, a thick layer of dust covers every surface and the police tape from last time it still stuck to the verandah bearers.

My heart sinks, I don't know what else to do. I slide down the side of my car and put my head in my hands. Mike walks over to me, crouches down, and places his hand on my shoulders. I look up into his concerned eyes. He clears his throat, "Look, dude, Kenz is strong. She will be fine. Let's head home, we need to be close by when we hear that Kenz and the munchkins are found and safe."

I'm too shaken to drive, so Mike guides me to the passenger side and I climb in. He drives us back to my place and just as we pull up, I get a text. I open up the message and stare at it in disbelief. It's from a number I don't recognise. It has two words,

UNKNOWN – *help me*

As soon as I finishing reading it, I drop my phone in shock. I know it's Kenz, but I don't know what to do. Snatching my phone back up, I immediately call Officer Hamilton. She picks up on the first ring. "Hamilton."

"Hey, it's Jordan. I just got a text from a number that I don't know saying, 'help me'. I'm pretty sure it's a cry for help from Kenz."

"Okay, that's great. Tell me the number and I'll see if tech can trace it."

"Sure." I give her the number.

"Thanks Jordan..."

Interrupting her, I ask, "So, what do we do now?"

"Leave it with me and I'll be in touch. Jordan, this is a great lead. Kenzie is strong, just keep remembering that."

"Yeah, thanks. I'll speak to you soon." Sighing, I hang up and slide my phone back into my pocket.

I look over, and Mike is staring at me and says, "See, it's going to be fine." He walks over to the fridge and grabs two Diet Cokes.

We head outside and sit at the Jack and Jill. After sitting in silence for about ten minutes, I jump up. "Fuu-uuuuuuck!" I yell in frustration towards the clear blue sky.

Sitting back down, I look towards Mike, "Dude, I feel so helpless. Kenz and my babies are out there, and I am sitting here doing nothing. I'm having a Goddamn freakin' Coke with my best mate. It's just not right."

Standing up, I lean over the railing and again I shout, "Fuuuuck!" I'm so frustrated that I can't do anything.

"Look, dude, I get it. You're annoyed, you feel useless and your fucking pissed off, but there is nothing we can do right now. I know it sucks donkey balls, but you need to remain calm and strong for Kenz. Why don't you go to Malt Me and tinker or brew some shit? It will take your mind off things and keep you busy. I can't be worrying about you, too."

I look towards Mike. "Shit, dude, when did you become the wise one?"

Mike fakes being hurt. "Listen here, asshat, I've always been wise and all that other shit. You are now just finally seeing me for all that I am."

"And there's the cocky Mike I know. Thanks dude, I appreciate the pep talk."

Mike says he's got to go and since we took my car, I offer to drive him home. We get to his place, just as De-Niece is pulling up. She races over and wraps her arms around Mike. "Any news?"

Mike shakes my head. "The cabin was a bust but asshat got a text."

De-Niece looks over at me confused. "From who?"

"No idea, I didn't recognise the number, but I'm sure it was Kenz reaching out for help. I called the police and they are trying to trace the number now. That was a few hours ago, so hopefully I'll hear something soon."

De-Niece looks really pissed. I guess she is just as worried as we are. Turning I slap Mike on the back.

"Thanks for today, dude, I'm going to head home, I'll keep you posted."

"Anytime, man, anytime. You keep me updated and just remember our girl is strong. She is one of the strongest peeps I know, she'll be fine, Jordan. I feel it in my bones."

"Thanks, Mike, I appreciate it and I fucking hope you're right. I'll keep you posted." Turning, I jump into my car and head home.

As soon as I get home, I collapse in a heap on sofa, and I let it all out. I crumble and cry.

I cry for Kenz.

I cry for our babies

Most of all, I cry because I've failed her...again.

52

KENZIE

THE DRIVE INTO TOWN TAKES US ABOUT TEN minutes. It's mid-afternoon on a Saturday and most of the shops are closed or starting to close; *I hope can pull this off*. The scenery is absolutely stunning, on one side of the road is a river and the other is a beautiful rainforest. It's secluded and peaceful, no wonder he chose to keep me here.

"Clint, it's absolutely beautiful here."

He glances towards me and smiles. Reaching over, he places his hand on my thigh and gives it a little squeeze. Inwardly I shudder at his touch, but to keep up my ruse, I look over at him and sweetly smile, before looking out the window again.

This is my chance to make my escape or at the very least get help.

We park the car outside the local supermarket and head in. To keep up the loving girlfriend ploy and make him think that I want to be with him, I grab his hand and put it over my shoulders, so I can put my arm around his waist. Slipping my hand into his back jeans pocket, I give his ass a squeeze, just like old times. Looking up at him I whisper, "I missed this," as I snuggle into him.

He sniffs my hair and I cringe, he hugs me closer and I start to tremble. Closing my eyes I take a deep breath, telling myself I can do this and to keep walking. Just put one foot in front of the other. My heart rate accelerates, as we get closer to the shop door. My mind goes into over-drive trying to figure out how I'm going to get out of here.

We race around the shop getting everything we need for the risotto, and not once do I see someone; just my luck. We get to the checkout and I place the groceries on the conveyor. I'm discretely trying to get the chick's atten-tion but she won't look up. *Goddam teenagers.* I guess that plan won't work, so I hope and pray that Jordan got my text.

Clint pays for our groceries, and I go to grab the bags but he places his hand on my arm. "I got it, Sweetcheeks." I secretly high five myself, I didn't shudder when he touched me.

"Thanks, baby, do you want to get a coffee before we head back? I'd kill for a latte and muffin right now. Maybe we could also take a walk through the park over there, when we are finished. It's so pretty here and it's a lovely day." If he agrees, I might be able to get away if I slip to the bathroom.

"Sounds good, Sweetcheeks, let's drop the bags off first." Turning around, I smile and walk out of the store with a little spring in my step. This is my chance, I just know it.

Clint receives a text on the way to the car, but as he

has the bags he can't read it. We get to the car; I open the boot so he can put the bags in. After closing it, I grab his hand, entwine my fingers with his, and we head towards the coffee shop.

As we are walking through the car park Clint pulls his phone out of his jeans pocket and checks the text.

TRAITOR – *he knows you have her*

Clint stops, lets go my hand, and I see his fist clenching by his side. He glares at me, and I know that whatever was in that text has pissed him off. "Is everything okay, baby?"

He looks back at his phone and then snaps his head up, glaring at me. In a split second, he lunges towards me but I jump back. "You bitch, you fucking lying whore bag bitch. You texted loverboy, and here I was going to let him live, but now you and he are both going to suffer, painfully."

I'm rooted on the spot.

I stare at him my mouth wide open.

I don't know how he knows but I'm screwed now.

My mind is racing, but I don't have the energy to come up with an excuse so I do that only thing that I can. I race towards him, swing my leg back, and with all my might, I stomp on his foot. Then I shove my knee into his balls and push him; he doubles over in pain.

This is my chance.

I take the opportunity and I run. I run through car park into the back street, and I don't stop; I run as fast as I can, turning down streets, doubling back. I just keep moving.

I don't stop.

I keep running.

Ducking and weaving down streets.

I don't look back.

After running for what feels like forever, I have to stop, I'm shattered and out of breath. It's becoming harder and harder to breathe. I'm lost. I have no idea where I am, or even which Goddamn town I'm in.

Ducking down an alleyway, I hide behind an old, beautiful brick building, which I think would be perfect building for a brewpub. Giggling, I shake my head, how on earth can I be thinking of beer at a time like this? Hiding behind the industrial bins out the back, bending over, I put my hands on my knees and take deep breaths.

Sliding down the wall, I rest my head on my knees and start to cry. I have no idea where I am. I have no money, and I have no fucking clue what to do next. What does one do when you have a fucking psycho looking for you?

When I look up again it's dark, I have no idea how long I've been sitting here. Taking a deep breath, I think it's now or never, so I sneak out from where I am.

Heading towards the road, sticking close to the building for cover, I

peek around the corner. I find I'm back at the main street that we drove in on. There's a streetlight on the other side of the road but the street is empty. This place is deserted. *Doesn't anyone live is the fucking town?* Looking up and down the street, I decide to head back towards the shopping precinct, surely someone will be around to help me.

Taking another deep breath, I pick up my pace and keep going. It takes me about five minutes to reach the supermarket. In that time, I have not seen one person, or even a single car; the lights in the shop are off and it's closed. "Damn smalls towns," I mumble to myself.

Taking another look around, I see headlights coming from the direction I was heading. I race onto the road to flag them down, but as the car gets closer I see that it's Clint's. "Fuck," I say to myself as I quickly turn and run across the road into the park.

Clint screeches to a stop, jumps out, leaving the engine running, and runs into the park after me. "I know you're here, bitch, you'll be leaving with me!" he shouts into the dark night sky. Before he adds, "Come out, come out, wherever you are." in a sinister voice.

I'm hiding under the slide when I hear him coming towards me, I hold my breath, and he stops right near my hiding place. My heart is beating erratically and I'm sure he can hear it. I think he's found me, and I start to give up, when I see that he's turning in circles. He's frustrated and looking around. He stops and shouts again, "I know you're here, bitch, and I'll find you. I've got all night bitch!"

Holding ever so still, not breathing for fear he will find me, I flinch when he kicks the slide in frustration, narrowly missing me. Turning, he runs further into the park. I sigh in relief.

I wait until I can't hear his footsteps and I sneak out. Taking a quick look around, I see a light on in the distance. I take off in that direction, trying to be as quiet as possible. As I get closer to the light, I can feel my heart beating; it feels like its going a million miles a minute. I'm about fifty meters from the house when, from behind a tree, Clint steps out. Stopping me, dead in my tracks, I quickly turn around to run away.

He lunges forward, grabbing me by my hair. "Got you now, you little bitch. " I squeal from the pain, my hair follicles tearing out. He yanks me roughly into him. Wrapping his arms tightly around me, as I kick and lunge my legs. Without thinking, I scream at the top of my lungs, hoping someone will hear me. Viciously, he spins me around and punches me in the face. Seeing stars, I drop to the ground like a sack of potatoes. I hold my cheek, the pain is excruciating; I start to cry. Blood begins to drip down my face. I sob harder.

Clint slaps me again. "Shut the fuck up, bitch." I'm lying on the ground; I immediately draw my legs up to protect the babies and myself. He grabs me by my hair and drags me back towards the car.

Kicking and screaming I keep pleading, "Please let me go, Clint. Please don't hurt me." Clint is mumbling to himself, but I can't make sense of what he's saying, he has completely spaced out and is babbling incoherently. As we pass under a light near the playground, he looks down at me. His face is void of any emotion and his eyes are dark with rage. I've never seen him like this. I have to get away; otherwise I will not survive.

Once again, I try to dig my heels into the ground, but it's no use, he's too strong. The anger coursing through his veins, gives him super human strength. He keeps dragging me towards the car. I'm so scared, I don't know what else to do.

We get to the car and he opens the boot to shove me in. As he is shoving me in, the light from behind him illuminates the tyre iron sitting there, in plain sight. I reach over and grab it. With all my might, I turn and swing. It connects with the side of Clint's head, and he loses his balance. With the hand that is holding the tyre iron, I shove him in the chest with everything that I have. He falls backwards, and I tumble back with him. I hear a crack as we both land on the bitumen with a thud.

Lifting my head, I look towards Clint; he's not moving and vacant eyes stare back at me, not blinking, he's dead. I start to scream as realisation sets in: he's dead. I continue to scream, as I see blue and red light coming towards us. Those lights are last thing I see, as everything goes black.

53

JORDAN

I'm at home, but I can't sit still, I can't concentrate on anything. I've never felt so lost or helpless in my entire life. I've failed to protect her again and this time there's the twins to think about.

"Shit! Fuck! Shit!" I yell.

I'd accepted that Kenz and I probably would never have kids. Now that she is pregnant, I'm over the moon. However, I'm now scared shitless that I'm going to lose them all.

Sitting on the couch, I stare at our wedding picture on the TV cabinet and I start to cry. I doze off, absolutely exhausted. I'm woken up by the sound of my phone ringing, I slide to answer and sleepily say, "Yeah?" Not caring that it sounds rude.

"Jordan, this is Officer Hamilton."

I immediately sit up, instantly, I'm wide-awake. "Did you find her?" I shout into the phone.

"Yes, we have her. She's currently on her way to

hospital to be assessed. I'm on my way there now, I'll meet you at the hospital."

"Okay, thanks, Officer Hamilton."

Hanging up I immediately call Mike. He answers on the first ring, "Any news, asshat?"

"They found her, she's on her way to hospital."

I hear him sigh in relief, "Swing by and get me, I want to see our girl."

"Okay, I'll be at yours in ten."

54

KENZIE

When I wake, I'm in a strange bed, again and I start to panic. But when I look around, I realise I'm in a hospital room. Jordan is beside me, with my hand resting under his head; he's sound asleep. A smile appears on my swollen, bruised face. I never thought I'd see him again.

With my free hand, I lift it up, and run it over his cheek. He stirs, so I continue to run my hand back and forth across his face. He opens his beautiful green eyes and stares up at me. His face immediately lights up when he registers I'm awake and grinning back at him.

"Hi, husband." I manage to squeak out before the tears begin to fall; the flood gates have opened and my face currently rivals Niagara Falls.

Jordan stands up and slides onto the bed next to me. I lean forward and he wraps his arms around me. Still crying, I snuggle into him and continue to cry. He rubs my arm soothingly, whispering, "Shhhh. You're safe now." He keeps placing gentle kisses to my forehead, while squeezing me tighter.

We are interrupted when Mike clears this throat. "Welcome back, Kenz!"

Looking towards Jordan, I hesitantly ask, "Did the police get him this time?"

Jordan looks at me confused, before looking towards Mike, who also has a perplexed look on his face. I look back and forth between the two of them. "Guys, am I missing something?"

Jordan sits up and takes my hands between his. "Kenz, what do you remember?"

Struggling to remember, I bite my fingernails as I think. "Umm, I remember running through the park, Clint dragging me and then him trying to put me in the boot. I managed to swing at him with something, and then seeing flashing lights. Then I woke up here."

My eyes pop wide open as it all comes flashing back to me.

Running.

Clint grabbing me.

Dragging me to the car.

Shoving me towards the boot.

Swinging the tyre iron.

Colliding with Clint's head.

Shoving him.

Falling.

Crunch.

His lifeless eyes.

Flashing lights.

My whole body starts shaking, and I scream. It becomes hard to breath and I start to hyperventilate. I took someone's life.

Tears are pouring down my cheeks, I'm gasping for breath, unable to breathe as the reality of what I did sinks in. Jordan is trying to console me but I'm beyond reasoning with.

I'm shaking, screaming and crying.

Shaking my head back and forth.

Screaming, "No! No! No!"

A nurse and doctor come rushing into the room. I hear them, but nothing registers.

I feel a prick in my arm.

Finally I feel calm and at peace.

I can't keep my eyes open.

Black.

———

I wake up a few hours later, Jordan is still by my bed, but this time Mike is gone. I see Mum and a Skye huddled together on the recliner. Mum and I lock eyes and we both start to cry. She jumps up, comes over to the bed, wrapping me in a Mum hug, and we cry together. This hug is exactly what I need.

Skye comes over, climbs onto the bed and joins our hug. The three of us sit here, crying, locked in each other's arms for a traditional Merlot family hug. Jordan steps back, but I grab his hand and he joins in on our hug too. We all sit there with our arms wrapped around each other.

My stomach growls, and I realise I haven't eaten in what feels like forever. We all burst out laughing as my tummy growls again. Jordan says, "Looks like our mummy-to-be is hungry?"

Mum's head pops up and she questioningly asks, "Mummy-to-be??"

"Surprise, we're pregnant," I say with a smile, looking at Mum. "With twins."

Skye yells, "Fuck me dead, said Foreskin Fred."

Mum smacks Skye in the arm, and scolds her, "Language, Skye."

I laugh.

Looking over at her, I say, "Skye, you need to stop hanging around Mike."

"Ohh, honey." Mum says as she envelopes me in another hug and through what I hope are happy tears blubbers, "Mac, I'm so happy for you." She reaches over towards Jordan and grabs his hand, giving it a squeeze. She draws back and grabs my cheeks, pulls me in and kisses my forehead. "You gave me such a fright, baby girl."

"I'm sorry Mum, I'm never planning on doing that again. Besides now that he's dead there's no one else to hurt me."

Mum looks up shocked. "What do you mean he's dead?"

Looking towards Jordan confused, I say, "You didn't tell her?"

Mum interrupts, "Tell me what?"

Taking a deep breath, I proceed to tell her what happened. We both have tears falling down our cheeks by time I've finished retelling what happened. I look to my lap and whisper, "Mum, I killed someone." Shyly I look up at her. "How do I live with that?"

Mum tilts my head towards her, wiping away my tears. "Now you listen to me, Mackenzie Merlot. He made his own bed and he now has to lie in it forever. You did what you needed to do to survive and to save those babies. If anyone thinks differently, then they will have me to deal with."

Staring at Mum in shock, I know she's right, if I hadn't done what I did, it would be me in the morgue instead of him. It's a hard to describe my feelings right at this moment. On one hand, I have relief. I'm relieved that I'm finally safe, but I also feel remorse. I'm remorseful, for killing someone, but I also feel sadness. I'm sad that someone is dead, even if he was a psychotic asshole douchehole.

We are all sitting in silence when there is a knock on the door. Officer Kincaid and Officer Hamilton come in. I take a deep breath as I think they are here to arrest me for killing Clint.

Officer Hamilton is the first to speak, "How are you feeling, Kenzie?"

Hesitantly, I reply, "Okay, I think. Relieved that he's dead and can't hurt me anymore. Scared that you're going to arrest me for killing him."

Officer Hamilton takes a seat. "I can assure you that we are not here to arrest you, but I do need to get your side of what happened, before we can officially rule his death as self-defense."

She sets up a tape recorder on the bed trolley and presses record to take my statement. Taking a deep breath, I recount everything that I remember. When I'm finished, they both look at each other, and I think to myself, "Ohh shit, I'm going to jail. My babies are going to be born in jail." I don't realise that someone is speaking to me until I hear my name being called; I shake my head. "Sorry, I missed what you said."

Officer Kincaid looks pissed that he has to repeat himself. "As I was saying, from what you have told us and the report from the coroner; the injury that Mr. MacNicholson received was not intentional. You pushed him away in self-defense and I might add; you have a mighty good left hook. The wound to the side of his head was pretty impressive." He smirks. "But you didn't hear that from me."

Officer Hamilton says, "Once you are released, we will need you to come down to the station to sign your statement. I'll type up what you've told us today, and then this matter will be finalised. Mr. MacNicholson doesn't have any family, except for a cousin that we are trying to track down. I doubt she'll contest any of this. The evidence is all there, and add in the previous history, there's no lawyer who would touch it. Rest up, Kenzie, and we'll see you in a few days."

Just after they leave, the doctor comes in. He wants to keep me in for another night, my blood pressure is still a little high and they want to ensure everything is okay.

Later that afternoon, Jordan and I lie in each other's arms, his palm gently resting on my belly. I look up into his eyes and for the first time in a long time I'm calm and relaxed. We are finally free...or so we thought.

———

Mum and Skye left this morning. I told them I'm fine and between Jordan, Mike, and occasionally Sarah hovering around me, I have someone with me at all times. It's quite overbearing to tell you the truth. I know they mean well, but I really want some alone time.

They have just pulled away when Jordan gets a call from one of the staff at Malt Me and he needs to head over there ASAP to sort an issue out. I'm secretly happy, finally I'll get alone time.

I grab my Kindle and head to the kitchen. Pouring a jug of soda water and lime, I grab a glass and head outside. I'm lying on the lounger when he comes downstairs. "I'll be back as soon as I can."

"There's no rush, babe. I have my Kindle and the babies and I are fine. Plus I know you, either Mike or Sarah have been summoned and will be here soon."

He leans down and places a gentle kiss on my lips and pulls back to rest his forehead on mine. "Maybe, I'll be back as soon as I can"

"I'm fine, babe, trust me."

"I'll be back as soon as I can. Text or call me if you need anything." He opens the side gate and heads to his Jeep.

Finally I'm alone, I lie back and instead of reading, I start playing Candy Crush. Hearing someone come down the driveway, I'm putting my money on Mike, but I'm surprised at who I see walk through the gate.

55

TRAITOR

I can't believe Clint is gone. He and I have always been there for each other, until he met her that is. Then his life became all about her. Mackenzie this. Sweetcheeks that. Fuck her!

When it comes down to it, I'm the only one who's ever been there for him, just like he was there for me when I needed him. Family always comes first, and that's why I have to end her, to get revenge for Clint.

Arriving at her place, I wait for Jordan to leave. I broke into the brewery last night and made a few little modifications, so he'd have no choice but to go.

Kenz is all alone now.

Getting out of my car, I make my way over to their house and I walk down the driveway. Reaching over, I open the gate and slam it shut; with the force of the slam, it pops open again.

She jumps when the gate bangs, looking up, she seems shocked that I am here. "Shit, De-Niece, you scared me,"

"Yeah, well, you get that," I spit. The dumb bitch looks at me confused, *fuck she is stupid*. With my hands on my hips, I stand there and stare at her. "You are one fucking stupid mole. You have everyone wrapped around your little finger, well not me. They'll drop everything to help you, when really you are just a stupid bitch. I mean, you let my cousin kidnap you; twice."

The look of shock on her face with that revelation is priceless. "And I'm here today to get payback for you taking him away from me. All he did was fall in love with you, and you killed him. As one final favour to him, you will not see tomorrow, your babies, or your precious Jor ever again."

Mackenzie stands up. "Yo...You're his cousin?"

"Oh My God, bitch, catch up. Yes, Clint's my cousin, but if you really cared about him you would know that."

She's just standing there, staring at me, so I take my chance and lunge for her. I knock her onto the lounger before we roll off with a thud onto the pavers. I manage to roll her onto her back and I straddle her chest. I start swinging, punching, and hitting any part of her body that I can. She lies there screaming. I spit, "This is for my cousin, you heartless fucking bitch." I swing my arm back for one final blow but my arm it is yanked back and I fly through the air. Crashing through the French doors, falling to the floor inside with a thud, in a shower of glass and splintered wood. There's an excruciating pain in my left side; I look down to see a splinter of wood and glass sticking out of my abdomen, blood pooling beneath me.

Everything starts to go fuzzy. Everything is dwindling

away. A cold numbing sensation rushes over my body, the pain subsiding. Rolling to my side I groan in agony and grunt, "See you all in hell," before everything goes black.

56

MIKE

It's my day off and I just kissed De-Niece goodbye as she races off to work. After making another coffee, I head to the lounge room. I sit in my brown leather recliner and relax to enjoy *Bold and the Beautiful*. It's my guilty pleasure, but I'll never admit it to anyone. It's just finished when I get a text.

JORDAN – *Hey asshat, any chance you can head over and check on Kenz? I've had to go to the brewery urgently*

ME – *Sure can, I'll grab her a dozen cheese-burgers and head over*

JORDAN – *Thanks man*

I finish my coffee, turn off the TV, place my coffee

mug in the sink. From the bench, I grab my wallet and keys and head over to hang with Kenzie.

When I pull up, I see De-Niece's car there, seeing her here makes me smile. I'm glad she's making an effort. I know she doesn't particularly like Kenz for some reason, which is weird cause everyone loves Kenz.

Getting out of my car I hear yelling coming from the backyard; it sounds like De-Niece is screaming at Kenz. Running down the driveway, I get to the gate and I see De-Niece straddling Kenz. She's screeching and my heart drops. I hear her yell, "This is for my cousin, you heartless fucking bitch."

She swings her arm back to lay into her again. I drop the food, run over and yank her back, pulling her off Kenz. She falls backwards, hurtling through the French doors with a crash.

Looking over, I see Kenz is barely breathing I grab my phone out of my pocket and dial triple zero. Cradling Kenz in my arms, as we wait for the ambulance, I rock us back and forth, mumbling, "No, no, no, I'm so sorry Kenz."

The ambos come down the driveway and they head towards De-Niece, I shout, "Not her, she's the one who did this. Help Kenz, please, she's pregnant, please help her." Stepping back, I let them attend to Kenz.

Looking up, I see Officer Hamilton and Officer Kincaid walk through the gate. Hamilton looks at everything with wide eyes and shock. Kincaid goes over and talks to the paramedics. Officer Hamilton comes over to me. "What the hell happened here?"

I'm staring at her, but it isn't until she touches my arm that I register she's talking to me. "Huh?"

"What happened here?"

I proceed to tell her what I walked in on, and then I look towards De-Niece just as the paramedic places a white sheet over her body. Stumbling backwards, I realise, she's dead.

My phone starts to play Jordan's tone, *Wash It All Away* by Five Finger Death Punch. I grab it from my pocket and answer, "Hey dude. You need to get here now."

"What the fuck?" he shouts through the phone.

"Ummm, De-Niece is dead and Kenz is in pretty bad shape." I manage to say before I drop my phone and vomit.

I collapse to my knees and proceed empty my stomach onto the lawn. Once I'm finished, I ease back onto my heels and I stare up at the sky. Shaking my head in disbelief at what I just walked in on.

Hearing Kenz moan shocks me back to reality, and I race over to her and grab her hand, squeezing it tightly. She looks towards me; her eyes well up with tears and she starts to sob. With my free hand, I push the hair on her face away. "It's okay, Kenz, Jordan is on his way. I'm so sorry. I had no idea."

She has a death grip on my hand, and just as I turn back towards her, Jordan barges through the gate. He freezes when he sees the sheet, but as soon as he sees Kenz on the stretcher, he races over to her. "Ohh, baby, I'm so sorry I wasn't here."

They've just taken Kenz away. I'm sitting on the

garden edging when I hear one of the officers say that it's okay to remove the body. It's when he says body that shock sets in.

Holy shit, I killed someone.

Holy shit, my girlfriend was working with the enemy.

57

JORDAN

As soon as I hang up from Mike, I race out to my Jeep and speed home. Luck must be on my side today as every light is green and traffic is light. Pulling onto our street, I see there are police cars and an ambulance outside our place.

Climbing out of my Jeep, I race down the driveway, and I immediately see a white sheet covering a body. My heart sinks, and then I hear Kenz groan. Racing over to her, I see the left side of her face is swollen and turning purple. Mike is holding her hand and throwing up. She sees me and starts to sob.

The ambo interrupts us, "Sorry, guys, but we really need to get Mrs. McRoberts to the hospital. You can ride with us or we can meet you there."

"Kenz, I'm coming with you. I'm just going to check on Mike, and I'll meet you in the ambulance." She nods her head.

Walking over to Mike, who is now sitting on the garden bed edge, I see that his face is green. He doesn't look too good. Reaching out, I squeeze his shoulder, "Dude, are you okay? What the fuck happened?"

He just sits there staring into space. I don't think he even realises I'm speaking to him. Shaking him, I shout, "Dude!" He finally looks up at me. "Are you okay, man?"

He shakes his head. "Dude, I killed De-Niece."

Now it's my turn to stare in shock, before I can say anything Mike says, "I got here and she was on top of Kenz, hitting and punching her. I grabbed her off Kenz, and she went through the French doors. I'm so sorry, Jordan, this is entirely my fault. I didn't know she was his cousin. I swear, I didn't know"

The ambo leans over the fence and says, "Mr. McRoberts we have to go now."

"Okay, I'll be right there." Crouching down, placing my hands on Mike's shoulder, I look into his eyes. "Dude, I have to go with Kenz. Are you going to be okay?"

He nods his head. "Yeah, yep, yeah. I'm okay. I have to wait here to give my statement. Go be with Kenz."

As I walk away, I worry about Mike.

58

KENZIE

I'M ADMITTED STRAIGHT AWAY AND IT'S NURSE TARA on duty. She walks over to my bed and smiles at me. "Well, well, well, we meet again, Mrs. McRoberts. If I remember correctly, you said we wouldn't be seeing each other until the birth of your lil' ones." She looks around the room. "And I don't see any little ones in this room so I'm guessing you told me a big fat porky." I can't help laughing but I cringe as my face hurts like a bitch when I do anything at the moment. She finishes my obs and leaves.

A few minutes' later, Jordan walks in, our eyes meet across the room. "Fuck me, Kenz...your face. Your arms. Are you okay?"

"Depends on your definition of okay," I laugh, "But apart from feeling like I was beaten up, I'm doing pretty well. I asked Tara to make an appointment with Jeannie. Dr. Greene is here delivering a baby, and she'll check in before she leaves."

Jordan sits on the bed holding my hand, gently stroking the back like he does to calm me down. Looking into his eyes, I see worry, and that scares me. Lifting my hand to his cheek, he leans into it. "Jor, I promise I'm okay. Things could be a lot worse. If Mike hadn't turned up when he did, who knows what would have happened? I guess we now know who Clint's missing cousin is. How did we not know? I just don't understand."

Jordan looks into my eyes. "I don't think we will ever know. Mike's pretty shaken up; he looked so broken when I left. He was waiting to make his statement, but the coroner turned up so the officers had to speak with her first."

I look at him confused, "Coroner, why is the coroner there?"

"When Mike pulled her off you, she went through the French doors. A piece glass and wood splintered off and went into her guts. She bled out and died."

"Holy fuck, are you serious? Oh My God! How's Mike?"

"Not sure, I haven't spoken to him since I arrived here."

"Babe, leave me and go and see Mike. He needs you now. I'm fine and the babies are fine, I'm just sleepy." To emphasize what I just said I lie back, close my eyes, and pretend snore. I smile when I hear Jordan laugh; it's that deep throaty one I love. "Okay, Faker McFakerson, I'll go and check on Mike, BUT if you need anything call me. I'll be back first thing tomorrow, and I'll bring a change of clothes."

"Sounds good to me. Now go check on Mike, he needs you now. I promise, I'm fine."

Jordan leans down and kisses my cheek. "Rest up, Kenz." Then he bends down to my belly and kisses it twice. "And you two lil' ones, be nice to Mummy. She's been through a lot, and even though she's a fighter, she needs her rest too." He kisses my belly again, twice, before leaving, closing the door quietly behind him.

A few moments later, the door swings opens, I presume Jordan has come back, but in walks Sarah with coffee and muffins. *God, I love this girl.* She smiles at me, as she kicks the door shut with her foot. "Seriously, girl, we need to stop hanging out here."

"But the beds are so comfortable." We both burst out laughing.

Sarah places the coffee and muffin on the bed trolley. I fill her in on all that went down this afternoon. When I finish, I look up at Sarah. Her mouth is hanging open and she has a shocked look on her face, "Fuck me dead, said Foreskin Fred."

"Seriously, Mike is rubbing off on everyone, but I agree. How did we not know?"

"I'm speechless. Umm, how's Mike doing? He must be devastated."

"Jordan is heading to be with him now." I sigh, "He saved me Sarah." A lone tear escapes my eye.

Sarah leans over and hugs me gently. "Poor Mike, I'm guessing that's where Jordan was off too? I passed him on my way in, he seemed happy that I was here."

"Yeah, he doesn't like leaving me alone at the moment. It's frustrating, I just want 'me' time, but there's always someone around. At least you've been giving me space."

Sarah looks agitated when I mention that she hasn't been around much, but I can't query her any further as Dr. Greene enters my room.

Sarah says goodbye and says she will pop round tomorrow when I'm released. Leaning over, she gives me another hug and leaves. Once she closes the door, Dr. Greene starts up the ultrasound machine; thankfully everything is fine with our munchkins.

Nurse Tara comes in and gives me an endone for the pain, which should help me sleep. Taking the tablet from Nurse Tara, I swallow it down. I'm so exhausted that I fall into a deep sleep and don't wake until just before sunrise the next morning. I'm stiff and sore, but I'm feeling good mentally, but not physically. Physically, I hurt all over.

My breakfast tray has just been cleared and in walks Jordan and Mike. Without thinking, I jump out of bed. I wince in pain because I did it too fast, but I need to hug Mike. "Thank you, Mike. If you hadn't got there when you did, I would not be here today. I'm sorry that I have caused all of this."

He kisses my cheek and hugs me back. "Kenz, this is not your fault. I'm just glad I got there when I did. Seeing her on top of you will be etched in my mind forever."

We end our hug and Mike helps me back to bed. "Besides Jordan has agreed that I get free beer for life. I mean that's the mandatory payment for saving you, and Mac and Cheese."

"Did you just call my babies, Mac and Cheese?"

"Yep, Mac and Cheese." He bends downs and whispers. "Hey Mac and Cheese, Unky Mike will also buy you beer when you're bigger. Well I'll get it free from your dad; he does own a brewery and all that other shit." He looks up at me and we all start to laugh.

KENZIE

...6 months later

TODAY IS THE DAY THAT WE GET TO BRING OUR BABIES home from hospital. Rory and Indi were prematurely born at thirty-two weeks. My blood pressure spiked and Dr. Green wasn't taking any chances. The girls were born via C-section later that day. And today, as a family, we get to head home together, for the first time.

The last two months have been hectic. We've been juggling our time between the hospital, the brewery, and being at home occasionally to sleep. Jordan has been my rock through everything, as usual.

Our girls are beautiful; they both have dazzling blue eyes. Rory has golden blonde locks like me, while Indi has curly sandy blonde hair like her dad; we still don't know where the curls come from though.

We sold the house we renovated, as it held too many uncomfortable memories. We bought a brand new brick home closer to the brewery. It has four bedrooms, ours with an ensuite and a humongous walk-in-robe, which rivals Carrie's from the *Sex and the City* movie. It has an office with a full wall of book shelves, that I may have filled, a guest room, media room, and an open plan kitchen/dining/living room, which leads out to a spectacular timber patio area that overlooks the most amazing pool area. It still has a beer shed for Jordan to experiment at home.

Jordan even built a cubby house for the girls, not that they'll be able to use it for a few years yet, but there was no stopping him. He would do anything for his girls, me included.

Smiling, I fondly remember a time when I was five months pregnant. Jordan and I were closing up at the brewery one Saturday night, everyone had just left and I was horny; I was a total nymphomaniac while I was pregnant. I couldn't get enough. I never thought I'd see the day that Jordan would tell me to back off, but that happened on quite a few occasions. I'd finally treated myself and bought some maternity lingerie from Hot Mumma and it had arrived.

Leaving Jordan out at the bar, I went into our office to tally the books for the night when I started to get that tingly feeling down below. I also realised that we had yet to officially christen the office; that thought only turned me on even more. That morning I decided to wear my new lingerie, and Jordan had yet to see it, so I stripped off. I was wearing my new navy and vivid blue microfiber bra and matching undies. Lying down on the office couch, I waited for Jordan to come and find me.

My heart was racing as I was hoping that he wouldn't

reject me, again. I knew it had been a bit much but I couldn't help it, those hormones were making me crazy. While waiting, I fell asleep, but I was pleasantly awoken to the feeling of Jordan running his fingers over the fabric of my undies. I moaned in pleasure as I rolled onto my back. Opening my eyes, I found Jordan standing next to me in only his boxer briefs. His eyes were full of lust and hunger. Sitting up, I kissed along his chin towards his delectable lips; I licked his lower lip before taking it into my mouth and sucking. I coaxed his mouth open, before plunging my tongue into his, moaning as he sucked it like a lollypop. I the connection and whispered, "Make love to me, Jordan."

He stood up and pulled his boxer briefs down, his cock sprang free. I flicked my tongue out over the tip as I grabbed onto his shaft and started stroking from base to tip. I took his cock deeper into my mouth, hollowing my cheeks to take him completely. His cock hit the back of my throat, I scraped my teeth along his shaft before sucking him back into my mouth. He ran his fingers through my hair as I was sucking. Before long, I felt the first spurt of hot salty cum hit the back of my throat. Sucking him dry before releasing him, he lowered his head and kissed me. He carefully lowered me, so I was lying down to the couch.

He kissed down my neck, sucking my breast through my bra before lowering the cup and biting my nipple. With his other hand he massaged my other breast and I moaned. Since becoming pregnant, I have loved having my breasts sucked and massaged, even more so than before. He reached around and unclasped my bra, lowering the straps before flinging it aside. He attacked my nipples and breasts with such vigor that my orgasm ripped through me without warning. I was still wriggling in ecstasy when he ran his hand down my body and rubbed my pussy through my now soaking, wet undies. He pushed the material to the side and ran his finger up my slit, before slipping it in. He was still sucking on my nipple, he added another finger, and I let out pleasurable moan.

Jordan pulled back, removing his fingers, and I cried out, but he grabbed the top of my undies and quickly removed them. Then he buried his face in my pussy. He nibbled and sucked on my clit. "Ohh, Jordan," I moaned, he then used his thumb and started massaging my clit. I could feel my orgasm building as he plunged his finger in, before sucking on my clit again. He slipped in another finger, causing my orgasm to peak. I crashed and tumbled over the edge.

Once my tremors stopped, he kissed his way up my body; paying attention extra to my sensitive breasts. Finally, he kissed me on the mouth, it was hot and heavy. The taste of my juices still on his lips. I felt his cock at my entrance and I lifted my hips as he penetrated me in one thrust. Due to my growing belly it was uncomfortable so he pulled out. He helped me up and then sat down, I lowered myself onto his rock hard cock. Lifting up onto my knees and I rode his cock like I was a jockey in the Melbourne Cup, impaling my self deeper and deeper each time. He grabbed my nipple and rolled it between his thumb and forefinger, leaning forward and sucking occasionally. I threw my head back and moaned. My orgasm erupted like a volcano, moments later, Jordan released his seed deep inside of me.

I eased myself off his lap and sat on the couch next to him. I looked over to him and ran my hand down the side of his face. "I love you, Jordan McRoberts."

Smiling he looked over to me and leaned into my palm, turning his head to place soft kiss there, "And I love you, Kenzie Louise McRoberts nee Merlot." He placed his hand on my belly and gently rubbed. "Mac and Cheese, I love you guys, too."

Yes, Mike's weird and wonderful name had stuck for the twins; even Dr. Green was using that name.

We've just arrived home from the hospital, and for the first time, it's just the four of us. Finally as a family, we are under the same roof. I'm standing in the doorway to the nursery staring at our beautiful girls, who are sound asleep in their cots, and I could not be happier.

Even though the road to this point was rough and definitely bumpy, I wouldn't change a thing. I am, whom I am today, due to what has happened to me. Its taken me a while to accept that, but there is no point in worrying about things that I cannot change, or the past.

I'm Kenzie Louise McRoberts nee Merlot.

I am strong,

I am a survivor.

EPILOGUE

...*2 months later*

It's been eight months since Clint and De-Niece tried to ruin our lives for the last time, but for me it's been eight months of growth. I've been through so much when it comes to Clint, but with the help of my family and friends, I'm a much stronger person.

There are no more pity stares, people treat me like the Kenzie from before any of this ever happened. In addition, I now have two adorable little girls to dote on. People finally see me for the that I am strong.

Everyone is over for a new tasting session. Everyone is laughing and having fun, but I look over to Mike and I notice that he's here, but not here. As much as he won't admit it, I know he is having a difficult time accepting what happened.

I really wish he'd let someone in. I see it in his eyes, I've been there before. He's struggling to move forward. To an extent, I think he blames himself, but there only two people to blame: Clint and De-Niece, and neither of them can hurt us anymore.

Mike used to talk to me about it, but he's closed himself off again. I worry about him and want my friend from before back.

Taking someone's life has an adverse effect on you and how you see the future. I know it did for me. Without the support of Jordan, Mike, Sarah, and Jeannie, I wouldn't be coping as well as I am. Mike helped to save me, now it's my turn to help save him.

THE END!!!

Mike's story will continue in Tequila Healing which is out now!

Read on for a sneak peek at his book....

PROLOGUE

It's my stupid dick's fault. I'm always thinking with my dick, and as a result, Kenz and Jordan nearly lost everything, including Mac and Cheese. All because of me, my dick, and a hot blonde piece of ass named Ho Bag Slutface, also known as De-Niece.

Never will I fall for another woman, too much happened last time, I can't risk it happening again.

My self-imposed dick purgatory; except for random pussy but that doesn't count, was going well until Savannah Blac got a job at my local bar, The Black Dungeon. I can't stop thinking about her. The curve of her tight ass, the way it swishes side to side as she walks, or the slight bounce of her perfect tits as she passes drinks across the bar.

Every time I close my eyes, I see her. I imagine her wavy, golden blonde locks wrapped around my fists, tugging her towards me as I sink myself balls deep into her tight pink pussy from behind. Her sapphire blue eyes sparkling under the dim bar light as I slam into her over and over, and she screams my name while I give her the best orgasm of her life. Before I take her back to my place and wake up next to her in my king-sized bed, our arms and limbs wrapped around each other, her eyes dazzling in the morning sunlight.

Shaking my head to clear those dirty sweet thoughts, I concentrate on what Jordan is saying and the tequila shooter in front of me. When I look up, I see Sav walking behind the bar after her break, and I can't help but smile. She has wormed her way into my heart, and I don't know how I feel about that.

Fuck, she's gorgeous; my dick is so hard right now. I really need to find another bar to drink at, but just the thought of not seeing her crushes my heart. Picking up the shot in front of me, I say a silent "cheers" to the world for bringing her into my life. With the next shot, I say a silent "fuck you" to the world for bring her into my life... why does the universe keep doing this to me?

Welcoming the burn of the tequila as it slides down my throat, I pick up the third shot, look to Jordan, and say, "Bottoms up!" After sinking the third shot, I signal Sav for more tequila and sambuca shots and two more beers for Jordan and me.

Seeing her smile makes me grin, but then I remember that chicks are nothing but trouble and cause nothing but strife, especially the super fucking hot ones.

Remembering that I promised myself I'll never go there again, I start to think about a naked grandma, with flabby wrinkly skin, and sagging boobs. Yeah, that works for about five seconds because Sav turns around and smiles at me; she fucking smiles and it's mesmerising. It brings back memories of our one time together. *I'm screwed*, I think to myself as I keep watching her.

Shaking my head, I again consider finding another bar to drink at, but just the thought of not seeing her crushes me; I can't do it, I'm a sucker for punishment. No, I deserve this punishment for all that has happened, this is my penance to pay.

Looking over at Jordan, I think, *how can he still be friends with me, after what's happened?* I start to think of Malt Me. I could always drink there, but everyone there knows...they know I'm partly to blame for De-Niece and all the shit that went down. They stare at me with their judgey eyes; I don't need them to add to my guilt. I already feel remorse, regret, and like shit, and any number of other words to describe feeling like an asshole fuckwit.

Looking over, I see Sav smiling and I find myself also grinning back. I realise that I only ever smile when I see her. Closing my eyes, I take a deep breath to try and shake those thoughts from entering my mind, but I can't. Savannah Blac is the most beautiful woman in the world. There's nowhere else I would rather drink, the pain from seeing her is my punishment, even though I deserve much more. Besides, I love this bar; it's my happy place.

It's simple; I just have to stop thinking about Savannah Blac, no matter how perfect she is. *Nope, nah uh, not going there...again with her, even though that night was amazing.*

Everything changed when I found the gorgeous, feisty woman broken and crying in the ally behind the bar. All bets were off, she needed me and I was more than willing to step up to the plate.

Looking down at her, I saw that she was frightened, broken, and fragile; my heart broke for her. Hearing me walk towards her, she looked up at me, with tears pouring down her cheeks. Taking a deep breath, with sad eyes, she whispered, "Please. Help me."

Tequila Healing, Book 2 in the Liquor Cabinet Series is now available.

ACKNOWLEDGMENTS

First of all I want to thank my husband **Troy** for giving me the courage to write this book. I had been tossing around the idea for a while and without your support I don't think I would have started to write this.

To my friend, **Amanda Browne**. You were the first person to read Malt Me and your feedback has been muchly appreciated. The wine is on me when we next catch up.

To the following authors for your words of encouragement throughout the writing process and answering all of my menial questions **Rebecca Rohman, Pepper Winters, Jodi Perry, Anita Gillham, Lyssa Layne, Elle Brookes, BJ Harvey, Amo Jones, TJ Hamilton, Michelle Dare, Angel Justice** and **Michele Stratton.**

To my beta readers **Amanda, Amy, Beth, Crissy, Elizabeth, Heather, Michelle, Patti,** and **Vicci** thank you for taking a chance on me and for giving me super honest feedback. I really appreciate it.

My editor **Karen**, thank you for taking the time to turn my baby into something amazing. After round one edits, I'm surprised you are still talking to me. You are not only my editor, but also a friend and I appreciate everything you have done for me on the authoring journey.

To my sister **Tara** for all your medical mumbo jumbo clarification and making me sound "smart" and my characters seem professional.

A special thank you to, **Anita Gillham** for allowing me to reference your series within my book and for your guidance and encouragement throughout the writing process.

...And lastly, **you, the reader**. Thanks for taking a chance on an unknown author.

MALT ME PLAYLIST

Israel's Son – Silverchair
Barbie Girl – Aqua
...Baby One More Time – Brittany Spears
Nothing Else Matters – Metallica
Dream On – Aerosmith
Lanterns – Birds of Tokyo
Runaway – The Corrs
This Life – Curtis Stigers
Ruby – Kaiser Chiefs
Stronger – Brittney Spears
Crazy – Seal
Chasing Cars – Snow Patrol
I Don't Want to Be – Gavin DeGraw
Wash it All Away – Five Finger Death Punch
Light My Fire – The Doors
Romeo And Juliet – Dire Straits
Until We Burn In the Sun (This Kids Just Want A Love
Song) – Bedouin Soundclash
Come Fly With Me – Frank Sinatra

Shut Your Mouth – Garbage
Addicted To You – Avicii
Walls Fall Down – Bedouin Soundclash
Lose Your Way – Sophie B. Hawkins
Never Tear Us Apart – INXS
Take Me To Church – Hozier
Halo – Beyoncé'
Love Shack – The B-52's
Pachelbel: Canon in D Major – Johan Pachelbel
(Everything I Do) I Do It For You – Bryan Adams

This playlist can be found on Spotify.

ABOUT THE AUTHOR

 DL Gallie is from Queensland, Australia, but she's lived in many different places all over the world, including the UK and Canada. She currently resides in Central Queensland with her husband and two munchkins. She and her husband have been together since she was sixteen, and although they drive each other crazy at times, she couldn't imagine her life without him.

Shortly after her son was born, DL began reading again. With encouragement from her husband, she picked up the pen and started writing, and now the voices in her head won't shut up.

DL enjoys listening to music, drinking white wine in the summer, red wine in the winter, and beer all year round. She's also never been known to turn down a cocktail, especially a margarita.